End of the Line

a novel

Janet Trull

blue denim press

End of the Line
Copyright © 2023 Janet Trull
All rights reserved
Published by Blue Denim Press Inc.
First Edition
ISBN 9781927882870
No part of this book may be used or reproduced in any manner whatsoever without written permission, except in the case of brief quotations embodied in critical articles or reviews.

This is a work of fiction. Resemblances to persons living or dead, or to organizations, are unintended and purely co-incidental.

Cover Design by Shane Joseph
Cover photography by Janet Trull

Library and Archives Canada Cataloguing in Publication
Title: End of the Line: a novel / Janet Trull.
Names: Trull, Janet, author.
Description: First edition.
Identifiers: Canadiana (print) 20230491863 | Canadiana (ebook) 20230491871 | ISBN 9781927882870 (softcover) | ISBN 9781927882887 (Kindle) | ISBN 9781927882894 (EPUB) | ISBN 9781927882900 (IngramSpark EPUB)
Subjects: LCGFT: Novels.
Classification: LCC PS8639.R844 E53 2023 | DDC C813/.6—dc23

Dedication:

To the ghosts who live among us in these high lands, too silent to be real.

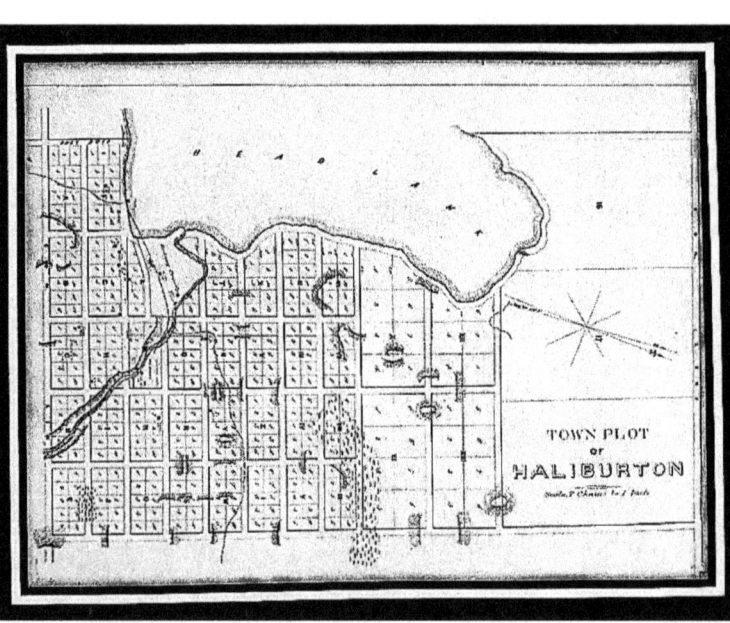

Prologue

The Stationmaster is not sixty yet, but looks eighty. A grey man. Grey hair, grey complected, crooked grey teeth. When I first saw who the railway hired to run Haliburton Station, I had to laugh. How did this old codger get the job? Crippled from years of hard labour, laying track. A navvy.

Like me, he was hired as a boy. He learned to swing a pick, hammer a spike, dig a grave.

Lefty is not the Stationmaster's real name. Most of us navvies were gifted with nicknames since our foreign monikers were too hard to pronounce, too hard to spell. Me, I was called Ladder all my working days because I was a tall man. Stood a head and a half above the other navvies.

How's the weather up there? Ha ha ha.

My first day on the job, the manager says, "I need a fuckin' ladder to look you in the eye, man." After that, I was Ladder. And that's what the boys carved into the beech tree where they laid me down. *Here Lies Ladder*. It's a fine resting place, on the ridge just above the train station. I can see the entire village of Haliburton. The inn, the barber shop, the mercantile, the church, the little homes on streets named after trees. But it's a lonely perch, especially in winter, with the wind soughing through bare branches above me. I'm prone to wander the midnight streets, seeking solace from the wakeful. I hear the thoughts of the troubled and feel the regrets of the sick and know the plans of the night workers. Midnight passes unbeknownst to most living men and women. But for the dead, midnight is bleak eternity.

Lefty was born Günther Plath. They called him Dutchie for years until he lost the use of his arm. He was a solitary man, unsentimental about the family he left behind in Amsterdam. Among his brothers and sisters, he had been noticeably smaller, darker, quieter than the rest. If they were living or dead, he did not know, and couldn't be bothered to write and find out.

Lefty moved his meager belongings into a back room of Haliburton Station. A room meant for storage. The manager told him, "You can't live here. You must stay at a boarding house."

"You better hire an extra man for the night shift, then," he said. "A watchman."

"Just lock the doors," the manager said.

Lefty nodded and ignored the manager, a man of no common sense.

He is a light sleeper. Lefty hears every mouse, every rattling windowpane. Every shift of ice on the roof. His lantern burns low by his cot and he does not even take his pants off, ready as he is to jump up and investigate the least little disturbance.

That is how he found me. A creaking floorboard as I crossed the room. I am nothing more than a wavering shadow to others, but Lefty looked up. Took the measure of me.

"A cold night in the grave, I expect," is what he said. Oh, it was gratifying to have a fellow see me, and I nodded. He retrieved a bottle of whiskey and two glasses. Two!

"A toast to the dead, my friend," he said. He drank deeply.

"A drink to the living," I countered.

He heard me. We did not speak again that night, only took comfort in the small pleasure of another's company, as navvies do.

We are opposites in many ways. He is old, I am forever young. He is short, I am tall.

But both of us are opinionated men. Observant men. Men who recognize a liar or a thief when we meet one. Men who witness.

Dead men, it is said, tell no tales. That is far from the truth. I am deeply interested in stories behind closed doors, hidden in dark hearts. I have read pages torn from a lover's diary and burned. I have listened in on plots, heard whispered confessions, commiserated with lunatics. There are stories that may surprise you about the people of Haliburton. Perhaps you know them? Perhaps you think you know them. Sit here beside me on the bench, if you are so inclined, and I will tell you what I have learned. The next train is delayed. We have time.

~1~

November 1885

The body of Alexander Smith washed up in the gut, a grassy narrows between Lake Kashagawigamog and Canning Lake. Two hunters who were tracking a moose along the shore caught sight of his red plaid waistcoat. Their dog, Angel, raced ahead and licked away some blood from the open mouth. Thanks to the cold weather, the body hadn't spoiled. It was secured between a rock and a fallen pine tree.

"This is the one went missing on Election Day. The one that run for Reeve." said Webby McGee.

"Who else but?" said his droopy-eyed brother, Murdoch. "Alexander Smith. Bank manager."

"Shot in the chest, looks like."

Murdoch squatted to have a closer look inside the bloody mouth. Blue lips curled back to reveal smashed teeth and something gold on the black tongue.

"That might be worth some money. Is it a tooth?"

"Nope."

"A coin?"

"Nope. Angel, girl! Back away! Sit!" Murdoch retrieved his pocket knife and wedged the blade under the oval medallion. "Come on, you little fucker," he mumbled.

"Don't be an eejit, brother! Leave him be. I don't like the way his eyes are staring at me. We could get blamed for this mess."

Murdoch worked at the gold piece until it popped free. "It's a tie pin. Here, have a look."

"Ach! Keep it away from me, Murdy. My stomach's delicate today as it is. I might boke."

"Somebody stuck it in good." Murdoch polished the piece on the bib of his overalls and laughed when he read the engraved letters. "A.S.S. Those initials suit him well." Murdoch's bad knee clicked painfully as he stood.

"Are you keeping it?"

"Aye. I know a gal who might like to know where it ended up."

"Shall we away, then? Alexander Sonuvabitch Smith ain't going nowhere."

The hunters marked the spot with a teepee of branches and carried on, hoping to have the hind end of the moose packed onto their sled before the sun disappeared. And, by golly, they got him, an older male with a misshapen rack. Crooked, like he'd been in a fight with another bull and lost. They butchered him on the beach and heaved out enough of the steaming rump to make two good sized roasts, then covered the carcass with cedar boughs.

It started snowing, wet and sloppy November snow, as they traipsed home.

The hunters waited until the next morning before they went over to Duncan Burns's place to report what they found. Dunc ran the post office out of his kitchen.

"He's been missing near a week," Dunc said.

"I doubt he's been dead a week," said Webby. "He looked pretty fresh, eh, Murdy?"

Murdoch mumbled agreement. Webster was the talky one in social situations.

"Hell of a thing, murder. Even for a right asshole like him. Wonder who done it?"

"I couldn't hazard a guess. Somebody who didn't want him to win the election, maybe?"

"No danger of that. He only got twenty-three votes. At least we know the new Reeve couldn't a done it."

"Aye. It's hard for a man with no fingers to shoot a gun."

Due to bad weather, freezing rain, it was two days before Clark Cook showed up at the McGee's place. Cook was as close to an undertaker as was available in Haliburton, so he got around. He'd driven by their laneway a dozen times, but this was his first chance to enter the stone gates and see for himself what the rough red-beards were up to. He was expecting to have a laugh at their expense. Hillbillies, people called them. But, goddammit!

Highland Golf Club

The sign hung from the front porch of an impressive log building. Clark climbed the steps and took in the splendid view all the way down Lake Kashagawigamog.

"Cold as a witch's tit today," a voice yelled from a smaller building around back.

"I'm the undertaker, sir. Clark Cook." He stepped off the porch and offered his hand for an introduction.

"I'm Webster McGee." The Scotsman's nose was a brilliant red, matching the length of tartan around his neck. "Are you a golfer Mr. Cook?"

"No, sir. But I want to try, come summer. Youse have done a lot of work up here."

"Aye. Ye are standing on the first tee box."

Clark Cook followed Webby's gaze up the hill, cleared of trees and not a stump in sight. Between outcroppings of granite, two sheep grazed on a clump of fescue in a sheltered spot not yet covered in snow. He whistled in admiration.

"We were raised on a golf course in Paisley, near Glasgow. Our fayther was Keeper of the Green."

"Word in town is that youse are butchers. Pig farmers."

"Oh, we're that, too. Leastwise my brother is. He believes pigs are intelligent creatures. Loves them. Here he comes now, he's just been back at the stable, slopping his beasts. Murdoch! Meet Mr. Cook."

Murdoch kept his hands in his pockets and nodded. There were yellow icicles hanging from his moustache.

"You fellas ready to show me where this body is at? Coroner's waiting at Doc Kennedy's office back in town."

The McGee brothers climbed into the horse-drawn hearse. They admired the suspension of the vehicle. It was a smooth ride considering the rutted state of the roads.

"This is the spot!" Webby called up to Clark when they reached the embankment.

"I'll wait up here with the horses," Clark said. "If you fellows don't mind, that is."

The brothers did not respond. They had already blamed each other over the foolishness of reporting the body in the first place. This particular dead man did not deserve the trouble.

"With any luck, the wolves have found him," Webby said as they skidded down the hill. But there he was, encased in three inches of ice.

"He's frozen solid, Murdy. Good thing you brung the hatchet."

Murdoch was a powerful man, and he found chopping to be satisfying work. The mid-section came away in a nice chunk. Webby peeled the ice back, pulling some blood-soaked fibres with it. He hurled it into the cattails, flushing a pair of ruffled grouse. The commotion startled Murdoch mid-chop, who missed his mark and put a nasty gash in the banker's scrawny throat.

"Well, shit. Nice work, brother!"

Murdoch swore and offered Webby the hatchet.

Clark yelled down at them and asked did they need anything.

"A length of rope! And a shovel if you have one," Webby called. Meanwhile, Murdoch grabbed hold of the banker's fancy leather boots and yanked as hard as he could. Ice cracked and water gurgled and Mr. Smith slipped out of his tomb. Most of him, anyway.

"Jesus! His noggin's still stuck in the ice!" Webby said.

Clark tossed a rope down the embankment. "I got 'er anchored to a tree. You boys tie him on and I'll haul him up."

Webby wound the rope around the dead man's ankles. "Okay. All set!"

Clark started pulling and the body ascended the embankment. Murdoch squatted down on his haunches. "I don't see a way to dislodge this head. Jesus. I wisht we woulda closed his eyes when we had the chance."

"Step aside," Webby said. He reached inside his britches and pulled out his pecker and let go with a nice hot stream of piss. Murdoch hooted and followed suit.

"Christ Almighty!" Clark yelled from up top. "Where's the bugger's head?"

"It's coming!" Webby assured him. "Ye wouldn't have a bucket in that fancy outfit would ye?"

"Hey, brother," Murdoch said. "Look at this. His hair comed off."

"It's a wig. And that looks like window putty on his scalp. Kept his hair from blowing away in the wind, I guess," Webby said, as a tin bucket landed near his feet. He scooped the bald head up, but the hair was iced in pretty good. "You got anything left in your bladder?"

"Nope."

Webby kicked at the clump of hair. "Not salvageable," he decided.

Clark Cook had recently expanded his livery business with the purchase of a hearse, a funeral sleigh for winter, and three luxury rental carriages, no thanks to Alexander Smith who had turned down his application for a business loan the previous spring.

"I'm sorry, Mr. Cook," Smith told him in a tone that did not sound sorrowful at all. "You don't qualify."

Hard work and ambition were not among the criteria for lending money at the Dominion Bank. Clark was dismissed but not dismayed. He managed to secure financial aid from another source. Now, as he looked upon Smith's head in the tin bucket, he allowed himself a small self-congratulatory smile.

The three men heaved the body onto a canvas tarp in the hearse, and placed the head above the shoulders.

"Jesus!" Clark Cook commented. "Them mean eyes! If looks could kill!" He put a cloth over the head and rubbed his hand hard across his mouth to stop from laughing. Then he folded the tarp over the stiff, and strapped him down.

"Just a little advice, lads," said Cook. "Don't mention nothing about his head coming off. I'll explain things to the doctor and the coroner and maybe it don't have to get around."

Murdoch snorted, choked on his plug of tobacco and horked it out rather violently. Webby pounded him on the back, and they both nodded in agreement to shut up about the incident. They weren't a gossipy pair anyways.

"Listen, lads, I'm terrible grateful for your help today. It's a grim task."

"We seen worse," Webby said.

"Still, you done a good job. Here's a couple dollars for your trouble."

"He got a family?" Murdoch asked.

"A wife and two children," Cook said.

"Give it to them."

"To be honest, fellows, Alexander Smith's wife has got lots of money. So, I want to pay you for your services. I won't take no for an answer."

Webby looked at Murdoch knowing he was thinking the same thing. No wolves had got to Mr. Smith. Their moose might be all right, too. Webby nodded and shoved the money inside his coat. They turned down the offer for a ride home and headed back across the gut.

Clark Cook watched them with a deep regret that Haliburton was losing the old ways, the ways of pitching in to do the hard things that needed doing. Duty. That's all it was, but there were men back in town, too many of them, who would have stolen Smith's wallet along with the silver cufflinks and the fine leather boots. As for Alexander Smith? He sincerely hoped this was one murder that would never be solved.

~ 2 ~

1878

Explosions shook the earth. Smoke rolled across the sky, leaving a sweet and lingering odour. Winona McLeod's heart ached as she witnessed flocks of birds, rising in panic from the canopy, chased by the shrapnel of their shattered nests. The deer and fox and wolf and beaver retreated far into the forest. From her lookout on the ridge, she watched the iron rails creep closer daily until the workers were in the valley directly below her. She learned the names of the men as they called out to each other. Luigi! Olav! Kostas! They shouted and sang and cussed. At sunset, they lit their fires, clustering together in groups of common lexicons. Cooking smells drifted up and surprised her with foreign savouries.

The world was encroaching on Gidaaki, a settlement established many generations ago. It was not an incorporated village. It was not acknowledged in the new way of places, which required legal documents and corporate seals and courts of law. Like snow melting in spring, the Michi Saagiig territory was disappearing.

Gidaaki still appeared on maps. Only they were now the wrong maps. Lost maps traced on granite, temporary maps drawn on birchbark, invisible maps, etched into the hearts of the dead.

Profiteers and savvy investors were filling Canada's backwoods with inhabitants. Soft-bellied, gout-legged and entitled, they gathered in drawing rooms across the ocean in England, naming towns after themselves and colouring the maps red. Red for British colonies. Red for bloody conquests. From a safe distance, they spilled red paint over tropical islands, great swaths of nomadic hunting grounds, territories of priceless natural resources, and entire continents. And Michi Saagiig territory, which they considered unclaimed wilderness. Free for the taking. Except for the tract of land stewarded by Winona McLeod. The high land. The land her grandmother called Gidaaki.

For centuries, Gidaaki provided temporary shelter to the original people of different tribes and clans who travelled along the five-lake chain following an abundance of wild game. It had been a meeting place for seasonal feasts and celebrations. But by 1878, Gidaaki was a community of women and children with nowhere else to go. The left behinds. Most of the folks who lived in the newly incorporated town of Haliburton ignored the granite castle up on the ridge. Surrounded by myth and mystery, the place was rumoured to be populated by whores and witches and squaws. No destination for Christians.

Not everyone kept their distance. Lumberjacks and trappers were among those drawn to the ridge for comfort services, and soon the place came to be known as the Nunnery.

"We're off up the hill to pay our respect to the nuns," they'd say as they downed their pints at Crooks Tavern after a day's labour.

Old Paddy Crook would cross himself. "Be sure to make a donation to the holy sisters in my name. Bless them."

Winona McLeod did not mind the harmless joking. She comported herself like something of a Prioress. Gidaaki was not so different from a convent. It was a charitable organization that saw to the feeding and clothing and sheltering of the poor. And, like nuns, the women of Gidaaki were not the marrying kind.

The day that Sunny Adams climbed the ridge to see for herself what manner of community was behind the granite parapet, she was met by a statuesque woman with greying hair and weathered skin and an inescapable gaze. A woman with a majesty about her, not unlike the formidable Queen of England.

"Call me Ona," she told Sunny. "Everyone does."

"Call me Sunny."

"The innkeeper."

Sunny smiled. Rarely did she get credit for running the business. Her husband's name was on the sign. "Loyalist Lodge, James Adams, Prop., Est. 1877"

"Your husband does not look like he is able to carry out the duties of a publican."

"How..." Sunny looked confused. "You know me?"

Ona took her by the hand and led her to a granite balcony that offered a view of Haliburton in the valley below. The mist was dissipating to reveal a clearing around Head Lake. The new steeple of St. Mark's, the partially constructed railway station, Crockett's Mercantile, Tucker's Sawmill, the bridge spanning the Drag River. And among the shops and homes on Queen Street, The Loyalist stood out with its freshly painted white clapboard, distinctive black trim around the windows, and decorative spindles along the second-floor balcony. How proud she felt.

"You have a bird's eye view. You must know everyone!"

Ona laughed. "Everyone we care to know. And we care to know you, Sunny Adams, if you would tell us your story. Come. Join us in the cloister."

"So! You really are nuns?"

"No, no. You'll see."

Some ancient geographical accident had created a protective granite wall along the north side of Gidaaki, and groupings of monolithic rocks formed a colonnade that opened onto a high meadow. Near the entrance were old women with leathery brown skin, their crooked fingers pulling quills from a porcupine hide. There were mothers breastfeeding babies, young girls kneeling in a circle combing each other's hair. Two young boys squatted over a game board. Ona offered Sunny a chair covered in bearskin.

"So," she said. "I understand you are an American."

"Yes, from Buffalo."

"I have been to Niagara, to see the great cataract. Buffalo is near to that, I think."

"It is. Down at the mouth of the Niagara River. On Lake Erie. My father was a fisherman."

"A hard way to support a family, no doubt."

"Indeed. He never learned the skill of putting money away for winter months or even the day after next," Sunny said. "'The Lord will provide,' he told Mother when she complained."

Sunny was handed a cup of fragrant tea. She sipped it and waited for others to speak. But this was a group of listening women, not inclined to comment or interrupt. They indicated their interest well enough with silent nods.

"My father fell through the ice trying to catch fish in December. My mother cursed his dead body when his mates carried him in the door and laid him out on the table. 'What are you waiting for,' she said to me and my brothers. 'Go out and find jobs.'"

Kateri, one of the crones, laughed aloud, and others chuckled along. These were women familiar with necessity, that hard-hearted taskmaster of the poor.

"My brothers went to work in the smelly bilge of the small canals, pulling boats back and forth like mules. I was lucky. I was hired into service in a fine home. The Adams had four children, all brats except for the eldest. James. Who, you might know, is now my husband."

Kateri spoke then, asking the question that all the women were probably pondering. "You married him before or after he lost his limbs?"

"After. His father caught us cuddling in the library once, before the war, and almost fired me. He had high expectations for James, being the eldest. And proud he was to see him in uniform. But when James was carried home from Fredericksburg in a wicker basket, it was a different story. He was happy to let me nurse him. I had no training for it, but nurses were in short supply. All the hospitals were full of ruined boys."

"You did a good job. It seems his convalescence was successful," Ona said with admiration.

"Yes. Better than anyone hoped for. Even James. Especially James."

"So how did you end up here in Haliburton?"

"James's father agreed to give his blessing to our marriage. On the condition we move to Canada where he had invested in some property."

Kateri cackled and laid her stitch-work aside. "Coward," she mumbled, and others spoke up.

"Sent you off into the wilderness of a foreign country."

"Like a Bible story."

"As if you hadn't suffered enough."

"Jamie was furious, of course," Sunny said. "We left under strained circumstances, as you may well imagine. But we are glad of it now."

Sunny looked up to find the sun had travelled a fair way across the sky.

"It must be near ten o'clock," she said. "I have to get back and start lunch."

Ona walks part way down the trail with Sunny and waves her off. As she turns to climb back, Mary's boys barrel past her accompanied by the new orphan lad, Buck. No doubt they are heading to the railway. They are fascinated by the industry of it all, teams of horses and oxen sweating in the heat, muscles straining and breaking under the impossible labour of laying steel tracks along a route not suited to straight lines.

"Where are you off to?"

Buck pretends he does not hear and keeps running. Peter, careless and rebellious, pauses and shrugs then follows Buck down the hill. Norman is the responsible one.

"We were offered work, Ona, fetching water for the railway workers," he says.

"Watch out for each other."

Raised up in a community of women, the boys are proving to be quick studies of the ways of men. Their boisterous play can become suddenly violent. Without formal lessons, they have acquired aggression that surprises them, as if their fists act on their own. Lately they have come home with bloody noses and unexplained bruises.

Evening comes and the boys return with seven men in tow, who take off their hats and awkwardly introduce themselves. Mary looks at Ona and shakes her head. Only an hour before, she had anticipated it.

"What do you think. Will any of them workers follow my boys home? Sniffing around for female company?"

"Very likely," Ona replies. "Regardless of nationality, men can figure it out. If there are boys, there must be mothers."

And sure enough, the men arrive, seeking services that women provide. There is a Frenchman with a bad limp, a swollen foot, and black toes. The Irishman has a stubborn infection.

"It feels like I'm pissing razor blades," he says.

Two of the men are from Iceland. In broken English, they describe the volcano that chased them off their native land. They are father and son, and both have swollen bleeding gums.

The others have no medical conditions, only sad and longing hearts.

End of the Line

"Do you have money?" Ona asks, rubbing her fingertips. "We must cover our own expenses, here." Ona learned long ago that, with men, the exchange of currency is essential. Charging for services earns respect. Helpless women, they think, require control.

The Icelander reaches in his pocket and pulls out a roll of bills.

"We can help," Ona tells them.

Twenty women, twelve children, and a newborn infant are living at Gidaaki in the summer of 1878. Their interests in the railway workers are varied, based on individual talents. Nila takes the Irishman by the hand and leads him away. She will supervise him as he drinks cranberry juice and then she will check his private parts for cankers. Nila has a square body and square face and thinning hair. Although she has suffered a great variety of derogatory names (harridan, battle axe) she is a competent nurse with knowledge of natural remedies and salves.

Mary takes a look at the Frenchman's foot and gets him to prop it up while she heats some water. Ona sends Norman down to Doc Kennedy's office. "You can ride Ginger. And ask Doc Kennedy to come up to the ridge when he has a chance. We may have to amputate a foot. I'd rather he do it, than me."

Norman nods. "It's an ugly looking thing, init? Stinks something awful."

"Away you go, then. Hurry."

The sun disappears behind the bush line and the temperature cools. Ona calls over to Molly, "Fix some raspberry tea for the men with scurvy, will you Molly?"

Molly wears a frilly apron over a gingham dress with long sleeves that cover surprisingly well-defined muscles. Her hair is pulled back tight into a snood at the nape of her neck. Sometimes Ona catches her pushing at her Adams apple as if she hopes to invert it. Molly nods and heads to the cloister. She is mute. By choice.

"There will be a wait," Ona tells the Icelanders. They do not complain. Birdie and Prit are keeping them company. They are Ona's best comfort girls, generous with attention in any language. Josie, Clare and Doll have taken charge of the lonely boys and disappeared.

Kateri and the old ones, the crones, do not rouse themselves from scraping the soft deer hides they are working on. They filled their quota of dealings with men long ago, and would just as soon spit on a man as save his life.

It is fascinating, really, how the presence of men brings an infusion of energy, as if the very air has been stirred by some invisible spoon. Sometimes, if a man is handsome, there is competition. Flirtation. Negotiation. Especially among the childless women. Girls, really, but most of them menstruating. Ona does not miss her monthlies, those cruel humiliations. Dull aches in the abdomen. Tenderness between the legs. Bloody undergarments.

In the bunkhouse, out by the high meadow, Ona's girls comfort a transient population of hunters, warriors, adventurers and loggers. Men of all ages and dispositions come for cures and whiskey and female services, but they do not stay long unless they follow Ona's code. Rough stuff is never tolerated. Sheaths are mandatory to avoid pregnancies and diseases. There is value in keeping men sated. A community of women require some male champions, lest they be seen as vulnerable.

In all the years since her grandfather died, Ona has only had to use his gun four times. She has only killed a man once. To put him out of his misery for a mind turned enemy. But times being as they are, Ona expects she'll be keeping it loaded from here on.

The first train passes through the valley under Gidaaki on November 24, 1878. It rattles bones and loosens teeth. Ona watches the black smoke ejaculating from the locomotive, and marks in her heart the end of an era.

Mary's boys are seven years old. Not twins, nor cousins, but uncle and nephew. Wild with excitement, they tumble down the ridge and chase the train all the way into town. A skittish hound dog they rescued from starvation is close on their heels. The orphan boy, Buck, is no longer with them. He was hired on with the railroad crew. Ona does not expect to see him again. Children must make their own way in the world. Buck proved to be a good worker, and the rail boss promised he would look out for him. Ona is relieved that he is gone. A thinly disguised malevolence festers in Buck's heart, eating away at him from the inside like a tapeworm. Mary's boys were starting to fall under his surly influence. They are disadvantaged enough in their dispositions, fathered as they were by a man who holds a position of influence in Haliburton. A man who has never acknowledged the boys. Scum.

As silence returns to Gidaaki, remnants of smoke drift up to join the low grey clouds. The women shrug and go back to stirring and tending and chopping, solemnly accepting this latest violation. They will learn to bear it, as needs must.

Lydia Kennedy, the doctor's wife, is lost in the forest, shivering as sleet comes out of nowhere to finish her off. She is sunk up to her knees in the marsh. Both her shoes are gone. Did she wear shoes? She can't remember. She only just stepped out her back door while Jane was having her afternoon nap. But a chattering red squirrel drew her to the bush line and a carpet of newly fallen leaves enticed her along the trail.

The red sun drops down through bare branches. Jane will be awake by now, wondering where Mommy is, and Lou will be angry when he returns from his office to find her gone again. Lydia's chest aches and her scalp tingles. She cannot feel her hands and feet. Her lips are numb. The harder she struggles, the deeper she is mired in cold, black goo. So it will end. They will be better off without her.

But wait. There are voices. Boys. So close she can hear them talking. A hound dog barks. Her pulse races with fear of being discovered. How foolish she will look. When they veer away, Lydia feels a flood of relief. Then screams explode out of her like vomit.

Back in the village, a neighbour raises the alarm about the doctor's wee girl, Jane. The mother is a wealthy woman who grew up with servants and has no talent for child care. That is none of Peggy Pemberton's business. With six children of her own, she has enough on her plate. But the ruckus has persisted longer than usual, so she calls her oldest daughter away from piano practice.

"Trudy! The little Kennedy girl is in some distress. Run over and see what's wrong."

Trudy is gone for twenty minutes and Peggy starts to fret, imagining the worst. Then she hears steps on the back porch. Trudy has Jane balanced on her hip, a child almost four years old, yet often mistaken for younger. Big eyes. Thumb in mouth. The face of a bairn who expects something bad to happen.

"She was all alone. Oh, Mum! The house! It's freezing cold inside. The back door was left open and a raccoon was in the larder. She's no housekeeper, that Lydia Kennedy. I had to dig through dirty laundry to find something warm for the poor poppin to wear."

"Hush. Don't speak ill of a neighbour. Here. Sit the girl on the bench and I'll get her a bite to eat." Peggy is broad in the beam but short. Not even five feet tall. Her eyes are squinty in her pudgy face. Her horrid brothers called her Piggy.

Peggy takes a look at Jane and tsk tsks. Puts her hands on her hips and considers how easy her life would be if she lived in the doctor's big brick house. Or if she only had the one bairn, a girl at that. She dips her apron in the dishwater and scrubs the snot off Jane's face. It is like dried glue and requires a good deal of rubbing but the girl takes the punishment.

"What was all that screaming for, Jane. Eh? Next time, instead of hollering, just come here. Understand?"

Jane nods.

"Can ye walk?"

Jane nods.

"Right, then. If ye find yourself alone, or if yer Mam is in trouble, just come get me. Okay love?"

Jane nods.

"Run to the store and fetch Mrs. Crockett, Trude," Peggy says, grabbing a hairbrush and lifting Jane's tangled rat's nest. "Eee gad!"

Trudy skips up the Victoria Street hill and turns right on Pine Street. She arranges her face to look solemn as befitting a bearer of bad news. The bell rings and Alma Crockett looks up from her place behind the cash drawer. She always appears to be cross, does Alma. That is just her way. Her face is set with disappointments. But when Trudy tells her Mrs. Kennedy has disappeared, she does not hesitate.

"Miles," she yells to her husband. "Come up here and watch the front. I have an errand to run." She retrieves her coat, taking care to button it up to her chin. Alma does not have a big wardrobe, but everything she owns is of good quality. She had the coat custom fitted by a reputable tailor in Peterborough and it has worn well. As she adjusts her hat, she glimpses Trudy in the mirror, eyeing the candies.

"Go ahead. Take a few sweets, then."

Trudy fills her apron pocket with a handful of humbugs and follows Alma out the door and down the hill. She can barely keep up with Alma's stride. When they get to the Pemberton's house, Alma does not wait to be invited in. She opens the kitchen door and kneels down in front of Lydia's little girl.

"Well, Jane," Alma says. "Where is Mummy this time?"

Jane shrugs.

"Her mother comes from money, is what I heard," Peggy says.

"Aye. Lydia's uncle is wealthy."

"Lydia is not right in the head."

"She is actually a brilliant woman. But she sometimes has spells."

"I should say! A maniac is what I heard."

"Where? Where did you hear that?"

"At the butcher's," Peggy whispers, realizing that Trudy is listening.

Alma shakes her head and is about to respond when there is urgent knocking at the door. It is Mary, from the Nunnery, with news. She throws her hood back and announces that Mrs. Kennedy has been found.

"She nearly died, poor thing. Wandered away from home without a coat. My boys found her in the marsh. Ona says we must keep her until she recovers." Mary glances at the girl on the bench. A miserable little thing with a pointy chin. She has been up to the ridge many times with her mother and Mary has no use for her, a child who does not take instruction.

"Can you care for the child?" Mary asks.

Peggy hesitates. There is applesauce on the stove needing canning and potatoes to peel for dinner.

"Of course," says Alma.

Trudy watches Mary carefully for signs of wickedness. The women at the Nunnery do bad things with men. But Mary seems calm and capable. Her hair is pulled back and plaited elaborately. She glances at Trudy and winks. Something fun and secret, and perhaps naughty. Trudy's heart skips.

"I can help," Trudy says.

"We'll bring Lydia home as soon as she feels like herself," Mary says. "And she will need some help, Trudy girl, so your offer is welcome. Not all mothers find it easy, you know, caring for a bairn."

Peggy swats at the fruit flies gathering over the apple bin, and takes a second or two to cough away the unbidden clutch of sympathy at her throat. She suffers after every child. Georgie especially, who cried and cried and would not let her sleep. She held a pillow over his head one night and, oh. The glorious silence. Through the window the moon was so bright. Purple shadows on snow. And a fox trotted up and sat under the apple tree her husband planted when they first arrived. Before he built the house, he planted that tree.

The fox looked at her. Witnessed her act. She lifted the pillow expecting to see a dead baby. But Georgie was wide-eyed. He made not a peep. He never cried again, that boy. To this day. And he is ten, now. Peggy knows Mary is right, that mothering can be hard, but no one tells you that when you need to hear it. She vows to take a more Christian attitude toward Lydia.

"I'll talk to Doctor Kennedy," Alma says. "He can surely afford to hire a housekeeper. I know a woman who could run the home efficiently. Thank you, Mary. Tell Ona we are grateful and tell your boys they must come to the store for some sweets."

~ 4 ~

As she lies on the cot in Ona's cabin, recovering, Lydia repeats her name over and over, hoping to identify herself in some way. Was she named for Lydia, in the Bible? That Lydia was humble, but independent. Did her pragmatic mother value those qualities?

"You'll be the death of me, yet," she often accused Lydia. "You almost killed me when you were born. I bled and bled. The bed was full of gore. Your father went out back and dug me a grave, that's how close I came to death's door. That's how hopeful he was of getting a new young wife."

Lydia rolls over and sees Ona, writing nearby at her desk, a quiet presence that makes her feel safe.

"Lydia. You are awake. Are you warm enough?"

"Yes. Thank you, Ona. What day is it?"

"Wednesday. The fifth of December. Are you ready to return home?"

Lydia sighs.

"What is it? What's troubling you?"

"When babies are born, is it possible they come into the world already black with sin?"

"Lord, no. Wherever did you get that idea?"

"My mother claimed I tried to kill her. Can a baby be a murderer?"

"I have attended the births of dozens of babes, Lydia. They are pure and innocent as wee lambs."

"Is there a way to do penance for a sin I don't remember? I feel as if God is punishing me for something."

Ona sits on the chair next to Lydia's cot and takes her hand. "Religion," she says, definitively, "is pure horse shit."

Lydia's Journal:

My husband believes I am not suited to Haliburton, but he is wrong. I love the wilderness. That is what I was promised. That is not what I got. Lou expects me to be a complacent homemaker and proper doctor's wife like his sainted mother. I do not think I ever led him to believe that was my expectation. I fell in love with his pioneering spirit and thought I might accompany him along the waterways in his canoe. I would sketch and paint while Lou paddled. We would make love in a tent while the kettle boiled over the campfire. Our baby would fall asleep in a cradle lined with moss. Lou wanted that life for himself. I thought he knew I wanted that too. But all the while, he was planning to imprison me in a brick house.

Was I not clear about my eagerness to escape my uncle's hollow mansion? Did Lou's mother not read him fairy tales? How many cautionary tales of unhappy princesses trapped behind stone walls does it take to get the point across?

I trusted Lou and allowed him to rescue me. But it turns out he is no valiant prince. He is a selfish ogre. I am to remain indoors with a child who exhausts me. To cook and clean and launder the linen as if I have the capacity of three women trained for these tasks. And what if the sun is shining on Head Lake? And rather than scrub pots on a summer's day I want to float in the water and gaze at the sky. What if the music down the rail line calls me to dance with the gypsies? What if the wind rises and whips the trees into a frenzied invitation? Calling, calling, calling with urgent voices.

What is wrong with the women in this village? They seem resolved to accept drudgery as their due. Bathing children who will only get dirty again. Acquiring goods that need polishing. Look! I want to tell the local ladies. When the lake is sparkling like a jewel, you must go down to the shore and take your shoes off. Instead, I see you washing windows and dressing them with lace curtains that are quickly soiled by flies and yellowed by smoke. Soon you must take them down and wash them again lest you appear slovenly. And why cover your floors with carpets that must be hung outside and beaten and then returned to collect more dirt? And china? My goodness. So many plates. Queen Victoria is the pattern Aunt Sophie selected for me, a botanical design. Dinner plates and salad plates and bread plates and serving platters and different cutlery for each.

There is another way to be in the world. Look up to the ridge. Look at Ona. Wise eyes in a wizened face. Words that are never hurried. Capable hands. She wears a layered wardrobe of practical invention, well suited to the climate and the task at hand. She maintains a shelter well suited to the terrain. She provides sustenance well suited to the abundance of fish and game and growing things. There is structure in her community, with room for freedom. There are processes with room for individual choice. Ona knows that necessity is dictator enough. No need to add the restraints of manmade rules and frivolities. She does as she pleases. Smokes a pipe and drinks whiskey like a man. She is strong like a man, too, and those who seek refuge with her are safe.

Local women look at me and think I am spoiled. Such a lovely home you have, they say, thinking all the time that I do not appreciate my great luck. Imagining how much the doctor's house could be improved with their domestic skills. That is what they call it. The Doctor's House. As if he is the only one living here. I am nothing but a troublesome tenant.

The locals have a way, here in Haliburton, of getting rid of nuisance bears. Back in the bush up behind the mill, you will see a metal washtub hanging on a tree. This is the bear baiting bucket. If a bear gets too familiar, stealing food and scaring people, it is time to fill the washtub with chopped up beaver carcass and pour some frying grease over the mess. Before long the bear comes along and the men shoot her. Sometimes there are cubs. They must shoot the cubs too, to be humane. Civilizing a wild territory can be brutal.

~ 5 ~

1879 -Spring

Every day, the train bullies its way into town. Loud and powerful and dirty, it rips leaves off bushes, trembles lake waters, sends animals fleeing. That's progress. Before it screeches to a stop, the stationmaster stuffs some cotton in ears that have been pretty much ruined by the constant racket. He is a skinny and stooped old fellow whose right arm hangs useless at his side ever since an accident on the TH&B line some years ago. Rather than pay compensation or pension him off, the rail boss sent him to the hinterland. He was not expected to last more than a few months. But Lefty is made of sterner stuff than one would suppose. He spent eight years in Lindsay and did not sicken or die, so they sent him to Haliburton. The end of the Victoria Rail Line.

Every passenger in the parade of arrivals must pass Lefty on their way to the village. Some with raggedy hobo sacks. Some with trunks of clothing and fine china from the old country. Some with the tools of their trade. Some bring strong backs. Some bring books. Some bring the word of the Lord. Lefty has the same poor opinion of all of them until they can prove otherwise. They come with stories of loss and woe. Some stories are true. The majority are convincing lies. He does feel a certain amount of sympathy for the suckers who've come for the free farmland. Only an idiot would look at this highland jumble of rock left by ancient retreating ice and think it possible to make anything grow here. Lefty knows something about the desperation of people with limited options.

The train goes in both directions. People come with various expectations, and lots are disappointed. Inhospitable weather. Inhospitable locals. Inhospitable geography. Inhospitable biting flies. Still, for every person who buys a ticket back to the city, two unload their worldly possessions at the Haliburton Station and ask Lefty for directions.

Lefty wishes he could place bets on who will pass muster and who will turn tail and run. He would be a rich man, wagering on the arrivals, because he is a good judge of character. If there is a shadow of violence or theft or deviancy in their pasts, he can see it in their eyes. Hear it in their voices. Recognize it in a man's stature. He is seldom wrong.

Does a man speak with rough language? Does he tip his hat to ladies and hold the door for them at the Mercantile? Does he drink and use tobacco in public? Does he cheat? Lie? Steal?

Appearance counts for little. Some wealthy toffs will fail to live up to the minimum of decency. Men who arrive dirty and unshod can earn respect through sheer hard work. Opportunities abound for the ambitious as well as the lazy. So much depends on the unfolding of events. Do they listen to advice? Are they kind to children and dogs and old people? Are they moral? Just? Purposeful? In a small village, a man is always under surveillance. Lefty knows a lot about the habits of men. Women he does not pretend to understand at all.

This April day, passengers enter a colder world than the one they left short hours ago. Winter is greedy here in Haliburton. It hangs on and on. Sunshine works hard to reach the muddy street. The granite ridge casts a long shadow from early morning to midday, making everything gloomy, like an abandoned church or a home without a woman.

"Well shit," Lefty says out loud, noticing the manager of the Victoria Railway stepping down from the dining car. Mr. Berger is a German with small hands and a tight ass. An ass so tight, it could turn a hunk of coal into a diamond in no time. He usually arrives with complaints about Lefty's unconventional record-keeping system.

"Send me a bookkeeper, then. I ain't got time for none of that," he told Berger last month. Lefty braces for new criticism, but today Mr. Berger walks right past him and climbs into a carriage. The coroner's carriage.

"Who died?" Sapper McMonies asks. He stuffs a plug of tobacco in his cheek.

"Damned if I know," Lefty says.

"Looks like your boss knows something about it. Must of found another body on railway property. How many is that now? Four?"

"Yep. Four found this side of Kinmount since the snow melted. Poor buggers. Building a rail line through granite and over muskeg. Helluva stupid idea."

"Somebody made money on it, I guess."

"Not you nor me."

A dog noses around a trash bin at the end of the platform and Lefty calls the cur with a whistle. Pats him on the head. Gives him some hardtack out of his pocket.

"Not all them bodies is rail workers," Lefty says. "One was found at that encampment up near Gould's Crossing."

"Tramps and thieves."

"And others, supposedly upstanding citizens."

"Moonshine?"

"Worse. Opium."

"That Chinese powder."

"It's poison, brother. Stay the hell away from it."

An ox cart rattles past on the main road.

"There goes the last of them Finnish settlers. Shameful dealings. Forced off their land like varmints."

Lefty nods. "Good luck to them. They were offered property up in Kennaway by Ona McLeod. I wish them well. I been here hardly four months and seen more lowdown shenanigans than ever I seen in the city."

"Well, it's all deemed legal in courts of law. Hardworking farmers forced off their homesteads because of some fine print in a language they can't even read. Criminal, if you ask me."

"Nobody's gonna ask you nothin', Sapper."

"That's the truth."

"Where I grew up, we had our ways to set things right. Midnight justice, we called it."

"Aye. There's no justice to be found in a court of law when a piece of paper means more than five years of back-breaking labour. Fields cleared, cabins built, barns raised."

"No use to protest. The law wins anyway," Sapper says, his mouth filling up with brown juice. They watch the evicted family head northeast, Mother and Father and young boy on the front bench, an old woman holding a baby in the box of the ox cart. A pile of household goods rattling around them.

"Might be a kindness to shoot them, that's how down and out they look."

"Makes me sick to my stomach." Sapper horks a great quivering gob into the spittoon near the ticket wicket as punctuation. Then he takes a stained linen handkerchief out of his pocket and wipes the dribble from his chin.

"A man would have to be mighty heartless," Lefty says, "to kick a fellow off of his own place where his people is buried out back."

My interest this day is to supervise the burial of one more nameless navvy. An unknown soldier in the war against the wilderness. Lefty, himself, is not long away from the grave. His joints are failing, but his memory is sharp. He sees the small-time swindlers and fornicators and thieves and pays them little mind. They will get sorted out soon enough. Bad luck and stupidity will catch up to them. The true devils rarely stand trial.

Them that's been wronged cannot expect justice. I wish I could help. I wish I could do more than watch folks struggle. All I can offer them is my blessing, although a dead man's blessing has no worth.

~ 6 ~

Reverend Dick Whitlock, singularly unsuccessful at inspiring Toronto congregations, agreed to take on the pastoral responsibilities of St. Mark's Anglican Church in the village of Haliburton. Bishop Marshall awarded him the position after a cursory interview that left Whitlock worrying he may have been hasty in his decision to leave the comforts of city life. But he was anxious to extricate himself from a loathsome incident regarding a missing collection plate and a frivolous accusation by his housekeeper's daughter. The whole affair had impacted his health, caused him to lose sleep, and the opportunity to go north presented a fresh start on the northern frontier.

Back in 1638, Brother Patrick and Father Jerome accompanied a Huron hunting party through Wendake territory, looking for a place to build a Christian mission. Along the way, in the largely uninhabited land of lakes that is now Haliburton County, the black robes drew maps and assigned bullshit names to the waterways. Kashagawigamog, Koshlong, Kawagama, Boshkung, Kushog. Their alphabet was woefully inadequate at translating the sounds of the Ojibwe language. Good-natured and patient, the guides had a laugh at the missionaries' expense. There was much to make fun of. The black robes were like babies in the forest, weak and clumsy.

The priests built their mission in Huronia but their influence was short lived. An Iroquois Shaman had a dream about marauding black crows. The Iroquois Nation didn't mess around. They were suspicious of the black robes, and attacked the mission repeatedly. Over the years that the mission operated, five priests were tortured and killed. They were recognized as martyrs for Catholicism.

Ancient history! The savages were assimilated or exterminated or banished years ago. The Reverend Dick Whitlock expected he had nothing to fear from the lowly immigrants and backwoods hicks of Haliburton.

On Sunday morning, the new bell in the steeple of St. Mark's Church drew Ona to the outcropping that afforded a good view of the village. Like ants to honey, people came from all directions.

Ona contributed a sum of money when the church was first proposed. Not because she had any plans of becoming an Episcopalian, but because Captain Tucker went to the trouble of climbing the trail to ask her, respectfully, if she could see her way to a ten-dollar donation. Ona was impressed by the Captain's vision. His ambitions went beyond personal wealth and success, to include the wellbeing of all. His greed was tempered by a moral code of which she approved.

The Captain wanted Haliburton to prosper. He and his wife, Aliza, had twelve children, a very good start to the population. He also had the distinction of being the village's first Reeve. Ona had some satisfying discussions with him about the factors required to attract and keep the right kind of people to build a thriving village.

"Wilderness requires religion," he told her. "Without a pure life, constant activity and a firm belief in God, nobody will be useful."

"I disagree," she said. "The Protestant work ethic is detrimental to success in this country, Captain. Nothing bad will happen if a day goes by without some accomplishment. If there is an old man in heaven keeping track of a person's productivity, do you not think he is more likely to reward those who respect all living things? Animals and trees and waterways?"

Captain Tucker owned a particularly destructive business, a sawmill. To be fair, he did not invent this process of clearing forests to make way for settlements. He did not invent the system of political and religious control over populations. For him, it all made sense. For him, the universe was unfolding as per God's plan and the new Government of Canada was supporting it by dedicating glebe land for clergy purposes, tax free.

As Ona presented her perspective, Captain Tucker filled his pipe with tobacco and tamped it thoughtfully. He lit it with a small twig from her fire. She liked that he did not answer straight away, giving her a chance to fill her own pipe, which he did not balk at in the slightest. Tobacco, she found, was a tremendous support in decision-making. A conduit for clear thinking. She grew it herself in the high meadow.

The Captain and Ona thought about what the other said and pondered quietly as the shadows lengthened and ferns unravelled under last year's dead leaves. Ona admired the Captain, though his thinking was arrogant like most men of some standing. He thought of the village as one of his children. A child that required his nurturing and protection and influence. She liked being in his company, a man with some education and worldly experience. He used his authority wisely, for the most part, and that was needed in a place where so many did not know each other. Caution and suspicion of neighbours could erupt into violence, especially when they communicated in foreign tongues. A man like the Captain was adept at resolving issues.

"One way to bring people together," he said, "is by building a church, a place of peace and reconciliation. Once a church is built and a pastor installed, the village will have a moral centre."

"Very well, let me offer my financial support. Just don't expect me to become part of the congregation," Ona said. "Follow me."

Captain Tucker ducked his head and entered the low doorway of her cabin. She lit the lamps, and he smiled. An amused sort of smile. Ona thought it was a childlike delight in the unexpected. He stood, hands behind his back, and studied the world maps adorning the walls, the collection of firearms over the mantle, the cabinet of stuffed owls, the shelves of books.

"My grandfather built this cabin in 1820," Ona told him. "Angus McLeod, was his name." She unlocked the top drawer of an oak desk and took out five four-dollar Upper Canada bank notes.

"I haven't heard of him."

"A legend, in his time. Dead near thirty years."

"I shall have the treasurer issue you a receipt for your donation," Captain Tucker said. He shook Ona's hand, as if they were business partners. Ona supposed he felt confident he had won her over, and so far as any man could win Ona McLeod over, he was not wrong.

Good to his word, a 16-by-24-foot log structure overlooking Head Lake was completed. But the church fell short of John Tucker's vision as a sanctuary.

Ona felt no satisfaction whatsoever in the disappointing outcome.

The January day that Captain John Tucker led the elders of St. Mark's Anglican Church to meet Reverend Whitlock at the train station, was clear and cold. He had been expected in time to perform the Christmas service, but a snowstorm made the tracks impassable. So it was that the Reverend, without boots or winter overcoat, slipped on the metal steps of the passenger car and landed unceremoniously on the icy platform. The church elders hurried to pick him up. They apologized profusely as he limped unhappily to the waiting horse-drawn sleigh, and shot worried looks at each other about the stamina of their new leader.

Reverend Dick Whitlock was not an impressive figure, even while standing behind a solid oak pulpit. Pale of complexion, he appeared to have spent too much time in a windowless cellar. His voice had a strangled, high-pitched timbre which made his pronouncements about heaven and hell unconvincing. Children wiggled. Men coughed and scratched and nodded off. Women cast their eyes down upon the floor and grieved a little in their hearts for the faith leader they had hoped for. John Tucker blamed himself for trusting the recommendation of the Bishop rather than travelling to Toronto and interviewing prospective candidates in person.

He expected an enlightened man who could bring culture to the region. A definitive man to settle disagreements. An energetic man, to stir tired souls. It was difficult, sometimes, to justify the Lord's plan when a cabin burned down, or when a child died of the fever, and it was clear, after only a few dreary sermons, that Reverend Whitlock's droning voice had no comfort for the bereaved.

"Fear not," he told the congregants in a timid voice that fooled no one. He, obviously, was the one among them who was afraid. The farmers in this congregation had no time to waste on fear. They were clearing the land of rocks and trees. Piling stones to make chimneys. Chopping wood. Raising barns. Planting crops around immovable boulders. Harvesting stunted little root vegetables that would not last through the winter. They were hungry. They were tired. Their souls were weary. But they were not afraid. When all your energy went into keeping your family warm and filling their bellies, there was no room at the table for fear.

Loggers, likewise, could not pause to be fearful. Death was as common as spit. Every winter in the bush made the grave seem like a welcome respite. The Reverend's stories about paradise sounded as believable as the brochures that lured them to this country with promises of unlimited bounty and self-sufficiency.

Captain John Tucker sat alone on a rough-hewn bench at the back of the empty church. He liked the quiet. His home was not quiet, what with twelve children and four of them not of school age as yet. His business was not quiet, what with the saws screaming through pine and spruce and maple and hemlock, and men's voices yelling over the din. This was a peaceful place.

A breeze crept in through the double doors, carrying with it the music of rustling poplars. John closed his eyes and prayed to God to ease the strain in his chest. Too many people counted on him. His family, his employees, the electorate.

John Tucker did not want to be Reeve, but it seemed there weren't many citizens willing to step up and take on municipal responsibilities. It required an even temperament, some vision, and literacy. The town was short on people who could read and write and calculate. That woman, Winona McLeod, she would make a good Reeve. If only she was a man. The rumours about the Nunnery as a place of ill repute were unfounded, as far as his own observations went. It seemed more like a house of charity to him.

As a young man serving in the Merchant Marines, John travelled widely, following one gold rush after another. He recognized a whore when he met one. And he met his fair share of atheists, too. Ona did not fit his idea of either. It seemed she had a primitive trust in nature, like the natives he met in Australia. Like the Eskimos he met in the far north. Like the Indians at Rice Lake near Peterborough. And yet she was clearly an educated woman with an interest in community matters. And she had money. Curious. Everyone in Haliburton had a past shrouded in a certain amount of secrecy. He tried to judge each man and woman by what he observed with his own eyes, not by the stories they told, or the stories told about them.

John Tucker admired reliable men. Men who took seriously their responsibilities. He could not abide a lazy man or a drunk or a man who couldn't keep himself clean. Even a poor man could jump in the river and scrub the day's labour off him. The stink of animals. The stain of the soil.

"Have some pride," he told slovenly employees. "Clean up or find other work."

But above all, John Tucker put store in generosity. In his experience, wealthy citizens were the least generous. The manager of the Dominion Bank gave nothing toward the church erection fund. Alexander Smith put John off with promises to donate something at a future date, implying that it would be worth the wait.

Meanwhile, others came forward with joy in their hearts. The Crocketts donated the stained glass window depicting St. Mark and his winged lion. A Mason and Hamlin organ was donated by the widow of Thomas Chandler Haliburton. A carved oak pulpit arrived all the way from Buffalo, New York, a gift from the parents of the innkeeper. Clark Cook bought the bell. Sapper McMonies, local jack-of-all-trades, travelled to an auction in Kingston and purchased twenty pews for twenty dollars. They were scorched but not destroyed during a catastrophic fire in the Wesleyan Church. Sapper sanded and varnished the burned bits. The pews looked brand new.

Everything went according to plan, except for the ill-advised hiring of Reverend Dick Whitlock whose collar and cassock hung loosely on his thin frame. A graduate of Knox College, Whitlock's application for the remote position was endorsed by the Lord Bishop of Toronto himself. On paper, he seemed the ideal candidate. Too late, John Tucker received a letter from an esteemed friend in Toronto with a list of concerns and cautions. Unfortunate to say the least. But John intended to fix his mistake. Every problem had a solution.

Reverend Dick Whitlock adjusted his tippet and entered the sanctuary. The congregation rose and opened the new hymnals to page three. Trudy Pemberton stomped on the pedals of the pump organ and played "Holy, Holy, Holy." The Reverend cringed as the girl hit a flat instead of a sharp, but she had a pretty curve to her lower spine that made up for mistakes.

The pews groaned as people took their seats. Dick waited for silence.

"The first reading is from Hebrews 3:7 to 14," he said. He tried to project his voice, as John Tucker had suggested, but it strained his vocal cords and he coughed. Paused. Took a sip of water.

"Do not harden your hearts, as happened in the Rebellion, on the Day of Temptation in the wilderness. Your ancestors challenged me and tested me. And so, in anger, I swore that not one would reach the place of rest I had for them."

The Reverend looked up, hoping to see nods of understanding, but instead his eyes landed on a frowning Alexander Smith, arms crossed in a challenging way.

"Take care, brothers, that there is not in any one of your community with a wicked mind. Keep encouraging one another so that none of you is hardened by the lure of sin."

He took another sip of water and replaced the bookmark in the Bible.

"The word of the Lord," he announced, hoping his voice carried to the back.

"Thanks be to God," the congregation responded.

Trudy started pumping the pedals and pulling the stops and the congregation rose once again to sing "Thine be the Glory."

Reverend Whitlock had taken a little too much nerve tonic that morning. His sermon echoed in his ears. The words were blurry on the page, and he missed an entire paragraph, but carried on. He was distracted by the oldest Tucker girl tatting lace in the front row. Her mother, Aliza, reached across two other siblings and grabbed it away. Behind the Tucker pew, were bankers and business owners. Further back were farming families and labourers. The Reverend finished his sermon, led the congregation in The Lord's Prayer, and nodded to Trudy who started pumping in preparation for the Offertory hymn.

Reverend Whitlock felt some resentment as he watched Captain Tucker passing the collection plate. The Captain had berated his sermon last week.

"It is not necessary, Reverend, to embarrass people with sermons about tithing. There is hardship in the community. People give as they are able. Ten percent of nothing is nothing."

"Do you not suspect," he had responded, "that there are those in the congregation, specifically the transient men in the back row, who may be helping themselves to a nickel now and then? A nickel that belongs to God? Why else would ruffians come to church?"

"I suspect, Reverend, that they miss their mothers in the old country. They miss her Bible stories of overcoming hardship. Jonah. Ruth. Job. Noah. Difficult journeys like the ones they had themselves. They come to church for reassurance, sir. You must give it to them."

"Tithing is God's law, Captain. Not mine."

John Tucker strode to the front with the collection plate and set it on the altar and returned to his seat thinking that the church had been a more welcoming place when it was a frame without a roof. When Jameson Bull played hymns on his accordion. For a time, he worried that St. Mark's was stuck with Reverend Whitlock, at least for the agreed upon term of four years. But that was before John Tucker followed the Reverend on his "pastoral visits." It seemed Dick Whitlock wasn't visiting the sick and lonely after all. He was visiting the squatters out at Gould's Crossing, availing himself of opium-laced tonics. At the upcoming church council meeting, John intended to share his discovery with the elders. They would begin the review process. He would put the Reverend on the train himself.

Alma Crockett was one of the first to hear about John Tucker. Dropped dead, so he did. Dr. Kennedy had just walked into the store. The bell jangled and then jangled again as John Junior came running in yelling, "My father's keeled over at the mill, Doc. You must come!"

~ 7 ~

1879 - Summer

Doctor Louis Kennedy was a small man. Five foot six, and slight. Even in his heartiest days when he was eating well, he weighed no more than one hundred and twenty pounds. As a swimmer, he struggled to stay afloat. There was not an ounce of fat on him.

Scrawny, you might say as a way of describing him. But only from a distance. Up close, he had a kind of intensity like a magic trick. Like candles that burn too brightly, people were drawn to him. Women, especially. Some got burned.

Louis Kennedy was a terrible husband. He was a negligent father. But he didn't know it. For a man with so many skills and abilities, you would think he could figure it out. But, alas. Domestic harmony was not something he considered to be his responsibility.

Things had always come easily to him. He completed his medical degree at Trinity College in two years, impressing the faculty with his diagnostic accuracy. He was an athlete, excelling in sports. He was a woodsman, enchanted since childhood with the adventure stories of Daniel Boone, the Kentucky pioneer who claimed never to be lost in the woods.

Not ever in his youthful fantasies, did Louis expect to become a doctor like his staid and judgmental father. He would surely be an adventurer, living by his wits in the unmapped Northern Territories.

Civilization was creeping onto the Canadian frontier at unprecedented rates, but young Louis expected he could outrun it.

It was his mother who suggested he should consider being a woodsman trained in the medical sciences. Someone bringing knowledge of modern healing to the backwoods. When he was twelve, she watched him save a stray dog after a horse stepped on him. Louis retrieved the suture kit from his father's black bag. He stitched the wound together with strips of bovine intestine. The dog survived, although the scar was a nasty one.

Louis Kennedy was not a personable boy. He was something of a loner at school, oblivious to the girls who sat close to him in study hall. Isobel was amused at the number of young ladies who happened to stroll past their Oakville home on weekends. Looking up from a book of poetry or an embroidery hoop, she would shrug and wave. Her only child was splashing through Sixteen Mile Creek, acting like a savage. Strange, she thought, how young girls seem to set their hearts on the most inappropriate suitors. It has always been that way. She herself was intrigued by the gardener's son when she was sixteen. She mistook his brooding for passion and only recognized her error after reading Wuthering Heights.

Isobel knew her only child would never amount to much of a family man. She hoped he would marry a strong-willed woman of independent interests and low expectations for conversation. Louis, her beloved son, was a boy with a faraway look in his eyes. A longing to be elsewhere. It was a constant worry for Isobel that she would look into his bedroom one morning and find a note on his desk. A farewell note. I am off to make my way in the wilderness, it would say. So she congratulated herself when Louis graduated from medical school at the top of his class, and went on to complete his residency at Hamilton General.

Then he married Lydia MacNab, a most inappropriate choice. Lou made the same fatal mistake as throngs of men before him;

thinking with his little head instead of his big head. Isobel saw nothing but struggle for the couple. The girl was smart enough, but fragile. An orphan. Her parents died and left an oozing sort of sore in her heart that Louis would never cure.

Doctor Louis Kennedy started his rounds early every morning. Everyone knew his wife was no cook and he was fed well enough in farmhouse kitchens. Patients often paid him in baked goods or preserves. They might leave a chicken at his office, or a pot of Irish stew at the side door of his home.

After his morning house calls, Louis went straight to his office, avoiding the drama of Lydia's hysterics. There were always people sitting on benches in his waiting room who managed to sort themselves out according to urgency. A mother carrying an unresponsive child, or a lad with a severed finger would get the spot closest to the examining room. Louis stayed until all were seen. Now that the train was delivering city people into the backwoods, he was locking his office door later and later.

One particularly beautiful July day when Louis would have preferred to launch his canoe and paddle along the quiet shores of Lake Kashagawigamog, he found himself trapped in his office, inundated with lacerations, infections, and summer fevers. It was seven o'clock when he ushered the last patient out of his examination room, only to find three women standing shoulder to shoulder in his waiting room. Alma Crockett, Winona McLeod and a woman he did not recognize. The women were all taller than him and together probably outweighed him by fifty pounds. Each one independently presented a force to be reckoned with. Together they looked like a stone wall. Lou understood that this was not a medical visit.

"May we take a few minutes of your time, Doctor Kennedy?" Ona said, pleasantly.

"Of course, ladies," Louis answered graciously, seeing no other option.

"This is Hannah Ogilvie. She has just arrived from Peterborough and seeks a position as a housekeeper."

Hannah extended her gloved hand and clasped the doctor's bare one. He had an elfin quality about him. Her first impression was of a man she could improve. He was dishevelled. Hannah considered how well he would look with a starched collar and pressed trousers.

"We are grateful in this town, Doc, for your services. But we feel you may be too occupied with your practice to understand the difficulties your wife is experiencing," Ona said.

"Ah. Yes," Louis looked down at his scuffed brogues. He was baffled by a wife who couldn't cook an egg or chop a bit of kindling to light the fire in the kitchen stove. Manual labour was not part of the adventurous life she envisioned when Lou brought her up to Haliburton. Perhaps she imagined herself as an Anglo Saxon Pocahontas, bringing beauty and art to the wilderness. Louis was captivated by her, a young woman who knew the names of all the trees and plants and flowers and birds and constellations. A woman with a hearty appetite for outdoor love-making.

"I appreciate your friendship with Lydia. She's not having an easy…"

Alma interrupted him. "You need a housekeeper. Lydia is unwell and Jane is neglected."

Hannah looked embarrassed, but Louis appreciated a plain speaker like Alma. He listened to enough mumbling in the course of a day and had no time for it.

"And, Hannah? You are available?" he asked without hesitation.

"Yes, sir, Doctor Kennedy. I am recently widowed and looking for a live-in position." She reached into her handbag. "I have references."

"The recommendation of these two ladies are all the reference I need," he said. "I apologize for my poor response to the crisis in my own house. I have been expecting Lydia to recover. My consultations with colleagues in Hamilton who specialize in women's health have not had the desired effect."

Alma glanced at Ona.

"If you will allow me, I can provide some herbal teas to calm Lydia's troubled mind."

"Yes. Of course. Thank you, Ona. Any natural remedies would be most appreciated. In fact, I would like to accompany you to where they grow so I can identify them. You must help me understand the doses. The cautions, if any."

"Of course. I am happy to collaborate, especially in the area of gynaecology."

"You have medical training?"

"She has been delivering babies since before you were born," Alma said.

The sound of the office door creaking open ended the meeting. Alma agreed to take Hannah to the doctor's house to introduce her to Lydia and get her settled in the extra bedroom intended for Louis's mother, should she ever visit. Off they went, passing an elderly man with rheumy eyes on their way out.

Lydia did not answer the door when Alma knocked. Darkness was creeping over the village and the lamps remained unlit in the doctor's house. Alma felt discouraged. She had visited earlier in the day to prepare her friend for Hannah's arrival. Anticipating Lydia's reaction, Alma was armed with a dozen reasons why a housekeeper would be helpful.

"You will be free to pursue your own interests," Alma promised as she filled the kettle and put fuel in the stove and started clearing the clutter on the kitchen counter. "Come, come. Let's freshen the sheets in the spare room for Hannah. She is an efficient woman, covering my place at the store as we speak. I trust her. You must trust her."

When she left the doctor's house at three o'clock, all was calm.

Much can happen in a few hours.

Hannah put her bag down. She crossed her hands in front of her, waiting to enter or retreat. Alma called out to Lydia and, hearing nothing, proceeded into the main room. There was a rustling behind the easy chair.

"Jane. Girl! You startled me. Where's Mama?"

"Gone to bed."

"Ah! Well. Mama must be tired. Come and meet Hannah, Jane. She is here to help."

Lydia's Journal:
September 1879

Now that Lou has hired Hannah to keep house, I have more time to get out, but I am lost in this village.

At Lou's suggestion, I started attending meetings at the Women's Institute. They are a formal group of ladies, quite concerned, it would seem, with appearances. I arrived bareheaded to my first meeting and it took me some time to interpret their disapproving glances. Peggy Pemberton drew me aside.

"Lydia," she whispered, "A hat is considered proper at these meetings.".

I laughed. And then covered my mouth and pretended to cough when I noticed the attention it drew. Heavens! A hat? Really? If only they knew how comical they looked under all those feathers and lace and bows and frippery.

I signed up to be a speaker at the next meeting, thinking that these ladies could benefit from a little loosening up. It was quite the disaster.

"Why exhaust yourselves with expectations set by your husbands?" I queried from the podium. "Is it not time to rebel against society's expectations? We might start by smashing our china dishes and organizing treks into the woods. We could take a field trip to The

Nunnery and learn about medicinal herbs that grow wild in the meadows and forests. Ona McLeod is a tremendous, unappreciated resource," I told them. "Think of the lovely opportunities that will open up to us once we denounce the time-wasting activities that occupy us. We might paddle up the lakes to sketch local landscapes," I said. I held up one of my watercolour paintings. A study of a jack-in-the-pulpit that I was particularly proud of.

The eyes of the women seated in front of me were empty of understanding. I was flushed with the passion of my topic until I noticed that the audience was looking at me as if I was speaking Greek. The only thing I convinced them of was the thing they suspected all along. That I was unbalanced. I gripped the podium, feeling dizzy. The president, Mrs. Prudence Bell, stood and thanked me for sharing my philosophy and then she went on to the next item on the agenda.

"Do you want to know how to get stains out of carpets? Blood? Ink? Oil?"

The ladies murmured and nodded at each other. Yes, indeed.

Peggy Pemberton rose from her chair in the last row as I headed for the cloakroom, and motioned that I should come sit beside her. I accepted her offer, knowing she imperilled her own reputation to make it. The comfort she provided by simply holding my hand cannot be described.

No, I thought. I do not want to learn how to get rid of stains. But I listened, nevertheless. Like an alien who must learn to survive on foreign shores, I forced myself to sit through a tedious discussion on a variety of remedies. Next, Mrs. Lawrence demonstrated a new crochet pattern for antimacassars. If the women found this presentation boring, they were very clever at disguising it. As for me, I wanted to grab Mrs. Lawrence's crochet hook and stick it in my eye.

Lydia's Journal

April, 1880

Despair, in the confines of my house, is crushing. After Lou leaves for his rounds, I head off. Jane has stopped asking to accompany me. She is quite content to help Hannah with the washing up. They get along like a house on fire, those two, and if I was a natural mother, I suppose I would be a little jealous of my housekeeper. But, oh! The relief that floods me as I walk away! If the weather is fine, I climb the ridge. The women at the Nunnery do not think it strange or wasteful of me to sketch a flower or a portrait. In fact, they all want a likeness of themselves and their children. I am encouraged by their sincere praise.

Sometimes I visit Alma, the shopkeeper. I sit with her behind the counter and we converse between customers. Alma agrees with my assessment of the women at the Institute. "Never mind those old hens," she says. I confide in her and feel better afterward, like lancing a boil.

My neighbour, Peggy, worries about me. She kindly allows me to sit in her kitchen.

"I am just about to put the kettle on," she calls across the yard if she sees me pacing on my porch. I try to think what is so comforting about her kitchen. It is small and cluttered, with jumbles of bowls and baskets on open shelves. But it feels safe. Peggy hums as she works. She kisses her youngest atop his head and bounces him on her lap then lets him down to crawl about with the blind old dog. And there is a ginger cat that comes and goes. A good mouser. There is always soup on the hob, and bread rising and a clock that ticks rather too loudly. Peggy has swollen ankles and her hips ache and she has a gentle reassuring way of complaining about life. Her observations about men make me laugh.

How dare they take credit for being good providers, she says. Who is providing warm meals? Clean clothes? Obedient children? And who is providing relief from the persistent discomfort in their bulging britches!

That last question troubles me. I have not been fulfilling my matrimonial duties. So. Who is providing relief for my husband's discomfort? I wonder.

Lydia's Journal
August 1880
Lou and Hannah have set my own daughter against me. I see how Jane looks at me, with fear in her eyes. I was a little afraid of my mother too. She was oddly hollow. Dark as a lamp without a wick. I suppose I wasn't an easy child, trying to provoke her out of her silence, but I longed for a kind word.

How difficult is it to say, "There, there, child. Everything will be all right." And yet, I do not seem capable of uttering these words to Jane.

I was twelve when my parents died. Father first. Halfway between the outhouse and the back door. Mother moaned and soiled her bed and turned blue. Cholera. Neighbours all along Stoney Creek were getting sick. Our farmhouse was haunted by soldiers who died nearby on the battlefield, and the ghosts of my parents rose from their dead bodies and walked among them. I crouched behind the barn, waiting for my guts to explode out of me.

Except for a little cramping in my stomach, nothing happened. I milked the cow. I scattered some feed for the chickens. A cart clattered by on the road and I thought to run after it but I let it pass. The sun was low in the sky when I opened the latch to the summer kitchen and gathered a supper of stale bread and a slice of ham.

I went down to the creek and ate my meal, thinking I might survive. The water was poisoned, I had heard the neighbour tell Mama. Long grasses floated under the surface like a drowned woman's hair.

After the moon rose, terror seized me. Perhaps I am the last living person on earth, I thought. I mounted Firefly and rode west on King Street toward Uncle's house. I was very relieved to see vagrants in Gore Park and a Constable on Patrol checking the doors of businesses on King Street to make sure they were locked.

The windows of Dundurn Castle reflected sunrise as I approached and the cook, Beasley, was up and about the day's baking.

"Oh! Lydia! Sweet Jesus! Look at you!"

Aunt Sophie and Uncle Alan had travelled to their country cottage. They would return when the epidemic was past. Beasley stripped me naked and dumped bucket after bucket of water over my head and scrubbed me with harsh soap and made me rinse my mouth with charcoal. She sequestered me in an empty bedroom in the staff quarters for the better part of a week.

A young Irish girl brought my tray and let me outside to get fresh air. She escorted me about the gardens, keeping a fair distance. We sat by the lake and watched the swans.

"I'm sorry for your troubles, Lass," she said. "I lost me Mum and Da when I was younger than you. It's a hard thing. But, sure, you'll be all right. Yer hardy and ye have a determination about you."

I was not accustomed to kind words. They angered me. How dare she? How dare she presume to know I would be all right? I was not all right. I was a wreck.

~ 8 ~

October 1880

The Tucker house was an imposing yellow brick structure, anchoring the corner of Maple and Mountain Streets. Captain John Tucker chose the strategic location for his large family, within walking distance of his business, a sawmill on the Drag River. But not so close as to be inconvenienced by the racket. Across the street in the other direction was the municipal building, where Tucker became the first to occupy the office of Reeve. He also served as the first Justice of the Peace. Human failings came knocking, even in the backwoods. Especially in the backwoods. Gamblers, drinkers, fighters and thieves must be disciplined. Most villagers were honest. Some were honest once but lost the taste for it. John was tough but fair.

Well-travelled and knowledgeable about the ways of the world, John Tucker learned a lot about human nature watching men squander their health and their morals and their very lives over a few gold nuggets in California and Australia. By 1860, he had his fill of adventuring. He wanted to build something far removed from wars and cruelty and he had a vision of raising a family in the wilderness where his influences would be absolute. John Tucker achieved all that successfully, and then dropped dead of a bad ticker.

Aliza Tucker collects a pile of her husband's clothing and selects two turkey pies from the larder. Her fine home is staffed by a housekeeper, a cook and a nanny. John left her with twelve children to raise, but he did not leave her destitute. She hitches the roan to the buckboard and follows Mountain Street to the end where it narrows and steepens. The wagon bumps along a segment of corduroy, and then the wheels hit a patch of switch grass. Finally, just past the half way point, Jenny and Pip speed up, their hooves clip-clopping along a familiar granite path. On the left, a cliff drops away down, down toward the Drag River, a river that raged and flooded last April. Now it moves lazily toward Head Lake.

Finally, near the summit, Aliza enters a golden corridor that marks the edge of the Nunnery. Bright yellow poplars. Parchment yellow beech trees. Orangey yellow maples. All fluttering against a blue sky. The entire area was like this when John and Aliza arrived eighteen years ago.

"Such harmony!" Aliza says as Molly guides the horses to an open-sided stable. Molly made Aliza uncomfortable when they were first introduced, but now her exaggerated feminine gestures, like those of an actor in a play, seem only to offer gentle hospitality.

Molly expresses her deepest sympathy for the passing of Captain Tucker by folding her hands together in a gesture of sorrow and looking skyward.

"Thank you, Molly," Aliza says. "It is nearly six months since he passed. I am not myself, yet, but I feel better every day. Especially days like this when the sun shines. Gloomy skies make me cry." It is curious, Aliza thinks, that she feels compelled to fill the silence between them. She most certainly does not want Molly to think she is feeling sorry for herself. She knows something of Molly's story and understands her suffering is far worse than anything Aliza has experienced. Molly and her older sister signed on as kitchen help at a lumber camp down Buckhorn way to escape a bad situation at home. But children raised in fear have a way of flinching and cringing that invites a cruel response out in the world. They are like beacons for evil-doers.

Aliza would like to know, but dares not ask, if Molly feels safer dressed as a woman, or more comfortable. Or what. Aliza's second-youngest son, Aubrey, is feminine in his preferences. He would rather cross-stitch than play kick ball with other boys. Last year, John disciplined him rather severely for putting rouge on his cheeks and strutting about in his sister's satin slip.

"It's for his own good," John said when Aliza protested. "He will be seven soon."

"Shall I take him to be counselled by Reverend Whitlock? Perhaps…"

"Lord, no! Keep the child away from that man."

But now John is gone and Aliza must use the resources available to her. Dick Whitlock is an odd one, to be sure. But he has been most supportive since she started taking Aubrey to the church for Bible study. Not every man need chop down trees, shoot bears, arm wrestle. Indeed, the world is filled with gentle men who prefer the arts. Writing, studying, theatre, music. What a relief! Aubrey shall pursue these things without wearing women's clothing. Shall he not? Every gentle boy does not end up like Molly.

"John Junior has developed some stomach troubles," Aliza says to Molly. "He is losing weight, but won't go to the doctor. I hope Ona has something to treat him. Here, Molly. Take these pies. The children might like them. My cook is very talented at making pastry."

Molly accepts Aliza's offering and goes off to find Ona.

While she waits, Aliza looks about her. Women come and go, crossing the cloister as if it were the quadrangle at Queens University in Kingston, a city where Aliza once hoped to live, but now cannot imagine existing amid so much hustle and bustle. Such silence here. Such peace. Birch branches shudder and leaves flutter down from above. A child with ginger curls comes and sits on her lap and rests a sleepy head on her breast. Boy or girl she cannot tell.

"Aliza," Ona says. "I have been thinking about you, in your troubles."

"I brought some of the Captain's things," Aliza says. "John Junior claims they are far too old-fashioned to suit him. But they are of good quality." She nods over to the wagon. "You know men in need...?"

"Yes. Always. They will be much appreciated. How is John Junior? You are worried about him."

"Only because of his reluctance to talk about his symptoms or seek treatment. I suspect he is trying too hard to fill his father's shoes, now that he has taken on an adult role at the sawmill. Poor lad. He is only fifteen. It may be too much for him. Everyone seems to feel it necessary to tell him he is the man of the family now."

Aliza waits while Ona retrieves a small brown bottle with a cork in the top.

"Bismuth salts," she explains, handing it over. "A tablespoon before dinner. Try it for a week and see if his digestion improves."

"Thank you, Ona." Aliza pulls a small beaded drawstring bag out of her coat pocket. "How much do I owe you for this?"

"Put your purse away. I have a favour to ask. I am concerned about Lydia Kennedy."

"The doctor's wife? Yes. I would say your concerns are valid. I have seen her, lately, traipsing past my house on her way to that gypsy encampment on the rail line."

"Yes. Well. I was treating her with St. John's wort. It seemed to improve her mood and her thinking. But she stopped coming. Then she appeared yesterday, dishevelled and jittery. She wanted to share her dreams, lucid imaginings that she believed to be true."

"Indeed. I have seen her conversing with ghosts. I worry that she is seeking relief for her troubles in dangerous ways."

"Could you possibly pay Lydia a visit? And let me know her current condition?"

"All right. Of course, Ona. Your intuition is often correct. I hope we can help her."

Aliza climbs up into her carriage and turns the horses toward home. It is a relief to share her burdens of concern with a woman such as Ona. The difficult thing about this town is the lack of family. An odd worry for a woman who has twelve children! But Aliza misses her sisters and her female cousins. If she was still living in Peterborough, she would benefit from their wisdom, and the reassurance of knowing that the children have women relatives nearby who can take on the mothering role should she sicken or die. Everyone in Haliburton has been separated from loved ones, of course. Grandparents are back in the old country, aunts and uncles scattered to the winds. Orphans are common. Her children will have the benefit of each other's company as they grow to adulthood. Their children will have cousins nearby. Dozens of cousins, she hopes. That is a comfort.

Aliza heads downhill in the waning light. Quiet now, after the first frost. The crickets are done their chirping for this season. Her heart quickens as a figure appears ahead. She worries about the travellers. Men who arrive ragged and alone, some of them appearing quite desperate. But she identifies this man as Sapper, a local handyman. Not someone to fear in the gathering darkness.

"Evening, Mrs. Tucker."

"Good evening to you, Mr. McMonies," she calls. The recent census has given her the advantage of knowing all the citizens in the village. She recorded their names in the official documents herself, in her best script.

"Enjoy your visit," she calls after him.

"I always do," he says, cheerfully.

~ 9 ~

Lydia's Journal:

November 1880

Lou claims Reverend Whitlock is not suited to the ministry, but I have had the opportunity of late to speak with him on a number of topics unrelated to religion. Like me, he feels limited living in a place such as this.

We are hemmed in, he complains. There is a lack of hidden places, ironically, now that great swaths of forest have been clear cut from Donald to Kennaway and down to Minden.

It is true. We are open to scrutiny wherever we go. My husband is given a report of my whereabouts by citizens who consider it their concern if I wander out toward Mud Lake, or climb the hill to the Nunnery. Or visit the gypsies at Gould's Crossing. It was Reverend Whitlock who recommended their energizing tonic.

"Just one teaspoon, Mrs. Kennedy, and it's like I've climbed out of a deep well. The very air is easier to breathe. Surely, Jesus would approve of such a miracle."

I agree.

But I have been careless and greedy and spent the housekeeping money and sold the rings Aunt Sophie gave me. My memory is bad. My nerves are very bad. And now I find myself confined in this brick house. I am draining. Like the doomed marshlands, diverted by dams to fuel the mills.

What benefit is there in morality? It is no escape from mortality.

It has been weeks now that Lydia has been confined to her room. She tries to draw in her sketchbook, but her hand won't hold the pencil. She is exhausted but cannot sleep. Some invisible evil is feeding on her like a hungry parasite.

The room feels hot but when she tries to open the window, she finds the casement locked.

"Where are my things? Where is my robe?"

There is a delicate rap at the bedroom door. It is not Hannah, rough and abrupt. It is not Jane, tentative and wary.

"Come in."

"Hello, Mrs. Kennedy. We met at the Women's Institute last June. At the Strawberry Social. My name is Aliza Tucker."

"Yes," Lydia says with a slight slur. "Pardon my appearance. I have been unwell." She props herself up in bed and looks pleased to have a visitor. Like an actress, she remembers her role and even retrieves her lines from some distant play.

"Please. Have a seat. May I offer you some refreshment?"

"No. Do not trouble yourself." Aliza smells unwashed hair and an overflowing piss pot. She arranges herself on the upholstered chair and discreetly pulls a perfumed hanky from her coat pocket.

"How is the Captain?"

"I am sorry to say that the Captain passed away some months ago."

"Oh. I apologize. I have been... out of circulation." Lydia looks around the room, searching for threats among the shadows. Satisfied they are alone, she scooches out from under the covers and sits on the edge of the bed, trying unsuccessfully to cover her thin, scaly legs with her twisted night-gown. "May I confide in you, Mrs. Tucker?"

"Please call me Aliza, Mrs. Kennedy."

"And you must call me Lydia."

"Lydia. You can be assured that anything you say to me will be held in strictest confidence."

"Aliza, I am being held prisoner here. You must help me." Her voice is an urgent whisper. "It may not appear so. I am not kept in chains. But my husband is poisoning me."

"It was Ona sent me to check on you. She is concerned about your wellbeing. How can we help?"

Lydia tries to stand and crumples to the floor. She is thin. Her fingernails are bitten to the quick. Aliza is wary, now. Lydia is clinging to her, like a desperate toddler.

"We must get you well, my dear. I will consult with Ona and then we will make a plan to..."

"Please. Take me with you."

"Not today. When you are stronger. I promise."

Aliza uncurls Lydia's fingers from her wrist.

Lydia has lost the gist of the conversation. Forgotten this lady's name. She reminds her of someone. The matron at Château Mont-Choisi where Lydia learned to paint pansies on porcelain tea cups.

"Am I dying? Please tell me. Am I dying?"

But the lady is gone and the door is locked.

Lydia drifts in and out. Back and forth through time. She is selecting a gown for an ostentatious party with wealthy young debutantes. She is playing whist with Aunt Sophia's card club. She is watching as her mother's coffin is lowered into a hole in Woodlawn Cemetery.

Always contrary. Always disobedient. Always flirting with catastrophe. A bad girl!

Lydia refused the romantic advances of the stuffy young men directed her way by Uncle Allan. She ignored the lectures by Aunt Sophia, about her growing reputation as a girl who was too fussy for her own good.

"Father and I did not invest in your education so that you could choose a husband at your leisure, Lydia. To date, you have spurned four bachelors of good breeding."

"Auntie, really. I couldn't bear to marry an accountant or a professor."

"Who, pray tell, could you bear to marry?"

"An adventurer."

"Adventurers do not make good husbands, Lydia. They are like pirates. A woman in every port. They do not make good fathers, either."

"An explorer, then. Like those friends of Uncle's who go off on expeditions. I could accompany my husband. Take notes. Write about the discoveries."

"I do not think you would care for the deprivations that one must suffer far from civilized society."

"Civilized society bores me," Lydia said.

That summer, Lydia was allowed greater freedoms. Or, as Aunt Sophie put it, enough rope to hang herself. She did exactly that when she boldly introduced herself to a young man who pulled his canoe onto the beach where she was reading Wordsworth. His description of the Northern Townships intrigued her and her bare feet intrigued him and they talked until the sun was low in the sky.

And, ah! Yes. Finally Lydia recognizes the floral wallpaper. She walks to the window on painful feet and pulls open the heavy drapes. A night without moon or stars. Another day has passed by. Lost. She flips the small wooden slat at the base of the window to reveal three round ventilation holes and presses her nose as close as she can to breathe some fresh air. She is so thirsty for it. Woodsmoke drifts in a haze above the dark houses. Down by the lake someone has a bonfire blazing.

"What time is it?"

When I first started roaming this village, I sensed morbid fear every time I crossed paths with the living. There goes Old Ladder, the ghost, I imagined them saying as they hurried past me through dark streets. Drunken loggers leered off in the opposite direction. Elderly ladies crossed themselves and begged for mercy. Children called for their mothers.

I have come to understand that the living do not fear me. They do not even see me. They see a guttering candle, a dance of dead leaves, a glimpse of regret. It is their own mortality they dread. But now, in this room, something has changed. The doctor's wife has traipsed beyond fear. She has arrived in a new country.

"What time is it?" she asks.

"Winter," I say.

Lydia nods without turning and scratches her name into the frosty glass with a ragged nail.

Lydia Kennedy is shivering on a snow-covered bench in mid January, her carpet bag at her side. Her travelling suit is of fine quality, yet buttoned unevenly. She wears no hat or gloves. Her long brown hair is tangled. Lefty, the stationmaster, has sent a young lad to find the doctor to fetch her home. Because Lydia is not right in the head. Dotty. She talks to herself and nods and even laughs occasionally. Disembarking passengers glance away.

Doctor Kennedy, reports the messenger, is delivering a baby up at Kennaway, but Mrs. Crockett is on her way and here she comes now, marching furiously, bosom bouncing.

"Here, here, Lydia. Come along, now. You'll catch your death."

"I'm waiting for the train, Alma. Uncle is sending someone to escort me."

"Yes, well plans have been changed, dear. He sent a telegram. Your trip is cancelled for today. Come on, up you get. Give me your bag."

Lefty did not like Alma Crockett when he first came to town, but he is warming up to her. His attempts to convince Mrs. Kennedy to go home only met with resistance. He doesn't get paid enough to get his eyes scratched out. Alma's firm words and the right amount of force have good results, and Lefty watches the women stroll up York Street arm in arm. He returns to his office and opens the ticket booth.

~ 10 ~

April 1881

Reverend Dick Whitlock is sure this climate will kill him. It is raw for April. The ground is still frozen. Snow is slow to melt out of the bush. He hires a man to install a lock on the vestry door as it seems certain members of the congregation think they can barge in anytime they want. As soon as he arrived in this hill town, the interruptions were so frequent that he had little time to study and write his sermons. And absolutely no time to indulge in the small comforts he craves. In the city he could disappear from time to time without notice. But here! The expectations of these people! That he should fill his weekday calendar with church suppers and choir practices, and still be available to counsel the down-hearted. Or pay visits to shut-ins. After spending much of his childhood in bed with lung infections, he is reluctant to bless the dying or comfort the sick. He fears contagion.

More than disease, he fears the mockery of women. Women of a certain age. His mother's age. They arrive in clusters like cackling hens and insist on cleaning the church. Sweeping, washing windows, polishing pews.

"Yooo hoo! The Cleaning Committee is here, Reverend. Unlock your door so we can air out your chamber," one of them calls in a high-pitched voice. The response to his silence is giggling. "Come now, open up! We'll gather your laundry and take away your dirty dishes and Peggy has a lovely meat pie for your lunch."

"Leave it at the door!" he calls back. "I'm working on Sunday's sermon." There is some mumbling. He assumes one of the sour-faced matrons is making a low comment about the quality of his sermons. An unwelcome chill rides up his spine.

"Now or never," says the harsh, unmistakable voice of Alma Crockett, the shopkeeper's wife. "These ladies have their own homes to clean, Reverend! And quite a few charity cases to visit as well. In fact, you might consider joining us. We're headed out to Ralph O'Connor's place. Him that lost his hand in the saw on Tuesday. He has requested your presence, as you well know."

Dick pushes the door open so hard that it slams against the wall and knocks over a mop. The women scatter and cower a bit, all except for Alma who stands firm with hands on her generous hips. "Well, well," she says. "Did I strike a nerve?"

"I insist on privacy!"

"I insist that you step out of our way while we complete our task. You know we clean on Friday mornings. In future, you may wish to vacate the premises so as not to aggravate yourself."

A shaft of sunlight finds its way through the stained glass window, bathing the Reverend in red. Unable to conceal the murderous expression on his face, he retrieves a small brown bottle from his desk and stomps past the committee.

"Keep ahold of that pie, Peggy, and we'll deliver it to the O'Connor house," Alma says in a booming voice before he reaches the door. "Looks to me like the Reverend is having a liquid lunch."

"It's medicine!" he yells over his shoulder.

Clarissa Smith reports to her husband, Alex, that the women of the church are crass and ignorant. She is quitting the Cleaning Committee. Alex Smith nods and accepts her complaints without argument. Her efforts to belong in this remote village have been meagre from the start. Eight years ago, when the Dominion Bank sent him here as manager, he hoped she would adjust. But she has not.

These latest criticisms are duly noted. Alex Smith understands why his wife wants to move back to Toronto, and he writes a letter annually, requesting a transfer. Apparently, the Dominion Bank does not have an excess of managers willing to re-locate to the Northern Townships. Smith does not mind so much. His bank is the most impressive building in town, designed to express wealth, integrity, endurance, and confidence. It features a classical pediment supported by faux Doric columns. There are gleaming marble floors. Brass bars over the teller wickets. And, unlike the modest home they owned in the wealthy enclave of Rosedale, his home in Haliburton is recognized as the finest.

Clarissa sends a letter on vellum stationary to Reverend Whitlock, with a dinner invitation. The Reverend, she suspects, could benefit from some direction. Perhaps some matchmaking advice, as well. Bachelors of his age are rather pathetic. His beard needs trimming. His nails need a manicure. If she takes him in hand, she will gain an ally and he will find his reputation much improved.

Reverend Dick Whitlock can come up with no viable excuse to turn down the dinner invitation at the bank manager's house. He arrives exactly on time, five o'clock, and raps on the front door. It is a beautiful home with a sprawling veranda overlooking Head Lake. The dining table is set with crisp Irish linens and silver cutlery and crystal goblets and bone china plates. He is seated between the Anderson sisters, Morag on his left, Beatrice on his right. Spinster schoolteachers. Pleasantries are exchanged and soup is served by Madelaine, a young woman in a starched black and white uniform.

Across from him, trying not at all to conceal their boredom, are the two Smith children. The boy is slouchy and sullen. The girl twirls one long ringlet around her finger.

"The children are home for Easter holidays," Clarissa explains. "They attend schools in Toronto. Percival goes to Upper Canada College and Alice goes to Bishop Marshall's School."

"What are your favourite subjects?" Morag asks.

Neither child responds.

"Percival? Alice? Answer Miss Anderson."

"Arithmetic," they both say at the same time.

Dick Whitlock looks over the heads of the children to a large painting. A seascape of French and British sailing ships engaged in battle. Madelaine clears away the soup bowls and serves the lamb.

"Madeleine used to work for the Langtry family in Toronto. They were our neighbours in Rosedale. You know the Langtry family, Reverend, I believe?"

Dick Whitlock colours and clears his throat and puts down his fork.

"No. No I don't know them."

Mrs. Smith taps the table to get Percival's attention. When he looks at her, she models an erect posture, shoulders back, chest out.

"That is most curious. I was certain Mrs. Langtry spoke of her acquaintance with you. We correspond regularly."

"Yes. Well of course I have a passing acquaintance with the Langtry family. I just would not presume to…" Whitlock looks up from his plate to see the bank manager looking at him as if he were a fraud.

"How did you come to be recommended for this post?" Alex Smith asks. "Does the placement suit you?" The bank manager's thin face is bracketed by mutton chop sideburns that do not match his hair in colour or texture. His nose is as sharp as an axe. Local boys joke that

Smith should have a leather sheath fashioned for the protection of bank customers.

"What Alex means," interrupts Clarissa, "is that we have struggled, ourselves, to fit in here. It is a hardscrabble place, do you not agree? We are happy to have… progressive company in our home."

A smirk on Percival's face disappears with a tap of his mother's fingernail. Alice sighs. She has eaten barely a thing. Dick Whitlock tries not to look directly at the girl, but he notices that she is only just moving the roasted potatoes around her plate. He supposes she is about twelve years old, still wearing her hair long and her skirts short. A lovely age. The end of childhood. The blush, unfortunately, will soon be off the peach.

"And I," said Reverend Whitlock, "am most happy to be invited. I am keen to learn more about you and your family. Where were you born, Mr. Smith?"

"I was educated at Eton." Smith undoes the buttons on his waistcoat and begins a long-winded recitation of his academic and athletic accomplishments. He explains the unfortunate circumstances that robbed him of his birthright.

"Skulduggery and betrayal cost me an Earldom and a sprawling estate of great value. My brother got everything," he says, finally.

Clarissa dismisses the children and invites the adults to sit in the parlour by the fire. Dick excuses himself and goes out the back door to find the privy. He sits for a minute to gather himself and sip at his tonic. By the time he returns, Clarissa is positioned behind a silver tea service.

"Tea or coffee, Reverend?"

"Tea. Please. One lump of sugar. No cream."

"We were just talking about the need for temperance work in this community," Miss Morag Anderson says, primly. Then she flinches. It seems that Beatrice may have pinched her sister.

"Indeed," says Miss Beatrice Anderson, in a tone of some affectation. "Our rooms are situated above the Dry Goods store, between Crook's Tavern and the Reeb House. Saturday evenings are noisy with much hooting and hollering."

Morag drops her spoon and bends to retrieve it, to hide what would appear to be a helpless giggle.

Dick Whitlock fears that the Smiths consider the Misses Anderson as potential love interests for him. They certainly look the part. Either one of them would, no doubt, make a suitable pastor's wife. He guesses their ages to be between twenty-five and thirty. Dick Whitlock himself is thirty-four, and he has been coached by Canons and Bishops as to how marriage could benefit his career. It is probably true. His mother deflected many problems from his father's office. But the price is too high. His independence is precious to him.

Mrs. Smith agrees with the Misses Anderson. "Thieving and swearing and fighting are ongoing trials here," she adds. "Women who were raised in decent Christian homes dare not venture uptown alone." Beatrice nods and covers her mouth with her serviette.

~ 11 ~

The Haliburton Railway Station is not a hotel, but Lefty has slept rough many times in his life and does not deny shelter to those desperate for it. What harm to look the other way when a tramp sneaks into an empty boxcar on a rainy night? He has invited dummies and cripples and other such outcasts to sleep in the waiting area when the temperature drops below freezing. They trouble no one and he sends them off at the crack of dawn with an egg sandwich.

He keeps his communication with women to a minimum. Being a bachelor, he has never figured them out. Not entirely. He especially does not like strident women. Imperious women like Clarissa Smith, wife of the bank manager. Him and her got off to a poor start. Mrs. Smith fully expected Lefty, with one good arm, to convey luggage and parcels to her waiting carriage. Her two able-bodied children, returning home for holidays from their hoity toity private schools, were apparently not strong enough to carry their own bags.

"No baggage boys in Haliburton," Lefty told her.

"Are you paid by the railway?"

"Paid to sell tickets, and weigh packages for tariffs and dispatch the trains on schedule."

"And paid to be insolent?"

"No, Ma'am. That, I do for free."

The bags were still sitting on the bench where she left them when Mr. Alexander Smith entered the station an hour later, purple with rage.

"Load these parcels into my carriage immediately!" he yelled.

Lefty looked up from his paperwork and laughed out loud. "I am no servant of yours, sir," he replied in a softly menacing tone. "And all bags left unattended will be returned on the next train. Which," he pulled his pocket watch from his vest, "arrives in twenty-five minutes."

Alex Smith thought to look around the station. He straightened his tie and assessed his bluster as reflected in the eyes of several onlookers.

"Do you know whom you are dealing with?" Smith asked in a more genial tone.

"Well, let me guess. King Shit?"

This was too much for Ike Finch, the local barber who was waiting for his daughter's arrival. He tried to swallow his laugh and erupted into hiccups and rushed outside for fresh air. Alexander Smith was not a customer of Ike's. Rumour was, his hair was fake. A toupée.

Three years before, Ike had applied for a business loan at the Dominion Bank. He wanted to open a barber shop. He had a vision for the sign: The Clipper Ship. With a painting of a ship in full sail. Clever, he thought. But Mr. Smith had turned him down cold.

Two days after his run-in with Mr. Smith, Lefty got a letter of discipline from his manager, the tight-assed Mr. Berger. The Victoria Railway, apparently, would not tolerate insolence from its employees. He was asked to apologize forthwith to the bank manager, Mr. A. S. Smith, Esquire, the gentleman who lodged the complaint. Or face the consequences.

Lefty scribbled, I BEG YOUR FOREGIVENESS SIR, in grease pencil on the bottom of the letter, and posted it on the public bulletin board in the station. When the bank manager caught wind of the insult, Lefty was disciplined by the railway and docked two week's pay.

He posted that letter also, and was rewarded when Ike Finch took up a collection at the barber shop to compensate him.

Alexander Smith told himself that the low-brow opinions of local hillbillies were of little consequence, but it seemed to him there was an increasing lack of respect in the village for his position. The Dominion Bank discouraged managers from becoming too familiar with clients and he took that directive seriously. No one should think that they deserved special favours when applying for loans, or making payments. It was, in fact, the bank's policy to move managers around every five years or so. From branch to branch. From town to town. Alex believed that his eight-year stretch here in Haliburton implied a level of trustworthiness that would one day secure him a position at head office. Still, he could not help but wonder at the code of camaraderie that came so easily to the men who sat around the stove at the Mercantile. Or the bonds that connected the men who frequented the Loyalist Lodge. Sometimes, he felt like the boy he once was, trying to break through the powerful ranks of linked arms in Red Rover, a game for ruffians that he hated.

"Why do you think it is, Clarissa, that I have not been invited to join the Orange Lodge?"

"I don't think you need an invitation to join the Orange Order, Alex," Clarissa says without looking up from her needlework. "You simply show up at a meeting and pay your fees and the registrar writes your name down. Heavens, are you really considering joining that bunch? Orangemen are involved with riots, and shady politics. It wouldn't be seemly for you to join." Clarissa puts down her hoop and looks at her husband. He is friendless, she realizes. And only now, at the age of forty, does he recognize this fact about himself. Other men join service clubs. They participate in sports teams. They gather to study.

Alex is a loner. He rides off after supper most evenings to take the air, he says. Or to perform some kind of charity work. He dismisses her inquiries with vague references to the poor, implying he wants no credit for his good deeds. The truth is, Clarissa is happy to have the house to herself. Alex's brooding presence makes her increasingly uncomfortable. Does he have a mistress? Unlikely. Does he play cards with the immigrants down the Bog Road? Possibly. But, no. His clothes don't stink of moonshine or cigar smoke.

"The ironmonger has been elected chairman of the financial committee at the church," Alex tells his wife. "I am a little disappointed that I wasn't approached for the position."

"Indeed. Did you make your interest known to the committee?"

"No. But a responsible committee should have done their due diligence. They ought to have considered the most appropriate person for such a position."

"Perhaps Reverend Whitlock could put in a word with the elders?"

Alex grunts. "Clarissa, dear! I do not want a position on any church committee. I'm merely pointing out their negligence in not considering me. Whitlock smells of unclean undergarments. His handshake is weak. Why would I align myself with him? The very idea!"

Clarissa is accustomed to negative responses to any and all of her ideas. But she has learned that they fester in Alex's thoughts and often, in a day or two, he presents them as his own and she congratulates him on his wisdom.

The Reverend Dick Whitlock is on Alex Smith's mind. The man could be useful. As a boy in school, Alex learned to make friends with unpopular fellows. He aligned himself with trustworthy lads who had campus privileges, wealthy lads who had extra spending money, clever lads who knew what questions would likely be on exams.

Up until recently, however, Alex felt he didn't need allies in this town. He had an oak desk and an imposing office and a salary that, if not grand, at least supplemented his wife's trust fund. He himself had been excised from his father's estate. Not because he was the second born son. But because his father discovered his unsavoury proclivities. The old man had him followed, and the detective had been quite thorough.

Clarissa cried and cried when he announced they would leave England and emigrate to one of the colonies. Canada was not his first choice. He was keen to go to New Zealand where the weather was more clement. But an opportunity at the Dominion Bank in Canada presented itself first. Indeed, Toronto was surprisingly civilized, their home in quiet, leafy Rosedale was comfortable, if not grand, and the neighbours upper class. Clarissa was busy and happy with two babies and a nanny and a cook. Alexander joined a gentleman's club, and occasionally, when the burden of job and family responsibilities became overwhelming, he would disappear in the humming, thrumming streets of The Ward.

St. John's Ward, home to immigrants of all creeds and colours, was a notorious slum. But Alex liked slumming it. He liked the bawdy women and the activities they would engage in for ten cents. There was no danger of his father looking over his shoulder. No chance of being recognized.

Until he was. A chance sighting and an anonymous report resulted in his transfer to Haliburton. It was all presented as a promotion. An opportunity to become a manager with his name etched on a glass door. He couldn't turn it down, he told Clarissa. A few years in the Northern Townships, and they would return to Toronto. He needed the experience. He needed her support.

But eight years have elapsed in this northern wasteland. Alex is edgy. Rumours are circulating about a new bank coming to town. Competition for the Dominion Bank. Alex knows his loan quotas are low. Embarrassingly low. Queries from the auditor's department at head office in Toronto have him concerned.

Alex would very much like to know more about the mysterious moneylender who has been financing the businesses he turns down. He drops by the Mercantile.

"Any of you fellows know about this fellow McLeod? The moneylender?" No one moves down the bench to offer him a place to sit. The men shrug and mutter about the weather and fill their pipes. Miles puts another log on the fire. As Smith turns and heads out the front door, he hears laughter.

Against his better judgment, Alex Smith goes to the Loyalist Lodge for lunch. He sits alone at a small table near the window. James Adams has a booming, confident voice for a gimp, and Alex listens as the American leads a lively debate about vigilante justice. The group of men at his table like to argue and the conversation gets quite aggressive at times. The volume rises and falls. Adams reads aloud from a Globe article about the Donnelly family of Lucan, Ontario. Five murdered in cold blood in the middle of the night, and their house set afire.

"A massacre, they call it," he says, looking up. "By a mob. Eye witnesses aplenty, yet no one has been found guilty of the crime."

"They were criminals themselves, the Donnellys," Clark Cook says. "Black Irish immigrants. Squatters who fought with their neighbours and had no use for the law."

"Like those gypsies up the rail line," James adds. "The same thing could happen here in Haliburton. We've no constables. Just that old drunkard of a Magistrate who drops by once a month. What do you make of all this, Mr. Smith?" James Adams calls over to the bank manager's table.

All eyes turn toward Alex Smith, who is unhappily reminded of the discomfort he once felt as a student when the teacher called upon him unexpectedly. He dribbles some soup on his shirt in his hurry to put his spoon down. It clatters into the saucer.

"I agree with Mr. Cook," he says.

"Well! There's a first time for everything!" Clark Cook responds, and the table erupts in laughter and table pounding.

"What I mean is, I have no use for squatters. The railway has delivered undesirables to Haliburton. Council is not doing enough to eradicate the problem." Alex feels he has made a salient point. Until Robert Bell, Councillor for Ward Two, turns to address him.

"You must attend the next Council Meeting, sir, and offer your solutions. We welcome any criticism as long as it is accompanied by a plan of action. The next public meeting is Monday evening. Can we expect to see you there?"

Alex pulls his watch from his vest and feigns alarm at the time. "Excuse me. I must get back to the bank."

"But you have not finished your meal," James says, as Alex rises from the table. Sunny comes through the kitchen door at that very moment, carrying a most delicious looking pork chop with mashed potatoes and beans and a thick slab of bread with butter.

"Sir?" she says, as Alex pulls on his overcoat.

"Unfortunately, I have only just now remembered a meeting scheduled for 12:30."

"May I wrap your lunch and deliver it to the bank?"

"Yes. Indeed. That would be much appreciated." He pulls out his wallet and leaves a dollar bill beside his soup bowl.

"May I get you some change?" Sunny asks.

"No," Alex says. He notices the splatters of red broth on the white linen tablecloth and feels he must leave a generous tip. "Keep the change."

As soon as he gets outside, he feels angry at Clarissa for encouraging him to build alliances with the businessmen who take lunch at The Loyalist. He regrets his comments about the transients.

Too late, he thinks of several clever comments he could have made about the immigrant problem. Those men are not customers of his. None of them have so much as a savings account with him. Some deal with banks in the city, and some, like Clark Cook, deal with McLeod, whoever he is. Smith does not like the fact that he has no status among them. He needs some leverage. As he crosses the alleyway between the Dry Goods Store and Crook's Tavern, he is almost run over by a delivery cart. He stops and waves a fist in the air, anticipating an apology from the driver that does not come.

Sunny returns to the kitchen and calls Mary away from the sink.

"Guess who has sneaked away without finishing his dinner? Mr. Alexander Smith, Esquire, that's who! And I have promised to have his meal delivered to the bank. Freshen up, Mary, my girl. Here's your chance!"

The colour rises in Mary's cheeks. What a beauty she is, Sunny thinks. And such a good reliable worker too.

"I'm not prepared, Sunny. The very sight of that man turns my stomach."

"All the more reason to get the money you deserve for raising Peter and Norman. Do it for those dear boys, Mary. We have rehearsed it enough. I'll be here waiting with a brandy when you are done. Now. Get out of that apron while I wrap the bastard's pork chop."

Mary walks in the front door of the Dominion Bank and nods pleasantly at the teller, Timothy Bailey, newly arrived from Nova Scotia.

"Dinner delivery for Mr. Smith," she says.

Mr. Bailey smiles and points her in the direction of the manager's office.

Alex Smith is hanging up his overcoat and adjusting his hair in the mirror. By the time he turns around, there is Mary.

"Your pork chop, Alex."

"Set it on my desk."

Mary curtsies as if she is taking orders from the king. Then she giggles and takes a seat.

Alex closes the door loud enough to let Mr. Bailey know he is not pleased with the interruption.

Mary arranges her hands prettily in her lap and boldly tells Alex Smith she wants to send the boys to school.

"I've come to discuss the education and financial support of your sons."

Except for a deep flush that rises from his collar, Alex makes no sign of understanding, though Mary's voice is clear.

"Peter and Norman," she explains. "They are clever boys, and will require a substantial amount of money," she says, calmly but definitively, like she is ordering a pound of sugar at the Mercantile and does not anticipate any delay in the fulfillment of the order.

"Please introduce yourself, Madam," Alex Smith says, stalling for time. His heart is quite in danger of quitting on him. His underarms leak down his sides. There is no doubt that this is little Mary, a twelve-year old when last he saw her. He expected that she died along with her mother. Glenda's body was found when the snow melted in the spring but there was no trace of Mary or the baby boy. Smith had every reason to believe the wolves got them. Of course, he could not inquire. It would have cast suspicion upon him. He didn't think there were any in the village who knew of his visits to see Glenda, widowed and isolated and dependent on his generosity. He was justified in believing that nature had done the kind thing.

"Mary Hammond," she says. "We've met."

Mary smiles, casting a spell she learned from her mother, thinks Alex. That Jezebel spell.

"I'm afraid you have me confused…"

"You are the father of two boys whom, currently, you do not acknowledge or support financially. My mother's child, Norman, and my own boy, Peter, born to me when I was just a child myself. I have retained the services of a lawyer, and I am acting on his advice."

"You have no proof for this ridiculous accusation."

"Ah! But I do, sir. My mother, may she rest in peace, left me a valuable keepsake. Proof of your relationship with her. With us. And now that the boys are working at the train station in town, it's surprising how often Norman is mistaken for your boy. Your other son. Percival is it? They look like brothers." She laughs. "Because they are!"

Smith is suddenly aware of the echoey silence beyond his door. The walls of his office do not extend to the ceiling. "Lower your voice."

"Of course, I will lower my voice when you open an account for me and make the first deposit."

Mary. Large as life and more beautiful than he could have imagined. Mary, whom he hadn't expected to survive. Mother of his son? He is momentarily distracted by a most inappropriate feeling of pride.

Smith considers his options. There is no sheriff to call for help. No police force. The Jezebels of the world are quite capable of making much ado in public, having little or no shame. The lawyer tactic is probably a bluff. But. Maybe not. Can he risk it? He opens his desk drawer and pulls out an application form. He puts his wire-rimmed spectacles on. He dips his pen in the inkwell.

"Name?"

"As I said. As you know."

Alex's hand has a noticeable tremor as he writes *Mary Hammond* at the top of the form.

"Age?"

"Eighteen."

"Address?"

Mary removes a piece of paper from the cuff of her sleeve and hands it to Smith. The handwriting is elegant. The paper, velum. It seems possible that the note originated in a legitimate attorney's office.

Smith copies the information and considers the address, the tract, the lot number. So. Mary lives on the ridge at the Nunnery. A community of whores like Clarissa has been saying all along. A scourge. Even as he fills out the paperwork, he is considering what he must do. The Reverend must play a role. The church will be required to take action for the sake of morality.

"Mr. Bailey will get you a receipt book."

Mary checks the amount, a deposit of two dollars. The minimum amount required to open an account. She hands it back to him.

"Add two zeros," she says. "Compensation is owing for seven years room and board."

Smith looks at her. Blond hair coiffed and crimped with alluring bangs and side curls. Clothes clean and pressed. Her appearance challenges his understanding of the Nunnery as a rough settlement. Nothing more than an old Indian encampment.

My god, she is lovely. Despite his wrath, he finds himself wanting her. The bulge in his pants requires a repositioning in his chair that he suspects is obvious to Mary. How did she survive in that cold cabin? He adjusts his spectacles, adds two zeros and hands the paper back to her.

"You said you'd be back with a sleigh. I waited. Nine months along, I was, and could not set out on my own, five miles to town in that blizzard."

"Shhh!" Smith spits on his desk.

"Mother was dead and Norman was trying to suckle her stiff breast. When the door opened after two days, I thought it was you. But it wasn't."

"I... I was sick. I took sick. By the time I came back, you were gone."

"You came back? Looking for something? Ah yes! And I will return that special keepsake to you one day as long as you continue to do right by Peter and Norman. They're good boys. You should be proud of the way I've raised them."

Alex Smith feels bile creeping up his throat. He pulls his linen handkerchief out of his pocket and holds it over his mouth. He did go back to Glenda's shack, weeks later, looking for the gold tie pin. Clarissa's wedding gift to him.

Mary loosens the drawstring on her purse and for a moment Alex wonders if the tie pin is in there. Will she return it to him? Instead, she tucks the receipt inside and stands and exits with more dignity than is deserving of a woman of her class.

"See you next month," she says, lightly over her shoulder. "Daddy."

Alex Smith cringes.

He did. He did ask her to call him Daddy. The ache in his crotch is crippling.

~ 12 ~

November 1881

Voices of women in the village have little weight. Like dead leaves falling in autumn, their concerns land in a pile and decompose. Alma Crockett, who deals regularly with local men from her position behind the counter at the Mercantile, has given up trying to knock some common sense into the fellows who spend the shoulder seasons jawing around the Quebec stove. November and April are the worst. They become shiftless, taking a holiday from labour, while their wives keep cooking and cleaning and caring for the bairns. Why is it, she wonders, that they must wait for their wives to die before they recognize how changed their home is. How bleak. Men remarry very quickly. Often before grass grows on Mother's grave.

Alma disapproves of men in general, but she is willing to put up with most of them. They run the show, make the rules and fight the wars. She has no time for gypsies and drunks. But they generally harm only themselves. Her true wrath is reserved for thieves and fornicators. Of thieves, there are three types. Petty thieves, she can deal with. Alma has caught them pocketing apples, or filling cans with lamp oil out back. If they are apologetic, she is not unkind. There is always wood to stack or floors to be swept in compensation.

Then, there is robbery. A hand in the cash drawer when she isn't looking. A twenty-pound bag of seed gone missing off the front porch. Finally, there are low down embezzlers. Alma is disgusted with the dirty birds who cheat people out of their savings, their property, their pay. She used to look the other way.

"None of our business, Alma," Miles says.

All well and good. Some folks deserve to be cheated. They are careless and stupid and they may as well wear targets on their backs. But Alma refuses to stand by watching the vulnerable get the shit kicked out of them. She is no judge and jury. Simply a citizen who doesn't mind speaking out, writing letters, and demanding responsibility. If you make a mistake, fix it. It was Alma who first encouraged young Mary to seek compensation from the bank manager. Fine for Ona to take in the left-behinds. But why should lechers get away scot-free? And her eyes are on the Reverend, now. It is only a matter of time, Alma thinks, before she hears of some corruption on his part. He was sniffing around for a donation for a new stained glass window. Suffer Little Children to Come Unto Me.

Indeed! Alma is highly suspicious of the number of weak and unwary souls going in and out of the vestry door. Widows, girls, young fatherless lads, simpletons. The Reverend and the bank manager are seen together quite often. Predictable! Men of degraded morals find each other and commit their atrocities in the warm glow of each other's approval.

Women around town know things but keep mum about broken hearts and tales of woe and violence. Even rape. Because no woman wants to admit she was lied to and tarnished. No woman wants to stand accused of being a temptress. Horse shit!

The Reverend is corrupt in some unspeakable way. And yet the ladies of the Cleaning Committee continue to tie on their aprons, sweeping and dusting around him as if he is a religious artifact. They do not question the order of things. God put men in charge and women must obey them. Instead of condemning the damn men in this town, they point fingers at Ona McLeod and her sanctuary. They have convinced the Reverend to banish them. When Alma heard that, she hiked up the ridge to warn Ona, but Ona just laughed.

"Oh, Alma. The Reverend has no such power. I own this property. No one can evict me."

"But the church ladies are accusing you of running a cathouse." Alma looks over at the young women peeling turnips. She looks at Molly, bent over a washtub, a freak doing a simple chore. She looks at the bare-bottomed toddlers running about like little savages. The lot of them would make quite a spectacle if they decided to parade down Queen Street.

"The church ladies make better cats than we do. They should come here themselves instead of sending a mouse. We'll chew the Reverend up and spit him out. Don't worry."

Alma is satisfied. No one tells Ona what to do. She sees the past and the future of this place and plants herself firmly in the present. Dealing with things as they occur. If she knows of some crime that has gone unpunished, she will set things right. Quietly. Like she did with the rapists at the lumber camp who stole Molly's voice.

Ona does not suffer fools. Foolish men especially, but women can also be fools. Too often, women think what men tell them to think. Some cover up crimes for their sons and husbands and point fingers at other women.

Of course, Ona knows there is a limit to what women can achieve. A man can punch the crap out of his wife if he chooses. He can kill her. The very person who planted and tended the kitchen garden, who sewed the curtains, who beat the rugs, who kept the hearth warm. That person can be dispatched. The law is on a man's side, for he is a citizen and womenfolk are mere chattel.

Ona learned from Nokomis and the aunties not to be a groveller. Her grandmother kept her grandfather sated. His basic needs met. Then she did as she pleased. If there were complaints, Nokomis withdrew services, and Angus McLeod learned who was really in charge.

When her grandfather died, Ona took over his log cabin behind the cloister, a cabin he organized to suit him, filled with mementos of his travels and exploits. Grandfather McLeod had received a universal education at the University of Aberdeen, and he owned a comprehensive library that Ona consumed with surprising alacrity. Angus McLeod did not expect his granddaughter to become a scholar. Literate, yes, he expected that. But few students can make connections between academic subjects like Ona did at a young age. She could reason, analyze and apply knowledge in original and astounding ways. Old McLeod was sometimes frustrated by her claims that some of his texts had outdated inconsistencies.

"Your library needs updating," she told him. It took a while but she wore him down. He eventually allowed her to join him on his bi-annual visits to Kingston so she could select the books that interested her from the Queens University bookshop.

Stingy with praise, he was, but Winona understood he was secretly proud of her. She overheard him telling his solicitor that his daughter was a canny McLeod through and through, woman or no.

It was not lost on Winona that Angus McLeod took all the credit for her education. Never did he acknowledge the contributions of Nokomis, who taught Ona just as much with more practical outcomes. The dialectal thinking that resulted was advantageous for solving problems.

Nokomis had lived with the other women in the longhouse and visited her husband's cabin only to fulfill matrimonial duties, as required. She lived out her life according to her own traditions, and though he never admitted it, Angus McLeod learned to love the land as she did. In a way that other settlers did not. When Nokomis died, his grief was terrible. She left no mark, other than the cairn he piled with stones. Gone, like last year's wildflowers. Without a trace. Except for a collection of quilled boxes, and stories unlike those in text books. Stories to explain the creation of the world, the mystery of the stars, the reason there are seasons. The oral tradition of her people was steeped in myth and magic and memory and dreams.

Gidaaki was Ona's inheritance from both parents in very different ways. Angus McLeod left her a deed that named her as owner. Never mind land rights. Never mind treaties made in good faith. The past was erased. Overruled. Renamed. Resolved to the liking of a new order.

Gidaaki, was a name from the Wendat language. Literally, it meant high land. But, as guardian and steward of Gidaaki, Ona knew it meant much more. It meant layer upon layer of stone and soil and fire and flood and time. Animal bones and fish scales and lost creatures and spirits. Ona understood all that, and kept it in her heart, but her heart would stop one day. The earth would swallow her and Gidakki would go to the highest bidder. How would she protect it after she died?

Gidaaki spreads out like a campus with buildings that have undergone many renovations and extensions over the years. There is a longhouse for communal living, and a bunkhouse that served as a seasonal hunt camp in earlier times. There is a wash house, a four-seater privy, a kiln house and a cookhouse. There is a barn-like hall with tables and chairs, where Ona has been known to host events with measured amounts of good quality whiskey. No bathtub gin that can render a man blind. No moonshine. No mind-numbing powders.

Some of the nuns are card sharps, but they play for fun, not competition. Winners do not make money, but they might be awarded with a dance. Yes, there is music. Fiddles and mouth organs and the like. Ballads from the old country that make men cry. Folk songs. Hymns. Jigs and waltzes and reels. Sometimes one of the men might step out with a nun, to look at the stars. They might sneak along the shadowy stone wall to the bunkhouse with privacy curtains made out of animal skins.

Ona runs her business according to a strict code. Men agree to her rules. They have seen her escort noncompliant patrons off the property at the end of her long rifle. They have heard stories about unmarked graves in the meadow behind her cabin.

"Take your bad manners to Crook's Tavern," she tells men who want to fight. But Joe Crook has got no ladies, and lumbermen love female company. The so-called nuns are women from society's tattered margins. They come and go. Some are scrappy young girls who have lived their entire lives defensively. Defiance and meanness have been their survival tools. They behave badly and then cower, expecting punishment. When met with tolerance, they adapt and stay for a time. But as it is with those raised in meanness, they find harmony difficult and move on, looking for a fight.

Ona's nuns have histories that remain, for the most part, untold. Like small treasures sewn into their hearts, they keep their losses to themselves. A good thing, lest the flood of grief drown them all. The women contribute as they are able. Trapping, hunting, fishing, gathering, making garments, cooking, washing up. There are domestic animals to tend. Crops to plant. Babies to birth. And there are women among them who are skilled in the oldest profession.

"Comfort means different things to different people," Ona acknowledges when a few zealous parishioners send Reverend Whitlock up the hill to raise objections for the public good. For decency.

Reverend Dick Whitlock has repeatedly ignored requests to "do something" about the den of iniquity on the hill. He refuses until Alexander Smith asks for a favour. One that Whitlock cannot say no to. He sets out early to climb the ridge, wearing boots and an overcoat, gifts from Clarissa Smith. Her husband purchased new winter attire in the latest fashion from Eaton's on Yonge Street in Toronto.

The haze of woodsmoke dissipates as the Reverend climbs the trail that diverges at the end of Mountain Street. Though not so far from the village, he feels a change in the atmosphere. Ona greets him at the summit. She notes the self-loathing seeping out of skin ulcers on his sunken cheeks.

"Welcome, Dick," she says.

"You may call me Reverend Whitlock."

"May I? Thank you. It is a great privilege. Call me Ona. Everyone does."

"I am here at the request of church members who take exception to your immoral activities."

"Slow down, Reverend Whitlock. We can discuss this misunderstanding in a civil way. Sit here." Ona takes a blanket from her shoulders and places it on a chair.

"Reserved for dignitaries," she says. "Make yourself comfortable. I shall be back momentarily."

Dick finds no comfort here. He is aware of how aggressive the chickadees sound. Like little sentinels prepared to report his behaviour to the queen. He realizes his knee is bouncing, a nervous habit, and plants both heels firmly on the ground.

"Tea!" Ona announces upon her return. "For your skin condition."

Dick would prefer to refuse this backhanded hospitality, but cannot think how to do it. He takes the steaming cup and, finding no place to set it down, balances it in his lap.

"So. You are here to lodge a complaint about immorality?"

"It is no longer in the interest of the village to allow you to occupy a tract of land so close to the village. Times are changing. Civilization has come to the Northern Townships. Heathen behaviour will not be tolerated."

Ona leans forward. "Describe what you mean by heathen behaviour, Reverend Whitlock."

Dick looks around. The cloister is filling up with women and children. "I would think that is self-evident."

"The evidence being the care and feeding of orphans? The rescue and shelter of young women fleeing abuse? The operation of a successful comfort business?"

"There, yes," Dick says. "That's it. You must cease and desist forthwith," he declares. "Under the authority given me by the Holy Church, I hearby serve you with an eviction notice. The time has come for you to leave this township. I'll grant you until the end of the month."

"That sounds quite intimidating. My goodness. But, Reverend Whitlock, are you not in the comfort business, yourself? I cannot imagine you would wish to deny comfort to those whose needs are physical, rather than ethereal," she says.

Dick silently curses Alex Smith. He is the one with bastard children living up on this ridge. He is the one who should be here. This woman is no cowering half-breed as Alex led him to believe. He cannot think of a reply worthy of her statement. Instead, he rubs the tips of his fingers together and longs for the authority of his position which he seems to have left at the church. He thinks of his tippet, hanging on the back of his vestry door and wishes for the weight of it around his neck. A boy with dirty britches approaches and squats at his feet and whittles away at a small carving.

Suffer the Little Children, Dick thinks. Jesus would smile at the child and open his arms. But images of the Jesuit martyrs intrude. Christianity is a bright light that dims substantially in certain corners of the globe. Heathens and cannibals. And witches, here, in this coven upon the hill.

"May the Lord be with you," is all the Reverend can think to reply to her measured words.

"And also with you," Ona says, proving some education in the Christian scriptures.

Old Kateri cackles from her place by the fire pit. She glares at the Reverend through rheumy eyes. Like an accidental framework of discarded twigs, her body resembles a collection of bones from vandalized graves.

"Men miss their Mamas," Kateri says in a voice as faint as oak leaves skittering across crusty snow. "But you didn't have a loving Mama, did you, son? No kindness there."

"You must not call yourself Nuns!" he stutters. "It is a travesty."

The women enjoy his outburst and clap their hands.

"You misjudge us, Reverend," Ona says. "We do not call ourselves nuns. We do not call this place the Nunnery like a women's prison for some religious order. That is a name bestowed upon us by others."

A woman comes forward and kneels before the Reverend. She kisses the young boy. "Off you go, Norman," she tells him. Dick is suddenly quite sure this blonde woman is Alex's Mary. The blackmailer. The one he needs rid of.

"Nuns are married to Jesus," Mary says. "We are single ladies." She lifts a blue shawl from her shoulders and wraps it over her hair. The Reverend leans away, thinking her an unholy Magdalen.

"You're afraid?"

"Of course not," he says. But his heart is racing.

Mary waits until Norman is a safe distance away before she asks, "Do you think my boy looks like your friend? Mr. Alex Smith?"

It is true he does have some resemblance to Percival Smith. The high forehead. The wide set eyes. Reverend Whitlock undoes the buttons on his wool coat, and smells his own fetid perspiration.

"Whoremongers and adulterers God will judge," Mary says in such a sweet way that the Reverend almost misses the accusation. The Bible is his weapon and his shield and when he recognizes this quote from Corinthians, he feels humiliated. How do you defend yourself against a wrongful interpretation of scripture?

"Feeding the soul," he says, "is more important than answering the animal urges of the flesh." He rises from his chair but slips and crumbles to the ground, his muscles weakened by the climb uphill and also, somehow, by these brazen harlots who watch him scramble awkwardly to hands and knees and then cautiously to his feet.

"You aren't leaving so soon, I hope," Ona says. "You have not explained how you will banish us from this place. Will you chase us away in the dead of night with pitchforks and torches?" Dick has no idea what she is talking about. He has never read a novel in his life.

Furious with Alexander Smith for sending him on this humiliating mission, Dick retreats, tossing a Biblical verse over his shoulder, as a defeated bully might toss a stone before running away.

"Do not profane your daughter by making her a prostitute."

Ona and Mary follow him to the trail and watch as he stumbles down the slippery path as if the devil is chasing him.

"Leviticus," Mary calls after him. "Go in peace, oh perfect one."

As he descends, his open coat and fluttering robes give the impression of a wounded crow. He glances up. Ona waves.

"Poor soul. Never look back, Reverend," she whispers and Mary almost expects to see the man turn into a pillar of salt.

Much of the town can be seen from this aerie, including the white steeple of the church. Ona knows when someone is trespassing on someone else's land. She knows where fires are burning and who tends the flames, when fish are jumping and who catches them, when school lets out for the day and who goes straight home and who does not. If you think you can get away with something without the nuns knowing about it, you are sadly mistaken.

"I don't mind being called a nun, Mary," Ona says. "It is an old word. An ancient word. It means grandmother."

"I mind. When it comes out of his mouth, I mind."

"Mmm. Did he finish his tea?"

"No. He spilled it."
"Ah, well. There are other cures."

~ 13 ~

Louis Kennedy knows it is wrong to ignore Lydia's increasing needs. Even with Hannah to clean and cook and take care of Jane, she is not getting better. One solution is to pack up his family and return to the city. He could easily get a placement at a hospital. A month does not go by without a letter from a colleague, enticing him with a position. Or he could open a private practice in Oakville and be close to his mother. She would be a great support in raising children.

As he makes his solitary rounds down the backroads and up the trails to visit isolated families, he tries to picture himself as a doctor in Oakville. As his father had been. But. No. He rejects that image every time. He does not want to be his father. He does not want the predictability of it. Rising at seven. Toast and marmalade and a boiled egg for breakfast. There is something wild inside him. Not wild like Lydia is wild, uncontrolled and uncontrollable. Instead, he has a restless spirit. It is satisfying to him, this life. Arriving at an emergency. Assessing it. Analyzing the options.

Louis Kennedy likes the way people depend on him for more than doctoring. He sorts out all kinds of problems, except the problem of an incorrigible wife. Her unpredictable behaviour puts people at risk! Someone could die while he chases after Lydia. And Jane's safety is sometimes compromised. She is a child, vulnerable and often fearful of her own mother. The truth is, he is afraid of Lydia, too. The transients she befriended gave her "healing powders." They filled her head with strange lore and incantations, giving weight to her own paranoia. She caught a nasty lung infection visiting that railway encampment and spent Christmas, and much of January, in her room.

1882 begins quietly. Lydia gradually gains her strength back. Her appetite improves. She shows an interest in getting dressed and going out of doors in March, but both Lou and Hannah are loathe to let her wander. In the interest of domestic harmony, Lou increases the low doses of laudanum. He doubles them, actually, to a satisfactory effect. Springtime is known to awaken hibernating manias.

Doctors often play God. It is part of the job. Dr. Kennedy has smothered newborns with deformities. He has performed euthanasia on disease ridden patients to end their suffering. A doctor is called upon to hasten the inevitable.

So, when Lydia's suffering becomes too much, Lou travels to Hamilton to consult with some colleagues, experts in the field of hysteria. They strongly recommend he commit his wife to Century Manor, a newly built insane asylum on Hamilton Mountain. With the full support of Lydia's relatives, Lou signs the legal documents. He expresses his appreciation for their financial contribution.

"Of course," Aunt Sophia tells Lou. "We have long considered Lydia to be at risk of hysteria. She was a flighty girl and a disobedient student. We sent her to finishing school in Switzerland, you know. And she embarrassed herself on several occasions."

"How so?"

"You needn't know the details."

"It might be helpful for her medical history."

"I doubt it very much. In any case, I do not want a record of her lascivious behaviour made public." Sophia retrieves a small fan from her cuff and waves it under her chin as if the very thought of whatever transpired has her on the verge of a fainting spell. She actually refuted the accusations of the school. Much ado was made over some innocent nude bathing. Classical painters love the subject, she told the head mistress. The other girls involved, more knowledgeable about the ways of the world, apologized and accepted their punishment graciously. Lydia refused to apologize and called the head mistress a crusty old sapphist. She was expelled.

"There was an incident that sparked some kind of rebellion in Lydia," Sophia finally admits. "She carried a burden of injustice with her, as if her suffering was greater than that of others. It was unseemly. Unladylike. In all the years she lived with us, she never once apologized for any transgression. No punishment could force her to say she was sorry."

Lou does not like Sophia. He thinks the woman never had Lydia's best interests at heart. He also wonders at her lack of hesitation in writing a cheque in support of Lydia's involuntary hospitalization. Fleetingly, he considers that there may be details about the estate of Lydia's parents and her uncle that have been kept from her? Is she owed some kind of allowance? Was her inheritance deferred or mismanaged? He resolves to look into it.

Sophia hurries Lou through his explanation, outlining Lydia's course of treatment.

"You're the doctor. I trust your judgment. No need to tell me every detail."

Lou quickly describes the need for medications, safety restraints, and confinement as required. Sophia winces a bit as he begins to explain gynaecological manipulation. She holds up a hand to stop him.

"It's a common treatment for Lydia's condition," he says.

"Yes, yes. I suppose there must be evidence to support it."

"Also," Lou says with hesitation. "There have been recent medical advances in brain surgery." He is not entirely convinced himself that it is wise to sign off on this innovative procedure, but he cannot help being intrigued by the possibility of a cure. "A way to manipulate the frontal lobe of the brain that can improve the moods and behaviours of maniacs, particularly women. It is still in the experimental stages but, with our consent, they will consider Lydia for the surgery." Lou points to the place in the document that requires her signature.

"Of course," Sophia says, signing her name with a flourish. "Surely she can be no worse off than she is."

With Lydia gone, Dr. Kennedy embraces a heroic dedication to backwoods emergencies. This is how fast an accident happens. One minute a man is working and getting a bit peckish, thinking about lunch and then his attention strays to swat a black fly. His sleeve catches in the teeth of the saw and the flesh of his arm is torn open all the way to his shoulder and halfway down his back.

When Lou arrives, the hearse wagon is already there. The sight of the undertaker, pale and retching into the ditch, indicates the level of trauma that awaits in the mill.

"He's a goner, Doc," John Tucker Jr. says as they follow a blood trail to a cot where Joe Cooper lies, severed from stem to stern. Lou opens his bag and starts suturing. He talks calmly to Coop about what he is doing and Coop says later that he heard every word. The talking tethered him to Earth. Lou sends for Julia Cooper, the wife. She holds her husband's head steady, as a nurse would have done in the city hospital or on a field of war.

Lou administers a large dose of morphine, notes with amazement that Coop's heart continues to beat, and keeps sewing like a tailor with a deadline, using his curved needle first, suturing the arteries with fine wire. Then he stitches up the muscles along the ribs, using tiny forceps to hold the tissue together. The man is still alive, and he has used all the suture thread in his kit. Julia runs up the street to Aliza Tucker's house to fetch sewing thread.

"The strongest thread I have is red," Aliza apologizes. "He will look like the Modern Prometheus."

Over the shoulder and down the arm, Lou works. Julia stays in attendance in the makeshift operating theatre that smells of fresh cut wood. Sawdust drifts in the afternoon sun. Young John shoos flies away.

It takes four hours to sew Joe Cooper up. Lou never questions the surge of adrenaline that keeps him focused through long surgeries, but this day he collapses afterward and sleeps deeply on the bench beside his patient. He awakes to find that someone has pulled a blanket over him and tucked a pillow under his head. Julia, upright and stoic, sits beside her husband with her hand on his forehead. Such a wife, Lou thought, would be good to have.

The next day, Lou has his patient transferred from the sawmill to his cabin on the Barry Line. It is rough but clean. They lay him on his bed and Lou gives Julia a bottle of morphine with strict instructions for its administration. One drop, every four hours.

Still, Lou does not expect Coop to live. A week goes by, and Coop refuses the doses of morphine.

"I can stand the pain, Doc," he says, "but I cannot stand the bugs climbing up and down the walls."

"Hallucinations," Lou says. "A common side effect."

"Just a bit of whiskey instead of that medicine, if that's okay."

"Of course."

Lou knows that Joe Cooper has months of immobility ahead, and worries that his muscles will atrophy. So, he fashions a board to go at the foot of Coop's bed.

"Push your feet on that board," Lou tells Coop. "As if you are walking. Right, left, right, left, right, left. That's it." Lou sits back on the little bench under the window and lights his pipe, supervising his patient as he lifts his knees and marches like a supine soldier.

After Coop falls asleep, Lou makes to leave for home. Julia follows him out to his waiting horse and carriage. She holds out a demand note from the bank.

End of the Line

"They're calling in the mortgage, Doc," she said with a scratchy voice. "A hundred and twenty dollars, due Friday."

"Who? Who's calling in your mortgage?"

"Mr. Smith at the Dominion Bank. The sawmill gave us a month's pay and I got ten dollars left from that. How soon do you think it'll be before Joe is able to get back to work?"

"Five, six months, Julia. Leave this to me." Lou folds the crisp note and tucks it in his jacket pocket.

"I don't want to trouble you, Doc," she says, purely out of politeness. Indeed, she hasn't any other options.

"No trouble, Julia. This will be a pleasure."

Lou enters the bank as soon as Timothy Bailey unlocks the door at ten o'clock. Banker's hours! A soft job, Lou thinks as he walks directly towards the manager's office.

"Do you have an appointment, sir?" Timothy calls after him. He has been admonished about who, and who not, to let into Alex Smith's office.

"Don't need one!" Lou calls back over his shoulder.

Smith is closing his office door. Lou sticks his foot in the crack.

"I'm a busy man, Doc," he says. "Is this urgent?"

"In fact, it is." Lou takes the demand note from his pocket. "One of my patients needs a grace period before he can resume payments on this loan."

"Ah. A lien on his property, I see. Unfortunate."

"Indeed. It was an unfortunate thing that a saw nearly ripped his arm clean off. Painful. But the good news is, he's going to survive, because he's a tough son-of-a-bitch. He'll be back on the job in six months, I'd say."

"Well. If he had purchased our insurance for instances such as this, he would be covered for that period. I'm very sorry to say that bank policy..."

"How much is the insurance?"

"It cannot be purchased after an accident."

"That's not what I asked. I asked how much is the insurance?"

Alex Smith sighs, as if he is about to go to a great deal of trouble. He takes a large volume down from the shelf behind his desk and makes a show of calculating some complicated logarithms.

"Seven dollars and seventy cents per annum."

Lou nods. He reaches in his pocket and pulls out a handful of bills and coins.

"You fix this. Make it so the Cooper family won't lose their house."

"I could have you charged with…"

"Keep the change, Squire," Lou says, slamming the door hard enough to rattle the glass. He nods at Timothy Bailey as he leaves. Both men smile, sharing barely contained hilarity at the 'keep the change' line. After Alex Smith embarrassed himself at The Loyalist Lodge, it became a widely circulated phrase in the village, used to make fun of cheapskates. The bank manager was likely the only person in Haliburton oblivious to the joke.

Alexander Smith sits looking out the window to the right of his desk for a long time after the doctor leaves. It is a tall window, designed to maximize sunlight and save on gas lighting costs. But the ledge is high. Shoulder height when he is standing. So, from his chair, all Alex can see are the tips of golden tamaracks climbing the Queen Street hill. As his racing heart slows, he thinks how much he hates Dr. Louis Kennedy. How much he despises underhanded tactics, disguised as moral codes.

Society would not last long if the liberal-minded were allowed to interfere with the economy. The Northern Townships, populated by immigrants and criminals and imbeciles, require strict rules. Lawful enforcement. Visionary politicians unswayed by society's low-lifes. Nature's weaklings must be weeded out. Only the strong must survive.

Town Council, floundering under the interim leadership of an ineffective Deputy Reeve, is susceptible to liberal thinking. There are rumblings about social welfare. Financial assistance for needy families. Houses of refuge funded by taxpayers. Rubbish!

Alexander Smith is tempted to run for office. He has ideas that could elevate this village to greatness. First off, he would lobby the railway magnates. He would get the Victoria Rail line extended to Ottawa where it would connect with the trans-continental rail system. Haliburton would not be the end of the line, It would be a hub from which a person could travel to the Atlantic or the Pacific. Sea to sea.

~ 14 ~

Dr. Louis Kennedy invested a lot of time familiarizing himself with the tracts and outposts and camps that surrounded the village. He created a system to alert him of emergencies, engaging the help of woodsmen and farmers and shantymen; anyone who would benefit from a way to communicate a cry for help. A certain number of gunshots fired in sequence acted as a type of telegraph that represented the sectors of the outlying regions. Each lake had a code and a designated guardian. Each guardian was responsible for relaying messages along roads that crept through the dense bush of the county like pencil lines. Pencil lines that could easily be erased by spring floods and winter storms.

Young Peter Hammond, Mary's son, knocks on the doctor's back door early on Christmas morning, 1882.

"Four gunshots heard from the ridge," Peter tells Hannah. She wraps two slices of bacon in warm bread and hands it to the lad with thanks. She wakens Dr. Kennedy and relays the message.

Without knowing what to expect at his destination, Lou heads in the direction of the Sawyer Settlement. An Italian man with a fur hat meets him at the Sawyer Road cutoff and guides him to a tilting shack, half hidden by a snowdrift. A young man stands by the entrance, smacking himself on the forehead. His thick Irish accent is difficult even for Lou, with Irish ancestry, to understand.

"I am Gordon Murphy," he says, grabbing the doctor's arm. "My wife is dying."

"What is her name?"

"Catharine."

Lou seldom has to duck his head to get under a door jamb, short as he is, but this is a lowly shack. Desperate is the woman in labour, thankfully oblivious to her surroundings. Sinking to his knees, Lou thrusts his fingers into the gaping cervix and grabs hold of a tiny foot.

Gordon Murphy paces outside, making a mucky track in the snow. He longs for some tobacco or whiskey. Preferably both. Earlier, before the doctor's arrival, in that space between wakefulness and deep sleep, he heard a cow bellowing to be milked and cursed the lazy drunk of a neighbour who left her suffering. Gordon considered getting up to milk the cow himself. Some warm milk would satisfy the burning hunger in his gut. But, by Jeezus, it was too cold to leave his bed.

Slowly his consciousness shifted. The cow was in his house. He opened his eyes. He was not in Ulster. He was not in the wee croft where he spent his boyhood. Closing his eyes, he wished himself back there, into the poverty of Church Lane. Which, by comparison to this Canadian hell, was not poverty at all. The cow bellowed again and Gordon sat up.

Catharine was bent over the smokey remnants of last night's fire, retching and moaning like a dying animal.

"Is it the baby, Cath?" Gordon asked. "Is the baby coming?"

Gordon has never witnessed a human birth. That messy business is left to women. But here in the backwoods of the northern townships, the closest neighbours are half a mile down the road, some kind of foreigners. The woman came last week with a loaf of bread and made a fuss over Catharine's belly, but he couldn't understand a word she said. Still, she probably knew better than him how to get the baby out.

It seemed likely that Catharine was dying, would die alone if he left her here, would die anyway if he stayed, would die either way. Sweat poured down her face, even though the log walls were rimed with frost. As she howled, bile dribbled out of her mouth.

Gordon forced his legs into stiff pants and pulled on his boots and grabbed his coat off the peg by the door and cursed his pecker for the damage it had wrought.

The neighbour knew immediately what Gordon was on about. He grabbed his gun. Gordon tried to indicate that no gun was necessary.

"*Bambino! Bebè!*" The woman cried to let him know that she knew what was happening, but in his deranged state, Gordon thought the man intended harm.

The man yelled at him. "*Medico! Dottore!*" He shoved Gordon out of the way and went outside to fire off four shots into the frozen sunshine.

Catharine, Gordon believes, cannot survive this. She is screaming as if she is being gored by a bull over and over. He looks inside and sees that the doctor has hoisted her up onto her hands and knees. Crawling position. The full impact of his own incompetence makes Gordon shake with shame. He dragged Catharine here under false pretenses, claiming he was as good a farmer as ever there was. Farming is easy, he told her. Anyone with half a brain can do it.

Gordon's father called him a sapskull every day of his youth. And look, he went and proved his father right.

Catharine Ross, seventeen and pregnant, was hopelessly in love with Gordon Murphy, a black-eyed Irishman with a mean streak. He punched her father and knocked down her brother when they tried to stop him from marrying Catharine. After the dust-up, Gordon grabbed Catharine by the arm, rather too roughly, she thought, and they headed north following a map with directions that led them to ninety-eight acres on the Sawyer Road, four miles east of the new village of Haliburton.

Somehow, Catharine let Gordon convince her that clearing trees and building a cabin was an entirely possible achievement. Gordon had an axe. Catharine had a picture in her mind of a simple "but and ben." Table and chairs in the front room, a cradle and bed in the back. She visualized Gordon whittling toys for the children by the fireplace. It was cozy. She was safe.

But there was nothing cozy or safe about the hovel that Gordon managed to erect in the fall before the first snow. By the end of November, he was forced to trade his tired horse and wagon for winter supplies. Flour, sugar, tea, blankets, a pot. Even then, when it was clear they were in trouble, the baby was something abstract to Gordon. Something to worry about in the future. He didn't imagine the reality of a living creature, purple and angry, oozing out between his young wife's thin white thighs onto a pile of hay and thistles. Like a dog throwing pups.

The Italian woman made herself useful, wiping Catharine's brow, kneeling behind her to raise her, working in tandem with the doctor as if they spoke the same language. All the while she murmured.

Ave, o Maria, piena di grazia, il Signore č con te.
Tu sei benedetta fra le donne e benedetto č il frutto del tuo seno,
Gesù Santa Maria, Madre di Dio,
prega per noi peccatoti,
adesso e nell'ora della nostra morte. Amen.

And then it was done.

"Not even a manger for this little one," the doctor scolded.

"Is it really Christmas Day?"

"It is, little Mother. And you have given the world a lovely gift. A beautiful girl. Maria has wrapped her warmly. Just give me a push so we can get the rest of this afterbirth. Lovely. That's a brave strong lass. What will you call the wee girl?"

Catharine looked at Gordon, his head hanging between his shoulders. Did he want to name her after his mother? He had never said as much. "Gloria," Catharine decided.

"In Excelsis Deo," the doctor said, smiling. He indicated to Maria that she could place the babe at the mother's breast. Mouth discovered nipple.

The doctor tidied up his implements. Maria only spoke Italian, but she managed to communicate to the doctor that she would take the baby to her house. That it was too cold in this shack for a newborn. He patted his chest to assure her he agreed, but would take the family to his house. The pioneers who were well able to survive in the bush should not be made responsible for taking in the ones who were totally inept. Otherwise, they would soon starve themselves.

"Grazie, Maria," he said. He knew that she would have kept this sorry bunch all winter, feeding them and caring for the bambina. But he also knew that Lorenzo would want to send them packing. For their own good.

"Can you manage to carry your wife and child to my sleigh, Gordon? We need to get them to town where I can keep an eye on them. Childbirth has drained your wife's energy."

Gordon made an act of protesting, though he knew he had lost any say in what would happen next.

"Jesus would weep if I left your wife and baby here on his birthday," Lou said. "You must come along, too, lad. My housekeeper has a turkey in the oven and there will be far too much food for myself and my daughter. Favour me." And then in a lower voice, the doctor said, "Consider yourself lucky we are not headed to the cemetery."

Maria was left standing alone in front of the hovel. She waited until the sleigh was out of sight, before going back inside to retrieve the placenta and the umbilical cord.

The doctor was a competent sleigh driver. Gordon was surprised to find himself captivated by the journey through snow laden evergreens. Pine and spruce and hemlock. The woods were hushed and pristine. He gave himself over to the moment at hand and gazed thankfully at Catharine's frosted lashes and allowed himself a surge of pride to be a father.

Dr. Kennedy's house was built of red brick, wrapped with a green veranda. A festive wreath hung on the front door. Catharine woke and wept when she saw it, remembering childhood Christmases.

Hannah was plump and merry, and experienced with babies. She got the new mother settled in an upstairs bedroom, tucking her between fresh sheets. She pulled a drawer from the dresser and lined it with a soft blanket. She swaddled the baby and cooed over her before she went down to serve dinner. How much easier it is to be a competent housekeeper in a home such as this, Catharine thought before she let sleep overtake her.

Gordon lingered awkwardly in the bedroom doorway as if he did not deserve to be there. The difference in their circumstances between eight o'clock that morning and six o'clock in the evening was exactly that. Day and night. If he could have crept away and disappeared into the darkness, he would have done so. Instead, he left his humiliation upstairs and let his hunger guide him to a chair at the dining table across from a young girl who stared at him with eyes that told him she was happy for a Christmas Day diversion.

"This is my daughter, Jane. Jane, this is Mr. Murphy."

"Hello Jane. I am very glad to be here."

"Oh, Mr. Murphy. It is our pleasure. Your baby is the best present I received today."

"We're not keeping her, Jane," Hannah said, smiling.

Lou looked up from his place at the head of the table. "The Murphys will be staying with us for a while," he said. "At least until the New Year. We'll make sure Gloria has a good start in the world, won't we? Would you care to give the blessing, Mr. Murphy?"

Hannah raises her eyebrows. The doctor was not one to say grace on a regular basis. But it was Christmas Day and she was glad of it.

Gordon blushed.

"Only if it pleases you," Lou said.

Gordon nodded and bowed his head and folded his hands and called upon his mother's memory to help him. "Bless us, O Lord, and these Thy gifts, which we are about to receive from Thy bounty, through Christ our Lord."

"Amen," said Hannah. She rose to retrieve the gravy, staying hot on the stove, as Lou carved the bird. Turkeys were plentiful and dumb in this part of the country. The wild ones were not good eating. Stringy. Chewy. But Lou had a patient who kept them in a pen on his farm and fed them grain and fattened them properly. He gifted this one to the Kennedys in thanks for services rendered, and services yet to be required.

The juices ran clear and the slices of white meat smelled delicious. Plates were heaped with mashed potatoes and turnip sweetened with maple syrup. There were green beans canned last August. And bright red cranberry sauce. If food ever tasted so good, Gordon could not remember.

After pudding was served, the house creaked in the wind and the freezing pellets started tapping against the windows. With despair, Gordon thought of the absolute impossibility of returning to the shanty he built and a sob escaped his throat.

"May I take a plate up to the new mother?" Jane asked. She did not want to be present if the man started crying in earnest.

"Of course," Lou said. "But do not disturb her if she is asleep. Leave the plate on the nightstand."

Hannah started the clearing away and Lou ushered Gordon into the front parlour. Gordon tried to find words to excuse how he arrived at this hopeless dead end. The doctor offered him a snifter of brandy.

"There is much to learn from failure, Gordon," Lou said.

Somehow, an upholstered wing chair and a fire in the grate made humility seem less bitter. Gordon surrendered himself to advice. Something he refused to do when advice was offered by his grandfather and his father and his mates at the pub back in Ulster.

"Your best bet is the lumber camp, son. You'll make a good wage. You can start your farm in the spring with enough money to buy some livestock. Your wife and bairn will be safe with me for the time being."

Catharine Ross heard the knock at the door but she had no energy to respond. Except for a lamp on the dresser, turned low, the room was dark. Dark and warm and clean. A young girl entered and left a plate of food. Then she crouched beside the baby and hummed a tune. Silent Night. Catharine owed her life to this girl's father. She was shocked that childbirth was so violent. Shocked that any woman survived it at all. Every muscle in her body ached. Her own Granny, back in Prestwick, had ten babies. Ten!

Granny had hugged her hard when she left Scotland and pinned the Ross clan crest on her paisley shawl. Spem Successus Alit, it said. Latin. "What does it mean, Gran?"

"Success nourishes hope." By the end of the long journey at sea, Catharine doubted that success awaited her in Canada. It took every bit of energy she had to nourish hope. She scraped the bottom of the hope barrel. Or so she thought. Until she met Gordon Murphy, the dark-eyed Irishman with stories and promises and a land grant of ninety-eight acres.

He was keen to get away. To a place where Irish immigrants weren't treated like shit. The man at the Land Office suggested they wait until spring to go north.

"I been there, Lad. It's rough territory. You won't get a shelter built before winter if you leave now."

But Gordon did not want to wait around. He convinced Catharine that they would marry in Haliburton. To delay their journey, he said, would be foolish. The day was warm and sunny. The Courtice Road was lined with goldenrod and screaming with crickets. The breeze from Lake Ontario was at their back. All lucky signs.

~ 15 ~

March 1883

I am Jane Kennedy and my father is the doctor. We have the third nicest house in town. The Tucker house is bigger and the Smith house has a better view. My mother doesn't live with us anymore. It will be a year this May since she went to the asylum, a place where she can be safe, Father says. She sees things that aren't there, and she tried to kill our housekeeper Hannah one night, with a kitchen knife, mistaking her for Satan.

Mother was suspicious of Hannah.

"Don't tell her anything, Jane," Mother told me. "Your father hired her to spy on me."

Mother wandered. Sometimes she had fits, and Father had to lock her in her room until she calmed down. I was afraid of her especially when her eyes went spooky. She'd make me hide for long hours in her closet or in the root cellar. And then she would forget she locked me away and I would have to scream until Hannah or Father found me. Her thoughts, Father said, were governed by voices we could not hear.

"Sometimes the brain gets sick," he said. "Like a bad heart or a burst appendix. It can make a person feel desperate like an animal caught in a trap. They might hurt themselves then, or hurt the people who try to help."

Father received many visits from "concerned citizens" who claimed she was stirring up trouble. Time after time, he tried to rescue her, only to be met with curses and kicks to the shins. Shameful performances, all acted out in public. Sometimes she scratched Father's face or ripped his clothes. Her strength was surprising during these episodes. The crashing and screaming behind her bedroom door was terrible.

Father gave her medicine that quieted her, but she got thin. She feared Hannah was putting poison in her soup. We thought she was better but then she took a turn and Father sent her away.

I expected that I was to go with her.

I dressed myself in my Sunday clothing, my best hat and coat and gloves and the delicate boots that had arrived as a birthday parcel from my Hamilton relatives. They were ridiculously inappropriate for walking in the brown gumbo of the village streets.

"Wave to your mother," Hannah suggested.

"But, am I not to accompany her?"

"No, my darling," Hannah said. "We need you here."

Mother looked every bit the invalid as Father carried her down the steps and tucked her into the carriage. She did not bid me farewell. Within an hour the train whistle blew and she was gone and the house was peaceful.

That evening, Father made an effort to engage me with stories about his patients, perhaps concerned that I may be missing Mother. And I did miss her for a while, like one misses an ornament that has been sitting on the mantel and you notice, every time you enter the parlour, that it is no longer there. Until someone thinks to replace it with a clock or a statuette or something different. And that different thing was a lovely woman called Catharine. Father rescued her and Baby Gloria from a rough lean-to on the Sawyer Road. As Catharine recovered from childbirth, the house lightened up. She helped me with my schoolwork. Together we memorized poems, practiced spelling words, and tested each other on the times tables. My performance improved so noticeably that my teacher, Miss Anderson, invited Catharine to be a tutor. There are two Miss Andersons at my school. Sisters. Miss Beatrice Anderson teaches the primary students and Miss Morag Anderson teaches the junior class.

Hannah was happy, she said, to have Baby Gloria to herself, and now Catharine walks to school with me and helps the little ones with reading.

I had almost forgotten about Gordon, her husband, out in the bush. Catharine and I were boiling down maple sap up behind the schoolhouse the day he returned. Hannah got him sorted out, but she pulled Catharine aside as soon as we walked in the door and whispered loud enough for me to hear.

"I had to peel the long-johns off of him," she said. "The skin on his private parts is putrid for want of fresh air."

Gordon seemed uncomfortable in Father's clothes, and wee Gloria would not let him hold her. She screamed and screamed which was not like her at all. She was a sweet, calm baby most of the time. Father came home and set us all at ease and excused Gloria's behaviour by saying she must be cutting a tooth. Gordon handed the baby back to Catharine and ate his dinner rather too fast. He ignored his napkin, using his shirtsleeve, Father's shirtsleeve, to wipe his mouth.

Hannah started clearing away the dishes as soon as pudding was done and Father lit a cigar. He offered one to Gordon. With downcast eyes, Catharine pardoned herself to attend to the baby and I pushed my chair back. Poor Gordon did not understand that he was about to get some advice.

Gordon didn't expect a parade or anything when he returned from the lumber camp, but he did expect a little recognition. He remembered some cold winters in Ireland, but nothing like the raw Canadian winter with chest deep snow drifts and cold that froze the hairs in his nostrils.

"You ain't sweating hard enough if you gotta wear your coat," the bosses yelled. "Coats are for sleeping, that's all."

Gordon did indeed sleep well after pushing and pulling on a crosscut saw all day. Even the horrible snoring of forty men couldn't keep him awake. He lasted the whole winter. Not all of the lumberjacks did. He was determined to earn enough cash to buy a cow. And some chickens. He did not want to spend next winter at the camp again, even though lots of men swore the same thing and returned year after year.

"Don't you recognize me, Hannah?" Gordon asked when the housekeeper handed him some buttered bread and told him to be on his way.

"Oh Lord, Gordon," she screamed. "I mistook you for a tramp. Strip off those bush clothes before you step foot inside! They'll be crawling with lice! You cannot let Catharine see you like this!"

She heated water and poured him a bath right in the back kitchen and scrubbed him with the stiff brush. She cut his hair and shaved his beard. Little Gloria watched from her bassinet with big blue eyes. By the time Catharine and Jane came laughing in the door from school, he was a new man. "Hello Gordon," Catharine said. She sounded formal, like the preacher had come to call.

Gordon had been dreaming about this moment for months. How would it be? Would they stay one night at the doctor's house? In a real bed with clean sheets? Or would Catharine be in a hurry to get home? But Catharine did not rush to embrace him. She could not even meet his gaze. It seemed neither of them could think how to act until Doc Kennedy came in the front door and offered a warm welcome.

"Gordon! What a fine surprise! Hannah we must celebrate the shanty man's return with a bottle of port." He clapped Gordon on the back.

"Tell us all about your experience! What of the other men? Were they good companions?"

Later, in the parlour, after Catharine and Gloria had gone up to bed, Lou leaned forward, like a father might.

"So, now. Tell me what plans you have for the spring."

Gordon stuttered the way he did when his own father peppered him with questions. "I will clear away the trees. And Catharine will plant a garden. I have saved enough money to buy a cow and some chickens."

Lou got up and opened a small cabinet under the front window to retrieve a bottle of Irish whiskey and two glasses. He went to his desk and found a notebook. He came back to the fireside and poured them both a generous portion and settled back into his chair with a deep sigh.

"How much did you come away with, then, after all the deductions for room and board? And I imagine Robert Bell charged you for the coat and boots."

"Yes. And leather mitts."

"So," Lou said, dipping his pen in a small bottle of ink. "What have you earned in total?"

Gordon was not happy to share this information. He did not believe this was any of the doctor's business. But, clearly, Lou had been feeding Catharine and Gloria since Christmas. He had given them warm and safe lodging. Gordon could not think of a way to refuse without seeming ignorant.

"One hundred eighty dollars after deductions."

Lou looked at Gordon. Paused. Put pen to paper. "I heard that wages were lower this year. The railway has brought more labourers, willing to work for less pay. I had hoped you would earn more. You need, at the very least, five hundred to get started. Think of it. A pair of oxen will cost a hundred dollars. A good saddle horse..."

Gordon cleared his throat as a way of interrupting. "One ox is all I need, with a plow. We have no need of a horse. I can walk to town in two hours. Or bring the ox and cart." He drained his glass.

"A cart, then, twenty dollars. A plow will run you fifty. A cow you can get for twenty-five. I'll get some chicks for you for free from Mrs. Cooper. You must start on a house to have it ready for next winter. And a shelter for your livestock."

"I plan on earning enough for all that by clearing my land. Bell says he'll buy all the maple I can cut."

Lou nods. What Gordon expects is no different than the expectations of so many other newcomers. Some are even successful. Most are not.

"Or…" Lou says, refilling Gordon's glass.

"Or?"

"Or you could sign on with the railway over Bancroft way. They are hiring yardmen and conductors and brakemen and the pay is quite good. Twenty dollars a week is what I heard."

Gordon is either angry, or sick with doubt. Lou cannot tell which. But the crease between the younger man's eyes has deepened and Lou realizes he has made his point.

"Time to call it a night, then," he said.

Gordon crept up the stairs to sleep with Catharine, wanting badly to make love to her. But she was sleeping soundly with the baby at her breast and he laid on the floor and listened to her breathing and thought about how such a wife was not going to be much help. She wasn't a farm wife. She had got spoiled.

~ 16 ~

April 1883

Night. There is a thunderstorm raging. Lydia Kennedy's temples throb with pressure like she is wearing a very tight hat. Her chest is bathed in sweat but the windows are closed against the driving rain. When lightning flashes, she gets eerie glimpses of the women up and down the rows. Sunken cheeks and sharp noses and open mouths with crooked teeth. No one, it seems, is awake but her. As the storm rumbles on, she slips one foot out from under the sheet and then the other. Such a relief it is, when both feet touch the cool tiles. She stands and steps away from her bed.

Years ago, she had laced up skates and learned to glide over ice on Lake Jojo in Dundas with other giggling girls. They pretended oblivion to the boys playing shinny and acted surprised when they were chased and caught and pulled along at dizzying speeds.

What a pleasure, she thinks, to skate past the night nurse as she writes by candlelight. Lydia is safely hidden in deep shadows, floating along corridors to the balcony. She expects the door to be locked but the handle turns easily. Only the wind makes it difficult to push the door open. Lydia makes herself skinny and squeezes through the crack. Her nightdress catches as the door shuts, so she pulls it off and leaves it behind, shedding it like snakeskin with no regrets. The night is wild, the sky turbulent. She gulps the air like a pint of beer. Chugs it down, reckless, knowing better but unable to stop herself. Her thirst!

The vine curls up and over the balustrade and it takes only a moment for Lydia to climb over the railing and find a foothold. The leaves are sticky. The thorns tear her flesh. When she reaches the ground, she squats against the stone foundation. Now what? Now where?

Down the mountain to the lake. Perhaps there will be a boat.

Across the lawn to the woods. Perhaps there will be a trail.

Up the laneway to the road. Perhaps a handsome highwayman will take her to his hideaway.

"Tsk, tsk!" says the warden. "Look who has gone and stripped off her nightgown again. Back on with it. Come now! No one wants to see your titties. Such a lewd one you are Mrs. Kennedy. I am losing my patience with you."

While Gordon Murphy was felling trees at the lumber camp, Catharine allowed herself to daydream that he would never return. She did not wish him dead exactly, but when he showed up at the doctor's house with cash in his pocket, full of hope, she wanted to be sick. She hid upstairs and cried into a towel.

"Come along," Lou whispered, when he found her weeping. "Get your coat on. Time to take a look at your property. Gordon is waiting in the carriage."

"But, Lou, I can't go back to that hovel."

"I won't leave you there. Trust me."

When he took her by the elbow, her heart thumped so hard, Catharine was sure the doctor could hear it.

The snow was shrinking out of the woods. The sap was running. The lakes were getting slushy. Sawyer Road was a canal of muddy gumbo and Lou left the horse and carriage out on the main road. The three of them, Lou and Gordon and Catharine, hiked through the woods until they reached the clearing. It was a gloomy day, and the cabin looked like an animal pen. Not fit for humans. Some critters had sheltered there, and it smelled of piss when Gordon opened the door. Lou did not say a word, letting Gordon come to his own conclusions. It was obvious to Catharine that a homestead was impossible, but Gordon refused to admit the obvious. He did agree, however, to let Catharine return to town. He would get to work. He would come for Catharine in a month or so.

It was April first, Catharine noted. Huntigowk Day. And the gowk was Gordon.

Spring comes late in the bush. Gordon slipped on the ice and fell hard enough to crack his tailbone one morning. Just on his way to take a piss and he was flat out. It hurt like a son of a bitch. It was slow to heal. He could hardly bend down to coax a fire out of the deadfall he managed to collect. Shitty hemlock, wet and green, that sizzled and smoked and burned his lungs.

The maple trees he considered potential income started to bud. He did not have the tools to cut them or the manpower, and soon they would be in full leaf. The season for felling trees was past. He had little to show for weeks of misery. It was a low point. The lowest of his life.

Gordon started walking. Away. Away from the trees and rocks and biting flies. Away from failure. He would go to town and sit in a tavern. He would treat himself to a hot meal and a beer. It cheered him up a bit to think he was not a prisoner on these ninety-eight acres. But then he met his neighbour, Lorenzo Salvatori. In broken English, Lorenzo managed to communicate that he thought Gordon's little family had gone back where they came from.

"*La Moglie? Bambino?*"

"In town," Gordon said, pointing uselessly up the road. "Haliburton."

"Okay?"

"Yes. They are both okay."

Lorenzo gave Gordon a tour around his property. The log walls of his cabin were square and chinked tight with clay from the crick. The roof was shingled with cedar shakes. Lorenzo was proud of his fireplace, and even Gordon could tell without any masonry experience, that the stones fit together harmoniously. There was a side oven with an iron door for baking bread. Envy was not a strong enough word to describe the feeling in Gordon's chest.

The Misses offered Gordon some hot oatmeal and he was grateful. He tried not to wolf it down. They sat at a pine table that Lorenzo had made during the winter, and the Misses brought him coffee. Gordon realized that he needed a woman to be successful in the bush. He relaxed a bit, knowing there was someone to blame for his sorry state. Catharine should have been there by his side.

Lorenzo showed Gordon his work shed, with a sharpening wheel for his axe and carving tools. The shed was much nicer than the piece of shit cabin Gordon lived in. There was a privy, too, beautifully constructed.

Gordon pointed to his nose.

"How do you keep it smelling fresh?"

Lorenzo showed him the box of cedar shavings and decomposing leaves, to be tossed down the hole as needed.

Catharine would be impressed by these clever innovations. At the chicken coop, Lorenzo gathered two eggs and handed them to Gordon. A gift. Gordon palmed the treasures and put one in each coat pocket. Lorenzo pointed out the area he tilled for a kitchen garden for Maria. Onions and garlic already coming up.

Gordon returned home and cracked the eggs and drank them raw. He walked to the crick and bathed and put on his good suit and started walking to town. The sun set before he got to the doctor's house but he was not thinking about time. He was only thinking about his wife.

It was well past ten o'clock in the evening when Gordon pounded on the doctor's door.

Doc opened the door himself, with the tousled look of someone awakened.

"I come to collect Catharine," Gordon said.

The doctor nodded. Moved aside. Invited Gordon into the front room where there were still some hot coals in the fireplace. Gordon accepted a tot of whiskey and took a seat.

"What's your plan?"

"I plan to collect my wife."

Lou knew that Gordon and Catharine were not, in fact, married. Catharine had explained that Gordon, in his haste to get away from Catharine's family, had convinced her to wait.

"All right. In the morning, I'll drive you both out there myself."

Gordon did not know what he expected, but he didn't expect this.

"Sleep here by the fire. I'll get you a pillow and a blanket and you'll be quite comfortable."

Gordon fell into an exhausted slumber and woke to hear Gloria crying and footsteps above him. He smelled coffee perking and bread baking and bacon frying. He washed up as well as he could in the summer kitchen out back and managed to make himself presentable for the dining room. Hannah heaped extra servings on his plate and he listened to conversations that were almost as foreign as Lorenzo's strange words. Jane was planning a geography presentation for school. Catharine was discussing baby food with Hannah. Gloria, propped up in a little basket, was rattling a toy and cooing happily.

The Doctor seemed oblivious to it all. He studied a folded newspaper and sipped coffee until, looking up, he demanded everyone's attention by simply clearing his throat. This, Gordon thought, is what is meant by the head of the household. All eyes turned toward Lou. Gordon put his fork down.

"Gordon," he said. "You've made progress on the Sawyer Road?"

"Well…" Gordon understood that the doctor meant to take inventory of his failures.

Catharine turned to look at him. What did she expect he had achieved out there in the bush, with no help from her, with no help from anyone?

"I need Catharine's help. My neighbour has a wife and he has accomplished… he is way further ahead of…"

"Let's ride out there and take a look. See what still needs to be done to prepare for the growing season."

Gordon pulled Catharine aside before they climbed into the doctor's carriage. He asked her why the baby wasn't coming and why she hadn't packed her things.

"Be reasonable, Gordon," Catharine whispered. "Hannah cares for Gloria. Infants cannot be pulled from their routines on a whim."

"We shall come back and get her later," he said, refusing to anticipate how the day might require a change in his plans.

Catharine climbed up into the carriage and tied the ribbons of her bonnet under her chin. A bonnet Gordon had not seen before. He noticed that she had a new dress. New shoes. And a cape. Perhaps they had belonged to the doctor's dead wife?

Catharine did not anticipate a miracle. But Gordon had been working for a month and she did expect more, much more, than the lopsided shanty that greeted them as they turned down the rutted laneway. Even Gordon, who saw it through Catharine's and Lou's eyes, was struck with discouragement. And yet, he hopped down and pointed out the improved chinking around the doorway. A small woodpile. Some sticks, laid sideways, from the cabin to the crick, making the muddy journey easier. He had built a table, of sorts. For food preparation.

Catharine broke down sobbing.

"I cannot live here, Gordon. I am sorry. I would rather go back to my uncle's dairy farm in Darlington County than subject our wee baby to a life in the bush."

Gordon stepped toward her, and she flinched, thinking that he meant to slap her. He was capable of it, she knew from experience. He had done so in the past when his temper got the better of him, and would have again if the doctor had not stepped forward.

"You've done well enough, Gordon, without help. Let me send a man out here to get this farm in order. I will pay his wages for a month or two. You cannot do this by yourself."

"That's why I need my wife here. With me. To cook and clean as Lorenzo's wife does. To make a home of all this."

"That she will. But not yet. Not with a baby to consider. Not without a well-built cabin and proper outbuildings. You ask too much of her. Let her stay in town with us until the weather is better."

It started to rain then. A hard, mean rain that quickly found its way through the holes in the roof. Catharine pulled her cape up over her bonnet and looked at Gordon, hoping for his approval, but not requiring it. She intended to return to town with Lou whether he agreed or not.

Lou pulled a tarp from the back of his carriage and climbed the homemade ladder and tacked it over the leaky roof. While he was up there, instead of helping him, Gordon backed Catharine against the wall and spoke through gritted teeth.

"You are my wife," he said.

"I am not."

"To your shame."

"'Tis you should be ashamed."

"What difference does it make?"

"It makes a difference to me. It makes a difference to God."

"Do you think God would approve of you residing with a widower instead of with the father of your child? People will talk. Your reputation will be ruined."

"The doctor," Catharine said, "is not a widower."

"What do you mean?"

"His wife is in a hospital for the mentally insane."

"I don't believe you."

"Ask him."

Above their heads, they could hear Lou adjusting the tarp. The incessant dripping was diverted, and then it stopped.

"All the more reason for you to come here and help me as you promised. Act like a wife if you want me to make you one. Prove your loyalty."

"Prove you can provide shelter and food and a safe place for our daughter to live. This shack is not fit for a gypsy."

He slapped her then. Hard, across the face. And the shame of it was shared with the doctor as he entered the low doorway. He did not say a word, only stepped between Gordon and Catharine and led her out. The ravens went wild with cautions as they climbed into the carriage.

Catharine was not proud of herself for climbing up and taking her place beside Lou. She knew Gordon was watching. She could feel the heat of his hatred on her back. She did not turn around. She did not trust that he could take care of her and Gloria. She would not marry him, even if he built her a castle. And she was not sorry.

Maria watched from the stand of tamaracks that divided her property from Gordon Murphy's. She could hear the voices rising and falling with emotion. Italians were an emotional people, but, even when they argued, Maria thought her language sounded not so ugly. Not so harsh.

Where was the baby? How did the mother come to be so well-dressed? What transpired since Christmas Day? Maria believed the little family had returned to where they came from. And she had not blamed them. If she had not suffered through the hell of New York City, she also might have fled to seek an easier life. But she was starting to feel at home here in the peaceful forest. The plentiful game. The fish in the creek.

People. Maria missed people, but people carried disease. They were violent and aggressive. They attracted rats. All she needed was a husband and bambinos and she could survive quite well here on the Sawyer Road.

The doctor was on the roof of the shack. The couple was arguing. Maria leaned on a tamarack trunk and sighed. Tamaracks have needles that turn brilliant yellow in the fall and drop away. Now, at the beginning of summer, the branches were growing tender green shoots.

This tree had many uses, as Maria discovered.

A few days after Gordon and Catharine disappeared last winter, a lone figure approached their shack. A man or a woman, Maria could not tell at first. It was a calm day after three days of snow and Maria made her way to the privy with difficulty. She was a short woman. Her squat legs were not designed for stepping through deep snow. From her vantage point, sitting atop her frosty throne, she saw the figure. Normally she would be frightened. Lorenzo had taken the sleigh to town. She was vulnerable, here, halfway through a bowel movement with bare frozen buttocks exposed for all the world to see. Maria never closed the outhouse door as she did her business. She preferred to watch the trees and the squirrels. The presence of an unfamiliar traveller should have alarmed her, but she was not afraid. The chickadees sang in the cedar trees, and somehow she felt it was important to call out before the stranger passed. Her curiosity was great.

"*Ciao!* Hello!"

"*Ciao! Vengo in pace, lo prometto!*"

Italian! Maria rushed to pull up her knickers and layers of woollens. She pushed the door to the outhouse closed behind her and turned the simple latch Lorenzo had designed that spun around on a nail.

"Mi chiamo Maria."

"Mi chiamo Ona."

Ona traipsed along the backroads after winter storms, checking on newly arrived immigrants, or cabins where women and children were on their own. Humans give up their locations with chimney smoke. From her ridge, she noticed when the smoke billowed, thick and black. A new settler trying to burn green wood. She noticed when the smoke rose straight up, a thin pillar on the coldest day of the year. She noticed when the smoke was absent. A frequent and worrying sign that the occupants were in trouble. When the smoke from Gordon's lean-to had ceased, Ona strapped on her pack of supplies to find out why.

Maria led Ona back to her own fireplace and offered her a bowl of the soup that was always on the hob. She wanted to learn so much from this bear of a woman. First of all, she wanted to know how to make the snow-walking shoes that Ona strapped to her boots. That is when she was introduced to the tamarack tree, a flexible wood perfect for making agimag.

Maria was not afraid of hard work. Especially hard work that yielded results. As a young woman she worked long days on her family's farm, trying to coax crops from the arid soil of Sicily. Peasants, they were, poor as the dirt. Her brother, Lorenzo, got fed up. He convinced his fiancée, Giulia, to board the big ship for America. They sewed coins and a few small heirlooms into the hems of their clothing and paid the steerage fare to cross the Atlantic. But the day before they were to sail, Giulia's father took sick and she refused to leave him. She would stay and care for her father as any good Italian daughter would. Lorenzo believed that Giulia's father would make a full recovery shortly after the ship disappeared from the horizon, but he could not convince her to choose him.

So, Maria took Giulia's ticket and watched Sicily recede, glittering in the early morning sun.

"*Buona liberazione,*" Lorenzo said.

Maria knelt at the railing, crying for her sisters.

New York City was a hell much worse than slaving under the hot sun of Sicily. Maria became pale and sick from long hours working in the chaos of the garment factory. It seemed she would die of consumption like so many who spent their days in the dark, lint-filled caverns. Lorenzo, for his part, prayed to the Virgin, lit candles, and begged forgiveness in the confessional at Our Lady of Sorrows.

The priest, an Italian, gave him light penance and called him figlio. He also gave Lorenzo a brochure, printed in Italian, calling for farmers in Canada. Free land. The priest drew him a map and directed him to the railway station where he and Maria could board a train for Niagara Falls.

Lorenzo and Maria left the rat-infested tenement and headed north, expecting, with all optimism, a better life. How could it be worse?

~ 17 ~

Girls fall in love with boys. They do not do a very thorough assessment about future prospects. If they did, there would be fewer marriages. Catharine ran off with the first man who held her tight. Gordon Murphy pushed her up against the brick wall of the schoolhouse after the All Saints Day dance and told her she was beautiful and that was enough.

Girls fall out of love when they realize they are not safe, but they don't always leave. Long after they fall out of love, long after they get used to feeling unsafe, they stay. Even when they realize their babies are not safe, still, sometimes they stay. Where would they go? Girls don't leave until someone offers them a lifeboat.

Gordon knew that the doctor was offering a lifeboat to Catharine. Gordon needed saving too, and the doctor obliged. He paid the wages of a carpenter to help him build a decent cabin. But a man doesn't necessarily want saving. Sometimes a man would rather die than admit to that need. Sometimes, a man would rather kill his wife, kill his entire family, rather than see them saved by someone other than himself.

Gordon saw how Catharine looked at the doctor and he understood he would never measure up and the despair in his heart was great.

The only thing that remained for Gordon was deciding how to end his life. He tried drowning first. He had watched a man jump off the boat after ten days travel in the stormy North Atlantic. The crowded conditions below deck were unbearable and jumping overboard was the only viable option of escape. This man had painful cankers and other personal troubles and he bid farewell and told the crew not to save him. It seemed at the time a heroic venture. But at the edge of Lake Kashagawigamog, Gordon found it impossible to wade far enough into the freezing waters to accomplish his goal.

On his way home, he found a piece of rope, which he took to be a sign from God. He tied the rope to a stick and tossed it over a sturdy oak branch. He wandered away to find something to stand on. When he returned, rolling a chunk of hemlock ahead of him, one that had been serving as a chair in his wee cabin, a red squirrel greeted him with a proper scolding. The rope was on the ground. Gordon sat on his hemlock stool and bawled. He tied the rope around his waist and returned to his cabin and slept very hard. The next day, Maria appeared, like a saint, and saved him from himself.

Lorenzo did not approve of his sister helping the dirty Irishman.

"Too bad!" she yelled. Maria could put red squirrels to shame in the scolding department. "You think you can boss me around? You forget I changed your pannolini when you were a baby?"

"He's stupido. Stay away from him, Maria."

Maria ignored him and carried a pot of stew through the woods. She paused and watched as the Irishman pissed behind his shack. He was attractive. Black hair. Black sad eyes. Too thin though. He turned and looked her way and she emerged from the shadows.

Holy Mother of God, she thought. Why is my heart beating so fast? Too long in the forest!

"Bear stew," she said, offering him the pot.

Lorenzo shot the animal when it broke into their corn crib. One bear. Many uses. Grease, food, fur. The Irishman fell on the stew like it was his last meal.

The cabin! What a mess! The bedding smelled like wet dog hair and no dog in sight. Maria gathered up the ticking and dragged it outside and draped it over the sorry excuse for a woodpile. She collected dirty pots and bowls and carried them to the creek. Gordon followed and watched as she pulled handfuls of pale green lichen and started scrubbing the dishes with it. Her generous bosom bounced enticingly as she worked.

"How long have you been married? To Lorenzo?" he asked, slow and loud as if that would help her understand English.

"No conjugal. Fratello! Non sono sposata."

"Fratello. Brother?"

"Fratello! Brother! *Sì!"*

"Not married?"

"No! *Lui non è mio marito.*" Maria shook her head and made a face to show she was horrified at the thought.

"And me," he admitted. "Not married."

"Non sono sposato. Catharine non è tua moglie?"

"Catharine. No. Not married."

"E la bambina picola?"

"Baby?"

"Baby. Gloria."

"No."

Maria did not believe him. Men lie. But if this handsome man claimed to be free from responsibilities, so be it. In these backwoods, people leave old selves behind like outgrown clothes.

Every morning from that day forward, Gordon walked over to the property line and waited. Maria brought him coffee and warm bread, and by August they were engaged to be married. Lorenzo was not convinced that Gordon would make a good husband for his sister, but she wanted her own home. Gordon was dim, but manageable, and their babies would be handsome.

~ 18 ~

Reverend Whitlock and Alex Smith spent more time together. Like the last two wallflowers at the prom, they reluctantly partnered up. It was either that or dance alone. Together, they developed a list of mutually supportive actions to leverage their influence in Haliburton. Alex Smith, nominated by the good Reverend, became an elder at St. Mark's. In return, the banker made sure that Dick Whitlock's placement at St. Mark's was extended for another four years.

After a few successes, each man relaxed his guarded behaviour, trusting in mutual discretion. Their reputations depended upon it. It must be said that Alexander Smith found the Reverend's self-aggrandizement loathsome. He was nothing like Jesus, as he would like to believe. His relationships with fatherless boys and naive little girls, Smith suspected, were not the least bit Christ-like.

Likewise, Dick Whitlock could not respect a man who dishonoured his wedding vows with such flagrant indiscretion. The Reverend was fond of Clarissa Smith, who was not a stupid woman. He was sure she was aware of Alexander's philandering. But she continued to see in her husband a level of accomplishment he did not deserve. Perhaps it was because he constantly demeaned her and made her feel unworthy. He could be cruel. Dick occasionally stood up for her when Alex went on about his wife's failures, but Alex only told him he wasn't qualified to speak about marriage. That stung. More so because it was true. Dick was starting to see how the right sort of wife could be an asset. He even dropped by the school and asked Morag Anderson to attend a church supper with him. She blushed and explained that she was now attending the new Lakeside Church.

"And, I am stepping out with Murdoch McGee," she said, as a further deterrent. Dick backed up, keen to escape the schoolmarm's earnest look of pity. "Watch out!" she said, too late, as he bumped into a bookcase and caused an avalanche of anthologies.

"I'm sorry," he said. "How clumsy of me." He bent to pick up the books and saw Miss Beatrice Anderson leaning in the doorway with an unmistakable grin of pure delight before she rushed to his aid. The bell rang just then, and Beatrice walked with him out to the main door where the children were lining up according to height and gender.

"Thank you," he said. "I don't suppose…"

"I have a beau." she said, rather too quickly.

Reverend Dick Whitlock hated himself profoundly. He was not normal. And he was not talented at pretending to be normal. He sometimes felt that the ability to play his role convincingly was within his grasp. But no. He knew himself to be a sham. A faker. He marched up the railway line to Gould's Crossing to purchase more tonic. He never bought enough, thinking each visit would be his last. It terrified him to cross the trestle bridge at Barnum Creek, lest a train come along when he was halfway over. He had seen boys jump off and roll in the bog below and he hoped never to be forced to do that himself. But, sure enough, a train whistle sounded when he was almost perfectly in the middle. Dick was a clumsy runner, hopelessly pigeon-toed. The tracks vibrated beneath his feet, the whistle blasted again, and he tripped. Caught his ankle between the ties. Panicky, he yanked his foot out of his shoe and crawled on hands and knees to the edge. He rolled off the side and crouched by the creek and howled in pain as the train passed above his head.

"Jesus help me," he begged.

Miraculously, Jesus sent Angel.

Dick Whitlock's mother hated dogs. A boy with a dog is never without a friend, something Dick could have benefited from. But no one argued with Mother. Angel had a thick red coat and a gentle muzzle.

"Are you in trouble, Reverend?" Came a voice from up on the bridge.

Oh Lord. Murdoch McGee. "Yes. I believe I am. This is your dog?"

"Angel. She's not mine exactly. More like I'm hers. Here. Let me have a look at your ankle."

And that is how Murdoch came to know Dick Whitlock, for it took some time to get the Reverend sorted out and back to the church. And then Murdoch kindly made a trip out to the gypsy settlement to get Dick some of the tonic he needed. Murdoch knew about tonic. He knew about pain. All kinds of pain, and he did not judge the suffering of others.

When the Reverend was comfortable with his foot elevated in his cot, Murdoch pulled up a chair.

"Can I get you anything else?"

"No. Thank you."

"Do you want Angel to stay the night?"

"Yes, please, if you can spare her. I am glad to know you better, sir. I took you at first for a…"

"A brute?"

"Yes. I was taken by surprise to hear you are acquainted with the schoolteacher. Morag Anderson. But now I see how you may be quite a suitable match."

Murdoch smiled. "She's far too good for me, but, yes. I'm lucky there aren't a lot of eligible bachelors in this town." Then he blushed, worried he may have offended the Reverend.

Dick just sipped on his tonic and nodded off and when he awoke, Murdoch was gone. But the dog, oh the dog was warm and her heartbeat was healing.

Dead of night. Dread of night. Dread of the dead. Dread of being dead. Once you are a ghost like me, you will chastise yourself for the time you wasted on fearfulness. Midnight is an unsettling place at St. Mark's Church. Hollow with unhallowed vapours. And yet I am often drawn here by the Reverend's cries. Painful cramps in his legs cause him to beg for grace like the newly crucified. But tonight, despite his injury, he rests well. Angel watches me incuriously, her soulful eyes half-hidden behind long lashes.

~ 19 ~

If the Loyalist Lodge was the place for lively discussions of philosophy and new ideologies, Crockett's Mercantile on Pine Street was the place to go for news. Working men came and went during the day, gathering alongside the crowd of old fellows whose days of labour were past. They all had differing versions of local history and current events.

"If you ain't heard a whopper by 10 a.m.," Miles Crockett claimed, "it's time to make one up."

There was strong coffee boiling on the Quebec stove and strong whiskey in a jug hidden behind the rat poison, depending on the occasion. And strong words, even fisticuffs if an argument needed settling. Sometimes a bloodied nose was the only way to shut a loud mouth. The men swore and smoked and spat and argued about property values and unfair wages and annoyed the hell out of Alma Crockett. She paid close attention to what was going on around the stove. How much coffee they consumed, how much cider they drank. Miles seemed to think they were running some kind of charity, so Alma had to be the taskmaster and ask the men to pay for what they consumed.

Miles believed she expected too much of folks.

"There needs to be a little give and take," he told and told her. "If I treat a fellow to a tot of whiskey on a bad day, that man might help me fix a busted window or a hole in the roof."

Miles was right, of course. Those men would do anything for him if he needed help. Whereas, she had few friends. She had become accustomed to being lonely, until the Kennedys moved to town.

A close friend was something new for Alma. The unexpected joy of a kindred spirit improved her whole outlook on the tedium of daily living.

Lydia, the doctor's wife, took Alma into her confidence, revealing ever so many secrets and so much sadness. And Alma could tell Lydia Kennedy anything. About the ache in her barren womb and the worrisome lump in her breast and her suspicions about prying neighbours. But Lydia took ill. Alma had no experience with the kind of sickness her friend had. Doc Kennedy, a man of advanced medical talents, did not have the means to cure her and he sent her away. Back to her people in Hamilton, he claimed.

And yet, in her apron pocket, Alma had a letter to prove that Mrs. Kennedy was not with her people at all, but locked away in an institution. The letter begged Alma to come and release her.

I know people gossip about us. Folks believe they have the right to speculate about their doctor's personal life, and as his daughter, I am all the time being questioned about what is going on at our house. It's been almost two years since Mother's been gone and so much has changed. Catharine has swept the house clean of fear with her sweet temperament. Talking to Baby Gloria, kissing me good morning, chatting at the breakfast table about small miracles like a sunny day or a comical blue jay in the yard.

"Come out on the porch, Jane," Catharine called last night. "The moon is rising! Can you see her face?"

"Is the moon a woman?" I asked.

"Most definitely!"

Catharine makes Hannah happy, too, simply by noticing her efforts and offering thanks for the simplest tasks, like ironing the pleats on the baby's gowns. Thank you. It becomes a habit in our house. Thank you for making this delicious bread, for calming the baby, for holding the door open. For offering a hand with the chores.

So, when Catharine started sharing Father's bed, Hannah and I did not like to comment upon it, lest we break the spell of happiness in the house. I knew. Hannah knew. I knew that Hannah knew and Hannah knew that I knew and we shared a look when there was some intimacy between them after dinner as they sat together on the settee by the fireplace, sharing stories in the newspaper. Hands brushing each other, voices lowered. It was nice to see Father enjoying Catharine's company after the struggle he endured with Mother.

I know it's wrong, of course. And there will be consequences, no doubt. This is a sin, spelled out very clearly in the seventh commandment. Thou shall not commit adultery. My mother and Catharine's husband are very much alive. But it does not seem fair, somehow, that people well-suited for each other should be kept apart.

And so we continue. I avert my eyes and read my lessons. Hannah sews or knits or darns. We are complicit in this sin against God. For all of Father's upbringing, he does not appear to be a religious man in any way. No prayer beads or Hail Marys. He does not take the train on Sunday mornings to attend mass at the Catholic Church in Lindsay, like some Catholics. Wendy Pemberton's family goes to St. Mark's every Sunday. Her older sister Trudy is the organist. "You are welcome to come with us," she says, "but I warn you, it is terribly boring."

I want to judge that for myself and tell Father, but he is adamant that I shall not darken the door of that church while Reverend Whitlock is in the pulpit.

I cry my frustrations to Wendy.

"Come with me after school," she says. "The front door is never locked. A thief would be struck dead if he stole from the church."

As soon as I entered the church, I felt relief. Perhaps it has something to do with the way sun shines through stained glass, soft and holy. St. Mark's blue robe, the lion's golden wings, the red and purple frame. I stop in every chance I get, now, to sit in a pew and pray for absolution. If Father and Catharine are going to hell, I do not intend to join them.

Reverend Whitlock noticed me last Thursday. He invited me to join him for tea. We sat in the sanctuary and he let me choose the opening hymn for Sunday.

"Abide With Me," I said. That is Hannah's favourite.

"Hymn number twenty-four," he said, and opened the hymnal to show me. Then he let me slide the hymnal numbers into the wooden bracket beside the pulpit. He held onto my waist tightly as I reached up to insert the numbers and I felt I could trust him. So I confided that I was half sick about God's judgment and I stumbled through an explanation about Father and Catharine. My face was red with shame but I persevered. He reassured me in the nicest way and helped me light a candle for saintly intercession, and kissed me on the forehead and called me Darling, and told me I should call him Dick, now that we are friends.

~ 20 ~

Webster and Murdoch McGee were happy to be quit of the lumberjack business. Behind them lay the forests of New Hampshire and Vermont and the Eastern Townships of Quebec. The brothers had sustained broken wrists, broken ankles, severe knocks to the head, innumerable bruises, and a few stab wounds too. Shanty men were a rough lot.

Weaned on Scottish fescue, there was only one occupation to consider after quitting the lumber trade. They would take up their father's profession and become keepers of the green.

Golf courses in Ontario were few and far between. Webster convinced Murdoch that Haliburton would make an ideal location. The hills reminded him of Scotland. He visualized a challenging course for tournament play. The brothers traipsed around the township of Dysart et al, looking for a picturesque property, and finally found the perfect spot on the south shore of Lake Kashagawigamog. They climbed to the lookout atop the highest ridge.

"This shall be the ninth tee box, Murdy." Webster tossed a feather-filled leather ball on the ground and took a mighty swing at it with an iron club. He had forged the club himself, with a curved hosel that sent the ball arching up over the trees.

"It's likely in the lake, Webster. Fayther would be gobsmacked. What a backswing ye have!"

"We'll build the clubhouse on that plateau, Murdoch. All that remains is to find the owner and negotiate a fair deal."

Alma, at the mercantile, could not help them. The old fellows who were gathered around the stove that afternoon sent the brothers over to the barbershop, but that was a dead end too. Lefty, at the station sent them to the Nunnery.

"By your description, it sounds like you are talking about land in the McLeod Tract. Go up the trail behind Town Hall until you reach the stone cloister. Ask for Winona."

"A woman?"

"A woman worth knowing."

"Hello!" Webby called as they approached. "Hello the place!"

Instantly Ona felt the familiarity, as one often does, when meeting those of similar heritage. The men offered their hands respectfully and she noted the scarred knuckles. Sensed that they were not fighting men, but loyal men.

She offered them highland whiskey from the Oban Distillery.

"So ye are a Scotswoman, then," Webby said.

"I'm a McLeod, aye. But I'm only half Scottish. My mother was Anishinaabe."

"Well, I am truly in love with you, Winona McLeod."

"Slàinte Mhath!" Ona said, topping up their glasses. "Call me Ona. Everyone does."

"What do you want for that property on the South Kashagawigamog Road, Ona? Me brother and I fancy building a golf course there. Tis a braw sight from the lookout."

"That's a pretty tract. I don't want it clear cut, lads."

"Och, nay. The trees give the course its character. Each hole will be named for a tree. The first hole will be called The Birches. The second will be Red Pine Valley. And so on."

"Do ye play?" asked Murdoch.

Ona led them to her cabin and showed them Old McLeod's mashies and niblicks and spoons. "Grandfather would swing at anything. Mushroom caps, chestnuts, acorns. If he thought that there would one day be a golf course on McLeod property, he would have been very pleased. I will gladly sign it over to you lads in exchange for a lifetime membership. And for occasional services rendered. Sometimes, we nuns need the help of braiff men. Not often, mind ye. We're a tough lot."

"We are happy to offer protection whenever it is needed. But I insist. We will pay for the property. We will compensate you for its full value."

Ona laughs and accepts a reasonable payment in exchange for the deed to the lakefront acreage. "I know better than to argue with a stubborn pair of Scotsmen," she says. "Old McLeod left me rich in property. The McLeod clan motto is 'Hold Fast'. He was greedy for land. And determined to keep it away from them that would covet it. The injustice of the Highland Clearances was drilled into him by his grandfather. He carried that anger, and expected me to carry it for him once he was gone."

The men nodded. No need to explain further. Revenge, they knew, can be centuries in the execution.

"Common decency, is all I expect, but there are men in this village who believe they are above that. They threaten us. And though I have medicine to cure many ills, I have not found a cure for a black heart."

Murdoch was the quiet one. He rarely said a word, but when he did it was definitive. "Your enemies are ours now. Do not let them trouble your mind one more minute. Call on us as needed."

Ona filled their cups with whiskey, the water of life, and they solemnly toasted to their new alliance.

~ 21 ~

Maria's mother taught her not to take any crap from anyone, and Gordon learns early on that it is in his best interest to follow his wife's orders. He is happy to fix things, dig trenches, improve the house he built with the help of the doctor's handyman. A fine solid cabin with a loft for sleeping and a stone fireplace with excellent draw.

Maria has the energy to do everything else, even with a newborn baby and another on the way. Joseph, she called her son, because it is a favourite boy's name in Italian and Irish. A swaddled babe is complacent, hanging on the fencepost under the red maple as she weeds and hoes and harvests. Peas and beans climb the wire strung from post to post. And grapes. Giulia, her sister-in-law whose old father finally died, brought a trunk packed with grape vines in Sicilian soil that she managed to keep moist all the way across the Atlantic, tending them like children. Haliburton soil is rich in places, but not distributed in rectangular fields. The best loam lies alongside creek beds in damp recessions where fiddleheads and wild leeks grow. Maria seeks out the secret wealth of good soil. It is a treasure hunt.

Some say Maria wears the pants. Her cousins and the other new Italian immigrants laugh at the way Gordon allows his wife to boss him around. Gordon understands more Italian than he lets on, but he owes his life to Maria and he doesn't care what a few *paesonos* say to amuse themselves. His root cellar is stocked with glass jars lined up as neatly as a store. Red tomatoes. Maple syrup. Pickled beets. Plus, baskets of turnips and squash and garlic and onions. They have more than they can eat. So much, they have extra to sell to the Mercantile. The Victoria Rail Line may have reversed the fortunes of many local farmers with competitively priced produce from farther south, but Maria's preserves and eggs remain in high demand.

"Bring your wife to town, next time," Alma Crockett tells Gordon when he delivers some lovely orange pumpkins.

"She's shy," he says. "Her English is not good. Come out to our place and I'll introduce you. But I warn you, she will insist on feeding you! Don't eat before you come."

Alma nods. "Thank you. I will." She does not get many invitations, and she takes Gordon's gesture kindly.

There was a time when Gordon felt only humiliation as he walked through town, supposing that everyone knew him to be a cuckold. But the acrimony which once poisoned his heart, seeped away. The memory of the young girl he had dragged up here, thinking she could be a farm wife, faded. If he chanced to see Catharine in town, he could nod genially and keep walking.

Sometimes, he caught a glimpse of his daughter. Gloria reminded him of his little sister in Ulster. Except that Gloria wore lovely frocks and a warm coat and real leather shoes. And she wasn't his to claim. She was known as Gloria Kennedy now. If Maria suspected that the bambolina who was born that Christmas Day was, in fact, Gordon's daughter, she never brought it up. Best left alone, that possibility.

Only a few people knew for certain. And the only one Gordon was forced to engage with was the Doctor. But Doc never let on that they had history. Gordon went to Lou's office one winter day when he had a terrible ache in his side and thought he might be dying. Doc treated him for a kidney infection and while he was recovering on the cot in the office, he was also treated to a fatherly conversation.

"I hope you will not take this the wrong way, Gordon. There are many young men in this township who have come to Haliburton, as you have, escaping some hardship or perceived ill treatment. Men who do not wish to be slaves in factories at wages that keep them poor. I have watched many young men fail, and return to that life they hated once, and are sure to hate again. I have seen men prosper, too. And the difference, it seems to me, is ambition."

Gordon felt the pain easing in his side as the dose of morphine took hold. He started breathing evenly. The release made him love this man. Or at least, forget his grudge. This was a man he once imagined killing with his axe.

The doctor tamped some tobacco into his pipe and lit it. The fragrant smell drifted across to Gordon, and the curling smoke shone in the rays of sunlight above his head like a halo.

"My advise then, is not for you alone, but for any young man who wants to try the pioneer life. Become an expert."

Gordon turned his head. The doctor sat on a stool, in a hunched way. A wiry man with an intense visage that erected an invisible boundary. Like a protective shield. It made him seem separate. It made his words seem important.

"I am an expert at medicine, for example, and if someone has a disease or an accident, they come to me. They seek my expertise. But, no less important is the barber. He studied haircuts and bought the right tools and opened a business. Sapper, if you know him, has learned to divert water through culverts to stop spring flooding and has more orders than he can fill."

The smoke from the pipe rose up to the ceiling, and Gordon felt himself drifting but also listening. And not only listening, but paying attention.

"What did your father do? For wages?"

"He was a digger."

"A digger."

"Coal. Ditches. Graves."

"It takes a strong back."

"He had one. But it didn't last forever."

"No. But consider this. He knew the business of digging. Would you agree that he was an expert on digging?"

"Yes. I suppose. But it was a lowly job."

"And yet, essential. Essential to any construction task. During all seasons."

"True. He was never without work even if it was shovelling horse shit."

"So. He knew the value of a day's digging, and probably understood what someone would be willing to pay. If your father had hired a team of shovelers, he would not have had to do the work himself. Do you see what I mean? He could have been the man to get digging contracts for the cemetery, the gravel pit, the coal yard. And paid men their wages, sparing his own back."

Gordon sat up and squinted. Doc pressed his tender side and he yelped.

"That stone will pass if you drink another gallon of water. You'll have blood in your piss for a day or two."

Gordon became passably fluent in Italian. He developed an ear for the sing-song language and Maria was an appreciative teacher, kissing him and hugging him whenever he repeated a phrase. He soon found himself in the middle of an Italian community, the lots on the Sawyer Road filling up with immigrants. *Paesanos.*

Gordon thought about his conversation with Doc whenever Maria bade him get his shovel. As he dug a drain. As he dug clay from the riverbed for bricks that Lorenzo was making and baking in his kiln. Before another year was out, he had a digging business. Italian men, new to the country, appreciated the opportunity to work. Doc hadn't been wrong about contracts. Gordon hustled at first to build a reputation. He was reliable and fair and soon he did not have to seek work. Work came to him. Digging basements and privy holes and waste lagoons and graves. He did not discriminate at first, but as time went on, he learned that the wealthy paid extra for work done on demand. He raised his prices and the poor either waited or did their own digging. Eventually, he was busy with only two clients. The Victoria Railway, which needed constant repair work, and the bank manager who had invested in properties abandoned by settlers unable to meet their financial obligations. Some of the digging jobs required discretion.

"I like that your workers keep to themselves," Alex Smith told him. "I like that they don't speak English."

Gordon did not like Alexander Smith. He stood too close as he gave vaguely threatening warnings. His breath was rancid, like a maggoty midden. He did not like some of the job sites, haunted by ghosts of human suffering. But he did like the money, deposited regularly, into his business account at the Dominion Bank.

Doc had stopped in one day after making a Sawyers Road house call.

"I see you're working for the bank manager, Gordon. Does he treat you all right? Does he pay his bills?"

"He does, Doc."

"Not every man you will work for will be honest," Doc said. "You're keeping records, just in case?"

"In case of what?"

"In case there is ever a question of legality."

Gordon knew exactly what Doc meant. Following Doc's advice, Gordon started keeping notes with sketches and measurements and illustrated maps of every work site.

~ 22 ~

The railway platform was a tapestry of humanity when the three o'clock train arrived from Lindsay. Disembarking passengers looked up at the ridge to get their bearings. Such a magnificent monolith of prehistoric stone. When the sun reflected off the quartz deposits, the Nunnery appeared to glow.

What the travellers could not see, was Ona McLeod and Mary Hammond looking back at them from the ridge..

"So many arrivals, Mary!"

"A blight on the landscape."

"That's an uncharitable thing for a nun to say," Ona said, chuckling.

"Tis the truth! Parasites, all of them, swarming like mosquitoes. Come to suck the blood out of the earth."

"Yet, look, there are your boys, hustling to make a profit."

"Just as well them as others." They watched Peter follow some travellers to a waiting carriage, his arms laden with bags. Norman piled boxes onto a barge at the town dock.

"Soon the lake will be frozen and the boats pulled ashore until spring," Mary said.

Ona sighed. She was picturing the ice road that would soon be busy with traffic crossing Head Lake. Last winter, Ona watched two horses and a sleigh filled with Hogmanay revellers disappear up beyond the narrows. Three cries for help, and then silence. The bodies were carried a long way under the ice by the current and were not found until May. People reported that they heard the three haunting cries echoing near the bridge on summer evenings.

"I'd best go and check on Kateri," Mary said.

Ona sat in stillness as the constellations appeared, one star at a time. She thought about the Sky Woman stories that Nokomis used to tell. Kateri was about to join the ancestors. The old woman stopped eating days ago, stopped taking water. She turned her face to the stone wall and distanced herself from the living world to complete this final labour alone. Dying was difficult work.

Ona expected Kateri's spirit would escape in the dark hour before dawn. Eyes sunken in skull, toes curled, skin like ink-stained parchment. With Kateri's passing, so passed the story of Ona's birth and childhood. Kateri was the only one left who remembered Ona's mother, Meg. The cloak of grief seemed heavier because of it.

When Grandfather McLeod died, Ona was a young woman of twenty. She missed his presence, large and impressive. But she did not miss his domination. In the year of his final illness, as Angus McLeod lay bedridden, Ona committed herself to acquiring the knowledge to manage his estate. She inherited wealth, but also duty. The duty to honour the teachings of both grandparents, even though the two legacies were difficult to reconcile.

Theories of ownership and economics were heavy but necessary burdens. From Ona's perspective, the great tracts of land she inherited were abstract. Always, the memory of Nokomis's voice made her question the purpose of claiming ownership of a lake. Of a forest. Of a mountain.

"The people who wander through this territory will soon be surprised that their seasonal shelters and traditional hunting grounds are no longer available to them," Grandfather McLeod told Ona in his final days. "They will find fences where there were none before. They will be denied access. You must own property," he said. "You must manage it wisely. You must be the one with the power to restrict the movement of others, not the other way 'round."

"It seems cruel to deny people access to such a vast wilderness."

"The world is cruel. History is full of examples of cruelties. Your grandmother's people lost everything. And my Scottish ancestors were burned out of their farms, starved out of their highland villages, forced to be beggars or thieves or warmongers. Much blood was shed. I decided long ago to be a land owner. Never a tenant. Never a slave."

On the wall of Angus McLeod's cabin hung a collection of maps. Ona studied the way the world was divided by borders. She memorized the boundaries of the McLeod Tract, invisible to the naked eye and significant only within men's minds and in their courts of law. Her heart felt cheated by the great losses suffered as land was exchanged for money. Currency her grandmother's people had limited access to.

It became Ona's responsibility to meet with solicitors. She learned to negotiate the complexities of nineteenth century economics, and found that her grandfather had not been wrong. It was far better to be rich than poor. Better to be the innkeeper, rather than his serving wench. Better to be a landlord. Better to be a man, or to pose as one. Registering her business and properties as "W. McLeod" took care of that.

To their credit, the solicitors never treated Ona like a lady. From her first introduction, it was all business. She came well prepared to meetings, having educated herself on commercial development potential in the Northern Townships. Her questions were always precise and her actions decisive.

Legal papers. Deeds. Policies. Maps. They all required different kinds of literacy.

"Your mother would not have been such a patient student," Kateri told Ona. "It was meant to be that you took over the old man's estate."

"But my mother was clever, you said."

"Oh! Yes. Meg was fearless in the woods, but quick to learn her letters and figures, too. The truth is, she knew her father would have preferred a son. He made no secret of that and she could not hide her resentment. When she ran away, I promised to care for you."

"I always hoped she might..."

"Come back for you? Yes. I did too. We don't know, do we, what became of her. It is a big world. And women are often forced to take paths not of their own choosing. But life is long, Winona. You may yet be reunited."

Ona startles awake. Her dream memory dims and recedes. The flap of leather in the roof stirs and stills. A barred owl calls. Ona imagines that there is a feather under her nose, and tries to breathe so softly that the feather will not move. A trick Kateri taught her when wolves were about.

"Be the forest, my child."

"Be the mountain."

"Be the lake."

Kateri is still.

Ona senses a shift in the atmosphere. She is alert to the significance of transition. She opens her heart to the memories and listens once more to Kateri's gentle voice.

"We did everything together, your mother and I. We were raised like sisters, but maybe we were cousins. How would I know? McLeod treated our mothers the same. He did not discriminate between them as long as his needs were met. If he was fed and warm, he didn't care which squaw was in attendance. Your father, Ona, he was a Frenchman. His name was Jacques, I think. They were all called Jacques, or Pierre. He was charming, like so many of the coureurs du bois, with their squeezeboxes and jaunty songs. Jacques gave Meg a locket and promised to marry her, but when the first frost came, he was gone. Those Frenchmen! They do not like to be tied down.

"You were born in April. McLeod returned from his travels to find Meg nursing a black-haired baby girl, and his fury fell hard. She loved you, Ona, but she had to leave."

Ona knows the fierce tug of maternity. She felt it herself, briefly, and she has watched women put themselves in deadly peril over it. Kateri, the only mother she knew, has reached the end of her earthly journey. Ona pulls the bear skin over her head.

As the morning sky brightens, Mary brings tea and bannock, prepared the way Kateri taught her.

A hush. A rustle of leaves. Norman digs the grave. The crones sing words to ensure safe passage, their voices weakened by loss and too many years.

~ 23 ~

In his work, Dr. Kennedy observes many ill-advised matches and disastrous marriages. Often the bridegroom knows full well what misery awaits him. There are jokes about impending servitude. Is it so difficult to select a suitable mate? Lou suspects this failure has more to do with smell, than anything else. The way animals behave in the spring. Cows bawling, birds flittering. Dogs fornicating in every alleyway. There is an invisible aroma that alerts animals to the proximity of sexual opportunity.

A messy thing, sex. Men take foolish risks to engage in it. Fully aware of the consequences, they risk their reputations and their health. The treatment of venereal diseases can be as agonizing as the symptoms. Mercury is a common cure for syphilis, but it has proven to be poisonous. And there are hundreds of quackery cures that are costly, available at every barbershop, but for the most part, ineffective. Still, the sexual act is a compulsion most men are unable to control. Like bowel movements, sex is a physical and unavoidable need.

Lou thought himself immune to the base instincts that other men found irresistible. Until he met Lydia. Perhaps it was her disdain for her upbringing. Perhaps it was her lonesomeness, orphaned at a young age as she was. She was smart and thoughtful. Slight in figure, but agile. She had a wild spirit and loved the outdoors. Her adventurous nature translated into desire and, after a few days of getting acquainted, she was open to his physical advances. Lydia was not shy disrobing for a swim. They embraced, slick and playful as otters, and made love. Over and over and over again.

Nymphomania, a diagnosis for overly sexual women, had been a topic in his psychiatry lectures. It garnered laughter from fellow students. Lou dismissed it completely in regard to Lydia's appetite. Childbirth seemed to have made her lose interest in the sex act. But then he started getting reports. She was seen embracing a foreigner at the transient settlement. And someone saw her walking arm in arm with Reverend Whitlock along the railway tracks. Others claimed she swam in her undergarments at Barnum Lake with the gypsies. He couldn't help but feel angry that she carried on so in the company of other men, yet treated him, her husband, with nothing but frigidity.

It was humiliating, but Lou had to admit he may have fallen into the same trap as so many before him. Lured and enraptured and then trapped in a loveless marriage. Still, he felt it his duty to save his wife from public scrutiny. He was right to send her away. If not for her own sake, then for Jane's.

Catharine has successfully entrenched herself in Lydia's place. Her clothing is folded in the drawers of Lydia's maple dresser. She sleeps on the right side of the double bed in the master's bedroom. She sits at Lydia's vanity dresser and occasionally dabs some Eau de Lilac perfume behind her ears. Hannah notices and scrunches up her nose, if not at the scent, then at the very idea that the new Misses is nervy enough to try such an intimate trick. So, Catharine uses it only after she retires for the evening. She puts on her nightgown and uses the silver hair brush and comb, and hand mirror set, all engraved with the letter L in curving calligraphy that Catharine has convinced herself is a C.

If Lou feels guilty, he does not ever talk about it. The facility where Lydia is lodged has lovely grounds and gardens along a scenic stretch of the escarpment in Hamilton.

"She will live a calm and peaceful existence, free from the demons that tortured her," Lou tells Catharine when she broaches the subject.

"Will she grant you a divorce?"

"A patient in an insane asylum cannot conduct any legal business. Our relationship, yours and mine, will remain what it is. One of personal commitment."

"So, I will forever be a fallen woman, our children bastards?"

"Children?"

"I am pregnant, Lou."

"Ah," said Lou, with as little emotion as a response about the weather.

If Lydia's death is the only thing that can free Lou from his matrimonial vows, then Catharine will pray for it. She pictures Lydia in a private room with all the comforts. And she starts to begrudge the fees Lou pays to keep his wife in such a lifestyle. Money that her own children will need in due time.

On Lydia's ward, there are women who carry baby dolls around with them. Some dolls are no more than stuffed pillowcases or rolled up towels. But one woman, Grace, carries a precious china doll with eyes that open and close. She is very protective of this doll, and no wonder. It must be quite valuable. She calls her Olive. Lydia is haunted more and more with memories of her own baby. Baby Jane. But she cannot recall holding her or nursing her or singing to her as Grace does to Olive. She wonders if Jane is safe. Who is caring for her? Who is protecting her? Like a drowning woman, Lydia let her daughter go. But there is something in her now that wants to float back to the surface and rescue Jane, or at least save her from repeating this history of helplessness.

Lydia has moments of clarity when she feels as if she could just put on her boots and coat and walk away from the asylum. She is not mad, like Grace and the other women are mad. She does not belong in this place. She longs for the forest.

"If anyone says something unkind to you, Jane, just tell them that people in glass houses shouldn't throw stones."

"What does that mean?" I asked Hannah.

"It means that every person in this village has sinned in some way. So, they better pray for their own souls."

Since I started getting my monthlies, Hannah has taken me into her confidence more and more, and I have come to enjoy the cozy winter evenings beside the stove in the kitchen. Catharine tires easily and retreats to her room after Gloria goes to sleep. If Father is around, she stays up. But he is often out until nine or ten, or sometimes he is attending a patient all night long.

"That is what you have to expect if you marry a doctor," Hannah let slip one evening when Catharine wondered at his long hours. We, all three of us, blushed and looked at the fire. Because, of course, it is a bit of a sore point that Catharine and Father are not married.

Hannah is more at her ease when it is just me and herself talking, the pendulum of the eight-day clock keeping time to her stitches. Knitting, darning, tatting. She has a basket beside the rocking chair and a hurricane lamp with a wide bright wick on the side table. Sometimes she curses her poor eyesight. She interrupts my lessons with apologies, and asks me to thread the needle for her. Father bought her some spectacles, but she says they make her dizzy. Though she is wearing them more often now, for close work.

Hannah tells me about her childhood. So many sadnesses. Her brother was born with a caul and turned out bad just as the midwife predicted. A gambler! And one spring, their barn burnt to the ground. Struck by lightning. Most tragic, however, she lost her one true love when he was trampled by a horse.

"It's hard to justify an accident," she said. "I never got over the idea that I could have prevented it somehow. What if, instead of going to choir practice, I had arranged to meet him. My mother said, no. Fate will find you if it's your time, but I don't believe that."

"So that happened before you met your husband?"

Hannah laughed. "Truth be told, I knew them both at the same time and there was a third boy sweet on me too. I was passably fair and there were not many girls in my wee town at the time."

"How did Mr. Ogilvie win your heart then?"

"He was a tinker. A travelling man who sold pots and brushes and household items. He won me over with bits of lace trim and a copy of Dr. Chase's Recipes."

"How did he die?"

"Well. That was another bit of bad luck, pet. He was shovelling snow and took a heart attack."

"I'm sorry."

"Yes. Me too."

Hannah's casual remarks about tragedies got me thinking about the way a person can boil their entire life story down to a few defining anecdotes. Like the bit of amber toffee that comes from gallons of maple sap. One sweet mouthful that melts on the tongue. After so much labour, you barely have time to savour it.

The kitchen is snug with the coals banked up in the stove and the cat curled in the corner and the blanket rolled up to prevent a draft coming under the back door. This night, Hannah chooses her words carefully. I can sense when she has something to tell me and wonder if I am about to be treated to advise, or chastisement, or a warning. But I know she cares about me and wants me to grow up to be stronger than my mother. She thinks my mother was raised to be a hot house flower.

"They are pretty. But they dinna last. As soon as they are exposed to the weather, they wilt. Life is a struggle, Jane."

I do not agree with her assessment. My mother longed to escape outdoors. She loved a windy day. Waves on the lake, leaves ripping off trees. She was more like a purple thistle, tough and prickly and tempest tossed. It was the hot house that wilted her.

"No one gets out of this world alive," Hannah is fond of saying when I complain about my lessons at school or a tummy ache. "Stop whining," she says. "You are starting to sound like your mother." Without Hannah, I might wallow in my own sorrows more than I do. I mightn't watch my sharp tongue. And my posture would be slouchy like Father's.

"I'm not one to tell tales," is how she starts a conversation that involves gossip. She keeps her eyes on her sewing. I mark my history text book with a playing card and glance over at her. She pulls a long thread through the material and ties a knot and bites it with her teeth. She is shy about bringing up matters that may embarrass me. Or at least she wants to appear that way.

"People are gossiping about your father. Not everyone, mind you. I am almost certain that Reverend Whitlock is behind it. He dislikes Papists and is happy to turn nasty rumours away from his own door by drawing attention to the imperfections of others."

"What are they saying?"

Hannah pauses. "They are saying that, for a small man, he has a huge appetite for romance. That he visits the houses of certain women who are not sick. Who do not require the services of a doctor."

"More than one?" What desperate women could be attracted to my grumpy father? His brow always furrowed. His demeanour intense. Not a romantic bone in his body!

"That's not important. Only that you should know."

"Does Catharine know?"

"Yes. Certain people in the village take pleasure in telling her. But you needn't feel sorry for Catharine. Her circumstances are much improved. She owes your father a lifetime debt of gratitude. It is a woman's fate, I suppose. Something you'll learn. Men come and go as they please. We depend on them entirely. Catharine is not so bad off as most women of her station. But now that she's pregnant, and tired all the time, the doctor must refresh himself after being with sick people."

"Refreshment in the form of…"

"I suppose you might call it lovemaking. That's not what the villagers call it, mind you."

I sigh, knowing the crude language she means.

"Don't let the gossipmongers trouble you, is all I'm saying. I would never fault the doctor, as you well know, Jane. Men are different than women, so they are, with their impulses and their needs, if you get my meaning."

Which I do not.

Well, perhaps I do. But I prefer not to think about it. I cross my legs and try to ignore the pulsating soreness down there. As if the tender aching and bloodied rags have nothing to do with this talk about relations between men and women. All my innocent flirtations of younger days now seem complicated and somehow sinful.

My father is always the picture of comportment. If he has depraved leanings, he does not reveal them in my presence. What might they be, these needs of men? I think she forgets sometimes that I am not yet a grown woman. Nor do I wish to be.

I don't remember being a toddler, cuddled on my mother's lap as Gloria cuddles with Catharine. I never thought I would miss my mother, but I feel a strange connection to her. If she was dead, I could take flowers to the cemetery and people would say kind things to me about my loss. But she is not dead.

Sometimes I wish for my wild mother back, with flashing eyes and rebellious threats. Mother should have run off to live in the woods rather than be imprisoned. I wish I could have done something. But my mother was like a shameful secret, and I kept it. Only Alma Crockett inquires after her now. Alma misses her desperately. Only last week she asked after her.

"How's your Mother?"

I answered her as I thought Father would wish. "She's fine," I said.

"Will she come home, then? Will she return to Haliburton?"

"I don't know."

To my great embarrassment, I burst into tears. And I couldn't stop crying, even after Alma sat me down and gave me a cup of tea with sugar.

"Don't worry, lass," she told me. "I intend to get to the bottom of this. I'm going to see her for myself."

"You dare not, Alma. Father wouldn't like it if you went to see her."

"No doubt. Men don't like women who won't shut up and do as they're told. But the sun does not rise and set on Dr. Kennedy," she told me. "I will do as I please. I've had my only true friend stolen from me and I will not abandon her. I should have intervened years ago. No more talk. I've made up my mind."

Alma reached behind her and untied her apron and I wondered if she meant to go directly to the train station.

"Perhaps, if you wish, Jane, you could accompany me?"

"Right now?"

"No. But soon."

I have completed Grade Six, which is often the end of a girl's education here in Haliburton. Father wants me to go on the next level and expects that I will attend Continuation School in Lindsay one day, a prerequisite for those who want to pursue careers. Single women are in high demand at the small schoolhouses in this county. I try to imagine myself at the front of a classroom with a pointer and a commanding voice, but it terrifies me, quite frankly, the thought of having so many eyes upon me, counting on my wisdom and guidance. And what if there are rough boys who do not obey? I am quite sure I could not beat anyone with a leather strap. Miss Anderson occasionally takes the strap out of her drawer and smacks it loudly on the edge of her desk, but she has never used it on a student. Of course, it helps that the older boys know she is engaged to the giant, Murdoch McGee.

"Twelve years old," Hannah says on my birthday, "and never been kissed."

That is what she thinks!

My first kiss was from poor Harold Schmidt during a game of spin the bottle in the willow grove next to Dugan's farm. The activity was exhilarating until it was my turn and then the humiliation of kissing Harold in front of my classmates almost killed me. I was not able to hide my feelings like some of the other girls who performed with comic poses and batting eyelashes. Hazel Vance raised a dainty hand to her brow like a maiden in distress. It was not funny to me, knowing that poor Harold was oblivious to their mocking. And, of course, I suffered in the school yard for months afterward with taunting rhymes and cruel innuendos. "Jane and Harold, sitting in a tree. K-I-S-S-I-N-G."

The next kiss was a private, stolen kiss. But equally painful. Andrew Cook is a fine lad, from a good home. He lives just down the street. We often walk to school together. He carries my books. I like him a lot and we have much in common. But he took me by surprise when he pulled me into the alley behind the Chinese laundry and kissed me hard, almost knocking my front teeth out. It felt like an ambush instead of what he intended, which was a declaration of true love. I did the worst thing possible. Screamed. And Mr. Lum came running out and swatted Andrew with a wet towel. Andrew ran off and did not stop for me the next morning on the way to school. He is sweet on Leah Bain, now.

So, you see, I will probably end up a spinster because I cannot control my emotions.

Now I am cautious with people my own age. It is too easy for me to say the wrong thing, blush at inappropriate times, make a fool of myself with wrong answers in class.

My third kiss was quite recent. This kiss was not on my lips and it did not come from a boy. All I can say is that it made me feel cherished. It may well be my destiny to fall in love with an older man. Someone already established in his career. Who could care about me and help me become a better person. Because Father is quite unavailable for such a commitment. He barely notices that I am growing up.

~ 24 ~

It was a quiet weekday that Alma chose to take the train to Hamilton. Miles tried to dissuade her.

"Nothing you can say will stop me from visiting my friend," she said. It was August and business was slow. The dog days. Too hot to shop. She would have to trust that Miles could run the store without her for two days. Tuesday morning, she rose early and, although Miles offered her a ride to the station, pulled on her walking shoes and tied them tightly. At the corner of Maple Street, she waited for Jane.

The girl was petite, like her mother, and determined like her, too.

"Hannah knows I am away with you to see Mother," she assured Alma as they walked down the slope toward the train station. "I'm old enough, she says, to do what I think is right."

What Hannah actually said was, "Go on and visit her, poor soul." She reached in the jar with the housekeeping money. "Here. Enough for your ticket and a room at the inn. God forgive us."

While they waited for the train, Alma took out a small book of poetry and posed herself in a way that she expected train travellers would sit. Jane noticed the rising sun, red and angry, and worried about bad weather. Red sky in the morning, sailors take warning.

When she heard the whistle at Gould's Crossing, Alma tucked her book away and stood and wondered how it would feel if she were leaving for good. Now that she was here at the station, she was ambivalent about what chaos might transpire at the store during her absence. Miles could give away all the whiskey he wanted. What did it matter?

"Come on, pet," she said.

Jane wondered if her mother had seen this softer side of Alma Crockett. Even Hannah called her a mean old biddy.

"I don't like having someone snap at me when I am spending my money," she said after a recent trip to the Mercantile.

Alma settled into an upholstered bench seat, facing forward and patted the window seat so Jane could get a good view. For the first time, Jane wondered why Alma had no children of her own. She gave her a smile to acknowledge the kindness, and Alma squeezed her hand.

Trees, marshland, lakes, little roads leading into the bush, startled deer running off through a meadow with their white tails waving. Jane's mind could barely take in one scene before it changed. A granite wall, speckled with brilliant quartz and, an instant later, a deep gorge as the train crossed a bridge. Her stomach dropped and rose with the geography.

"Sixty miles an hour, we are travelling," she heard a man say behind them. No wonder she felt queer.

At Lindsay, they changed trains. A large older woman with a cluster of moles on her forehead sat across from them. She was sweating in the humidity, and fanning herself with a folded newspaper. Once the train started, the woman introduced herself. Ruth was her name. It was a name Alma admired because Ruth in the Bible was a stranger in a strange land, like herself.

"Are you going to a funeral?" Ruth asked.

"No." Alma was alarmed by the supposition. "What makes you think that?"

"You look sad, the both of you."

"We are going to see a friend. In hospital."

"Nothing serious?"

Alma does not like nosy women, but there is something caring about this query. "Yes. I'm afraid it is serious. My friend has been committed to a facility for the insane."

"Not in Hamilton, I hope. It must be very serious indeed if she is at the Century Manor House."

"She is."

"Oh, my darling, you are in for a very difficult day. I am so sorry for your friend's troubles."

Alma leaned forward and whispered a warning before the woman said more.

"This lass is my friend's daughter."

Jane concentrated on the houses and shops as the train chugged away from the Lindsay station. She did not want her presence to change the tone of the conversation, curious as she was for facts.

"Do you have an appointment to see your friend?"

"Why, no. I did not think to make one."

"They do not like surprise visitors there. They may try to deter you from seeing her. Do not back down. The staff prefers to be prepared, you see, to make sure the patient is clean and dressed and appears to be well cared for."

"You are saying they may not be scrupulous about patient care?"

"There are stories that some patients are better cared for than others. That's all. If I may offer some advice?"

"Of course."

"Challenge them. Ask questions about her diet and exercise routines. Ask to see her medical records if you find her changed."

"Changed?"

"Impaired. She may have been the subject of some experimental... techniques."

"But how do you know this?"

"My son is a doctor. He did some training at the Hamilton facility. He does not support the procedures they are using. Especially on women of a certain temperament. He filed a report with the College of Surgeons, then moved to London, Ontario to work in the psychiatric wards there."

"Mother was brilliant and creative, if a little wild," Jane said.

"That, my darling, is just the kind of woman they try to cure."

It was just as Ruth described. The nurse at the front desk was brusque when Alma and Jane entered the asylum. Alma responded equally brusquely.

"We have travelled eight hours by train to see my sister and the young lady's mother," she declared. The nurse excused herself and brought the matron to the front desk.

"It has been some time since Mrs. Kennedy's last visitor," the matron said, accusingly.

"We intend to change those circumstances. We are anxious to see her."

The matron hesitated. "Won't you please be seated, ladies."

Alma and Jane took seats in the atrium. Was the nurse hustling Lydia into clean clothes?

"Follow me," the matron said upon her return. "I'm sorry for the wait. We weren't expecting you. We like to prepare our clients for visitors. Her benefactors have not been…"

Jane cringed at the implied neglect. "My father. And my great aunt. They signed the papers for Mother's…"

"Interment," Alma added.

The matron glared, but then softened her eyes and carried on.

"How long has it been, then? Since you have seen your… sister?"

"Too long, I'm afraid."

"Ah. Here we are. Hellooo Lydia! Look who is here to see you!"

The room was empty of any furniture save a few hard-backed chairs. There was a large window with curtains open to reveal rolling lawns and waving hollyhocks. Alma had prepared herself for a shock. But, oh.

"Lydia," she cried, dropping to her knees in front of the wheelchair. "Oh my dear, dear, girl. What have they done to you?"

Alma clasped Lydia's cold hands, brittle with disuse.

"Alma," Lydia said. "I've been abandoned, Alma. Are you here to take me home?"

The matron was visibly shaken. Lydia Kennedy had not uttered anything so coherent in some time.

"Who is this young lady, Alma?"

"Why, it's Jane, your daughter."

"No," Lydia whispered. "My daughter is a wee child."

~ 25 ~

Dick Whitlock filed the papers to nominate Alex Smith for the position of Reeve at the August General Meeting of Town Council. There appeared to be no other contenders. All he needed was twenty signatures of endorsement and, if no others stood for the office, he would be acclaimed.

But three days later, as irony would have it, Alexander Smith received a summons to meet with the president of the Dominion Bank, Elmer Austin, at Head Office on King Street in Toronto. Finally, Alex dared to hope his dedication had been recognized. Just as well, as it was not as easy as you might think, finding supporters willing to offer their signatures.

It was early in September, the beginning of the school year, so Alex accompanied his children to the city by train and waved them off at Union Station. Then he walked several blocks north to King Street, noticing with dismay how unaccustomed he had become to city life. His nerves jangled with the stink of horse shit, the clamour of street cars, and the harsh calls of vendors. His nerves were bad as it was, because of a complication in his private life. All the more reason to accept whatever position the bank president offered him, despite the potential disappointment of giving up a chance to be Reeve. He would happily move his family anywhere in the province as long as it meant he could extricate himself from the problem with Mary Hammond.

Alex Smith nodded to the doorman and entered the ostentatious atrium of the Dominion Bank Headquarters with high expectations. He rode an elevator for the first time, his sphincter contracting in fear all the way up to the fifth floor. An austere secretary led him to a club chair outside Mr. Austin's office where he was made to wait for half an hour. He picked at a ragged cuticle and silently practiced the small speech he had prepared to accept whatever position it was that Austin intended for him.

"Come in, Smith!" Elmer Austin hurried past him with another gentleman and opened the office door. "Have a seat."

Austin settled himself behind a huge oaken desk. Alex took a chair across from him, admiring the view over lower buildings all the way to sparkling Lake Ontario. He was made acutely aware of how his little office in Haliburton compared.

"Mr. Smith, this is my clerk, Mr Hartwick." Alex rose to shake hands. None were offered. He sat down again.

"The Chairman of the Board has brought it to my attention, Mr. Smith, that you have fallen far below your quota for new accounts and business loans. For the third consecutive year."

Alex's face reddened. He was vigilant when assessing applications for business loans. If a man could not present himself in a suit and clean the dirt under his fingernails for a meeting with the bank manager, well, that implied the man was not likely to make good on payments.

"The Bank of Ottawa is opening a new branch in Haliburton. The president is John Maclaren. A lumber baron from Quebec. He calls his bank the Lumberman's Bank, offering loans to sawmills, lumber camps and the like. Seems your area is burgeoning with opportunity. What's going on?"

"I am scrupulous in assessing loan applications, sir. Many back-woodsmen cannot produce proof of formal education. They are too often illiterate, or barely literate. I never risk the bank's money on half-baked schemes."

Austin is quiet. He steeples his hands. He nods at the clerk. The clerk hands a folder to Alex.

"You'll find a list of businesses in the folder who have applied for loans. From your branch of my bank. And been turned away. Look at the list now."

Alex did not like the tone of the bank president's voice, but he did as he was told.

"How many of those businesses on the list have been unsuccessful?"

Alex recognized every name, every venture. Admittedly, he was curious as to how they found alternative financing. A popular tavern, a butcher shop, a tannery, the livery and burial service. Even the barber, who spoke with a stutter, had attained enough money for his start up. And most notable, the Oblong Lake Lumber Company. All of the businesses on this list were thriving without money from The Dominion Bank.

"None of these businesses have failed, sir, but..."

Alex Smith finds himself on King Street, clutching a folder that contains damning evidence of his ineffectiveness. He is under review. He must demonstrate that the Haliburton branch of The Dominion Bank can compete with the Bank of Ottawa, which will be anchored on the corner across the street before Christmas. The less imposing edifice will make working men more comfortable.

"They will not have to knock the sawdust off their boots before they enter. They will not have to show proof of literacy. I don't care if they sign their names with an X," Austin said. "I want profits. The profits in the Northern Townships are connected to lumber money, and to small businesses where lumbermen spend their money. Like the damn barber shop. Everyone needs a haircut, am I right? All the businesses on that list are making money, am I right? I'll give you three months to turn your ship around. Three months to improve your profit margins. If it doesn't happen, I'll have to replace you with someone else."

"Would that mean I could return to a position with the bank here in Toronto?"

Austin rubbed the bridge of his nose, as if Alex was making his head ache.

"No. It means you would be well advised to seek other employment. You should know that your friend Langtry, who sits on our board, spoke up and asked that you be given a grace period to prove yourself. Otherwise. This would have been your last day."

George Langtry was Alex's former neighbour in Rosedale on Scarth Road. A quiet and protected enclave that Clarissa longed to return to. Smith hailed a carriage and gave the address and knocked on Langtry's door hoping to find George home early from the office. A servant answered and asked him to step into the parlour. She did not give him any indication whether or not Mr. Langtry was at home. He sat on an overstuffed settee and admired the decor of the front room. The heavy drapes. The flower arrangement in the window. The Turkish carpet. As it turned out, George was not at home. But Sarah Langtry greeted him, extending her hand and (was it his imagination?) greeted him with a coolness that suggested she knew of his poor performance as a bank manager.

"Alex. What a lovely surprise. George will be sorry to have missed you."

"Yes, well I was in the city and had a difficult meeting with Mr. Austin and I thought… I wanted to thank George for supporting me."

"I'm sorry, Alex. It must be terribly difficult to make a go of it in the Northern Townships. I know from Clarissa's letters that the village is crude and backward."

Alex Smith was flustered and suddenly needed the toilet urgently. Sarah rang a bell and the servant, an older woman, severe around the mouth, escorted him to a small indoor toilet off the kitchen. Rosedale homes were equipped with indoor plumbing, of course. His home, grand as it was by Haliburton standards, had a well-insulated outhouse, mere steps from the back door, but still it was an inconvenience especially in winter, especially in the middle of the night in winter.

His bowels exploded in a fearsome reaction to the stress of the day, and echoed in such a way that Alex suspected Sarah could hear the noise from the parlour. He bent double with gut pain and prayed to God for relief, and eventually he was able to stand and wipe himself and pull the chain that released a flood of water to evacuate the mess in the toilet. To his shame, the porcelain remained shockingly splattered with his excrement. He straightened himself up and exited with as much dignity as he could muster, considering the servant was waiting outside the door to escort him back to the parlour, and she could not disguise the disgust on her face.

Why did he come here?

Oh, yes.

"Sarah, I must be on my way. But if it's not too much trouble, George hinted in a recent correspondence that the bishop may have had reason to send Reverend Dick Whitlock up north. He is not well liked, I'm afraid, and there is some concern about his character. I, myself, am an elder at the Anglican Church, and any information you might have to help us understand his history would be much appreciated."

Sarah's face lit up. Her cheeks flushed.

"Alex. You must promise not to tell a soul where you heard this."

Smith nodded, solemnly.

"Clarissa is dear to me and you have a daughter the same age as my Annabel, so I warn you to keep them well away from the man. He. Is. A. Pervert," she whispered. And offered a few shocking details to prove her point.

Smith needed a drink very badly. A drink and a visit to The Ward. It had been too long. He had told Clarissa that he would not return home that night. That he would stay in Toronto. Probably, he hinted, he would be wined and dined by Elmer Austin to celebrate his new position. He would stay at Montgomery's Inn. He would return Tuesday afternoon.

He did not suspect in his wildest dreams that Clarissa was happy to spend the evening alone. In preparation, she sent her coachman out to Sawyers Road to buy six jars of red "cooking wine" from the Italians. "Keep one for yourself," she told the driver, to assure his discretion.

Alex returned home a bit peaked, Clarissa noticed, but then again, she was feeling delicate herself. They sat in the front room and he gave her his version of the bank president's threat.

"How dare he?"

"I suspect I have been the victim of some conspiracy," he told his wife. God, she looked old, he thought. She did not compare favourably to the city women. "I imagine Austin has some nephew or friend that he will replace me with. We must sell this house. This might be a good time to move to New Zealand."

Clarissa rubbed her throat, a long-standing habit that kept her from blurting out the things on her mind. Many impulsive thoughts were piled there and they did not dissolve until she thought of ways to rephrase her ideas to save Alex's pride. It was not easy for a man when his wife came from money.

"There is no rush, Alex. The children have only just started their academic terms."

"But, Clarissa, dear, I have no hope of reaching the goals outlined in this folder." He threw it down on the dining table. "See for yourself."

Clarissa read the contents of the folder while Alex reclined on the settee and closed his eyes. He started snoring almost immediately. She turned up the wick on her reading lamp and read the familiar names of people he had refused. Church people. Farmers. Journeymen. Shop owners. She felt sick as she realized the depth of her husband's vindictiveness. He was mean. Mean to her and mean to their children and mean to their neighbours.

No wonder she was lonely. No wonder women crossed the street to avoid a conversation with her. She looked at Alex now, dribble on his chin like a baby, his hair askew. What a weak man she had married. She rose and went to the sideboard and poured herself a glass of thick red syrup that looked like blood. She sat and sipped and refilled her glass. If, she thought, there was no chance of returning to Toronto, to the comfort of a proper home and her society friends, she would have to take charge. She would not be disgraced. Alex had let her down.

"Quit!" she yelled at him as soon as his eyelids started fluttering. "I will not be disgraced. I will not be humiliated by the Austins and the Langtrys. I will not stand for it!"

Alex sat up. Clarissa had his attention for the first time in a long time. Her colour was high. She was flushed like a schoolgirl. His wife was drunk!

"You must submit your resignation immediately, Alex. My income is more than enough for us to live on. I will not stand to have my family disrespected."

Yes, Alex was convinced his wife was drunk. He himself was hungover from the night before. A concoction of cheap gin, a specialty in The Ward, had his head pounding with familiar punishment. And he was sore in places that hadn't been exercised in some time. So, if Clarissa was on the sauce, he had no real objections.

"You must go ahead and take on the position of Reeve. Imagine how well you will look, wearing the Chain of Office. It could be the beginning of a new career, Alex. After a term, you will run for a provincial seat in parliament. We'll show them!" She poured a glass of wine and handed it to him and sat next to him. He drank it down in one gulp and grimaced.

"Where did you obtain this?"

"The Italians, out in the Sawyer Settlement."

"It's vile."

"I like it. It helps me think."

Alex chuckled. The wine actually did make him feel somewhat better. He pictured the arrogant luncheon bunch at the Loyalist Lodge. They would have to lobby him for the improvements they considered important. Better roads and sidewalks. A proper courthouse. A hospital. His name would appear in the Toronto Telegram. "Alexander Smith Meets with Provincial Premiere to Request Funding for Northern Townships." He could well end up in Ottawa, running for Prime Minister. But, first things first.

~ 26 ~

Ona didn't follow a calendar, but somehow, she was able to keep appointments with those who did. She had a sense of preparedness even without a pocket watch. The hours of the day, the days of the week, the months of the year, they were both abstract and distracting. Ona followed the phases of the moon and the cycles of the seasons. She was always exactly where she was supposed to be.

Over the years, Ona's wanderings have taken her in every direction. She has tramped the trails and paddled the waterways, losing herself between earth and sky. There are hundreds of lakes in Haliburton County, and they all have different personalities. Some placid. Some rough. Some moody. Some muscular. Water is alive and responsive. Ona used to keep her canoe in a shelter by the narrows between Head Lake and Grass Lake. But with newcomers helping themselves indiscriminately to resources under the tenet that "finders are keepers," she has rented space at the boathouse of a local ferryman.

Ona paddles along the newly denuded shorelines of Lake Kashagawigamog. Trees will grow again, the lumber barons claim. Liars. The ghosts of the huge white pines cry mournfully as high winds and damaging floods rage. Scraggly poplars and hemlocks take root among the stumps, but they will never replace the old growth.

Once raped, a woman is scraped raw. She curls into herself and hardens her heart. Once violated a forest is permanently scarred.

Every living thing is out of balance. Yes, there is beauty here still, but it cannot be sustained at this rate of "progress." Ona hates the word. The water is polluted with waste from saw mills and grist mills. Sewage and bleaches, dyes and potash, they spew into rivers, poisoning the animals, the waterfowl, and the fish.

Ona longs for the land to return to the way it was when she was a child. "Nokomis, I am sorry. Help me think of a way to slow this destruction." Nokomis, Ona knows, cannot help. Her people were forced to make way for "civilization." Farther and farther back into the forest they were pushed. Away from hunting grounds. Away from fertile soil. Away from the well-travelled waterways. Until they were cornered and caught and rounded up and sent to less coveted territories.

Ona is aware of her dichotomous nature. Her heart is ruled by a profound love of the natural world and her head is ruled by pragmatism. Equally strong and unstoppable. They are two strong rivers like the Drag and the Gull, both rivers coursing like bloodlines from Algonquin toward Lake Ontario.

Hundreds of years ago, humans had limited opportunities for mixed parentage. But people travelled. Foreign bloodlines were created. What liquid courses through her own veins? She is Scottish, French, and Anishinaabe, a mysterious new composition that does not seem to have any ill effects on her health. But there are those who would believe that mixing nationalities is detrimental. A dangerous theory. Ona has attended the births of babies of many colours and hues and shades and they are all perfect in her eyes. What characteristics are hidden within an infant's tiny mind as it rushes toward adulthood? What circumstances will divert its path? Some tributaries lead to Niagara Falls. Some dry up and die. Is it luck? Is it fate?

Ona paddles past familiar places, once the quiet denizens of beavers and muskrats and deer. But in the last twenty years, the wilderness disappeared, becoming a manicured frontier of simple cabins and pastoral farms. There are cows and corn fields and orchards and ornamental gardens, all divided by stone walls and root fences. There are pretty painted houses and barns. Neat and tidy properties, however, can be deceptive. Suffering happens in fine homes, too. Ona thinks of Lydia Kennedy.

She pulls her canoe up into a swamp at the end of Grass Lake, a place Nokomis once brought her to collect fiddleheads. Here, she feels her grandmother's spirit. Ona surveyed this tract herself and she knows exactly where the boundaries of her property are.

When Ona was sixteen, she did not see the purpose of dividing a forest with invisible lines. Grandfather McLeod sent her to supervise the surveying team as they plotted out his newest acquisition.

"The time of stepping off property lines with strides is long past," Old Mcleod told her. "A tall man ends up with a bigger lot than his short-legged neighbour. A fair and accurate system is required."

"Why not agree that our property begins at the water's edge and extends west to that stand of willow trees?"

"One day, years after ye are dead and gone, that stand of willow trees will be gone too."

"What should I care what happens after I die?"

"Your children will inherit the land, maid."

"I shan't have any children. Besides," Ona said, "it seems troublesome. And unfair. I won't stop a trapper or a hunter from coming on my land to feed his family."

Angus McLeod sighed. "Yes, lass. Ye will. Ye must. Men cannot be trusted to share the bounty of field and forest and lake equally. Greed always factors into the equation."

Thus began Ona's surveying education. Geometry and triangulation and measurement. She learned about the tools. The great lengths of surveyor chain for accuracy. All marked with metal rods driven into the ground for permanent reference. She learned how to measure slopes and grades.

Land management required knowledge in three worlds. Her grandmother's sensitive world. Her grandfather's defensive world. And the new hybrid world of science and mathematics and economics.

The lead surveyor's name was Christopher. He was not interested in teaching young Ona the surveying trade, but he tolerated her presence and eventually let down his guard. She was an apt student and a teacher too, skilled at massaging aching muscles at the end of the day, a mutually enjoyable activity that proved to be an excellent prerequisite for Ona's next area of study. Romantic love. Something of a concurrent education you might say. Ona was devoted to the surveyor in the usual way of first love, and the affair ended in the usual way. Christopher laughed when she claimed she would accompany him to his next job in Sault Ste. Marie.

"You must stay and I must go," he said. "You own this place. The stakes have been driven into the ground. But it does not end here. The lots will be divided again and again. Like pieces of pie at the Sunday picnic, the servings will get smaller and smaller. And, like wolves marking their territory, land owners will claim their little patches of earth and foul them in various ways, each to their own uses and tastes."

Ona stayed, vowing that the boundaries would not change. The land would not be sold for men to divvy up and profit from. She did not tell Christopher about the baby. Kateri gave her a tea of black root and cedar root and she stood waist deep in the Drag River and watched the blood seep out and curl into a whirlpool and become one with the water. The scars healed, of course, and she gave her heart to a more reliable lover. Ona lived to see a hundred young girls throw themselves on the same burning pyre as she had, to be scorched and hollowed out by unrequited devotion. Trees and lakes never betrayed her in that way.

~ 27 ~

Alma Crockett could not get the image of Lydia Kennedy out of her mind. She sometimes woke in the night, seeing the distress in her friend's eyes. The pleading. "Take me home, Alma."

She was prepared to act, and sent a message to Ona begging for a meeting without delay. As she waited, she watched a skiff of debris floating across the surface of Head Lake. Recently, there were voices of alarm about it. Pollution it was called. Dead fish washing ashore, flotsam and jetsam clogging rivers and streams. Human waste that could cause illnesses. Young boys used to jump off the town dock on days such as these. They have found more pristine swimming holes, Alma guessed.

Ona arrived and sat next to Alma on the wooden bench. "Tell me," is all she said.

"Oh, Lydia has been tampered with. Damaged. Her spark extinguished. They might better have killed her than leave her to sit in a chair staring mindlessly out the window. We need to seek justice for her. On her behalf."

"What can we do? You remember, Alma, if you are honest with yourself, how wild she was. How likely she was to get hurt somehow."

"That may be true. Only that I have promised Jane I will get her mother home."

Ona paused and took a letter from her vest pocket. "Look here. My solicitors have communicated the legal parameters of a woman committed to an insane asylum by her husband or guardian."

"And?"

"Not good. Dr. Kennedy was diligent in his documentation of professional opinions. Lydia was indeed incapable of caring for herself when she was admitted."

"So, she is destined to live out her days in that place?"

"Unless someone intervenes."

"Someone like..."

"Someone like her husband. With a change of heart."

"What are the chances that Dr. Kennedy would retract his statement at this point? He has a new woman. Not a wife. But, all the same, Catharine is installed as a replacement. I have even heard her introduce herself as Mrs. Kennedy. They have a child together."

"It would do no good, in any case, to release Lydia and have her imprisoned once again in a house that made her ill."

"True," Alma said. "She was unhappy there. And she was miserable in her uncle's home too."

"Yes," Ona said. "It's clear her relatives conspired with Lou on her placement."

"I will care for her. She can live with me until..."

"If she is damaged, as you say, Alma, you cannot take on that responsibility, as good as your intentions are. You cannot run the store and help her. There is no medical service in Haliburton for the care she needs."

"But she would be safer with me than where she is. Believe me. Lydia is not safe. Not at all. She may a victim of medical experimentation," Alma said.

"But, surely you see how risky it is. Unless..."

"Unless?"

"Dr. Kennedy suffered a great deal over the course of Lydia's illness. If his actions were harmful, I do not believe they were intentionally malicious. He is a reasonable sort of man. An idea has occurred to me, Alma."

Matron came for Lydia with a wheelchair. Lydia gasped, expecting to be taken to the Procedure Room. It had been some time since she had been selected. For the past week, she had endured many sweat-soaked nights and headaches and shaking fits. Something was very wrong, although she was feeling less foggy. Anticipating the ether mask, the treatment, and the long recovery that followed, Lydia gripped the arms of the chair in fear. But Matron did not take her down the windowless green hallway.

Lydia was wheeled out to the veranda, down a ramp, past the rose garden to a small ivy-covered cottage. Inside, a young woman bathed her with sweet smelling soap, and rubbed cream into the dry skin on her arms and legs. She was wrapped in a soft dressing gown and her hair was styled with a curling iron. Finally, Lydia was given a good quality travelling suit to wear. And stockings. And boots! Lydia loved the feeling of the boots, so firm and supportive around her thin ankles. The woman nodded and smiled at the transformation and led her to the atrium of Century Manor where Lou Kennedy was waiting for her in a chair by the desk. He stood and called her by name.

"Do I know you?"

"I'm Lou. Your husband."

Lydia did not recognize him, hunched like an old man with a crease of concern carved deep between his eyes. He was surprised at her appearance, too, her eyes hollow, her cheeks sunken.

"I'm sorry," he said, simply. And Lydia knew, by the catch in his voice, that he was. But she also knew he didn't come easily to that apology. She started to cry, and Lou had no idea how to comfort her.

He turned away to let her have a bit of privacy. When he felt she had been given enough time to gather herself, he began.

"Your Aunt Sophia and I have signed your release papers, Lydia." He held up a large envelope. "I was under the impression that she was contributing money for your care," he rushed on. "It was a generous sum." Lou had practiced this speech trying to absolve himself of responsibility, but it sounded lame and he knew it. "I became suspicious and agreed to have Ona McLeod's solicitors investigate on your behalf. As it turns out, Sophia was not using her own money."

Lydia experienced a sick feeling in her stomach at the reference to Aunt Sofia. Sophia had come to visit Lydia early on in her stay, unloading cruel accusations, accumulated over a lifetime. Nothing Lydia had ever done, it seemed, had been worthy of forgiveness. Every disobedience had been an attack on Sophia's reputation. In conclusion, Lydia was an ungrateful leech and deserved to rot in the madhouse.

Sophia left and did not return, though she lived only a short carriage ride away.

"The investigation revealed that Aunt Sophia has been accessing your inheritance," Lou continued. "Legally, it was within her right to do so, as your guardian. The intention was that she would transfer the endowment from your parents' estate to you when you reached the age of twenty-five."

Lydia hiccups. Lou thinks it is a giggle. He considers it an odd reaction. Essentially, he is explaining that she has been paying for her own imprisonment. But it will be a long time before this irony occurs to Lydia.

"Sophia had her guardianship extended, along with her control over your finances, when you were diagnosed as... What I mean is, several medical professionals concluded that you were not capable of managing..."

"I am not insane."

"No. The Director of Care has conducted a thorough examination and deemed you cured."

"I was never insane."

"You had a severe bout of melancholia. That is the official medical conclusion."

Lydia looked beyond Lou. There was some disturbance at the entrance to the dining hall. She was hungry. When she looked back at Lou, he had stopped talking. He was holding up the envelope again.

"With your discharge today, you are quite independent. Ona has made arrangements for your living quarters and a… companion." Lou tried to take her arm then, but she pulled it away. She would prefer to fall flat on her face rather than let him touch her. Indeed, that was a possibility. She was quite wobbly.

"Ah," Lou said. "Here comes the Director of Care now."

"Your wife will be more comfortable waiting here in the atrium while we talk," the man told Lou.

"Lydia will be privy to all information concerning her health in the future," Lou said. "Starting immediately."

This eased her hatred toward him. She could not help but feel disengaged, however, while the men talked about her "case." As if her best interests had been met, even exceeded. It was clear they needed to justify to each other, for the record, that they had been right to jail her in the asylum. Here is what they concluded: Lydia's behaviour was so extreme, so intolerable, so offensive to society, that she had to be incarcerated like a murderer. She sat quietly while the Director of Care referred to her as a maniac. An hysteric. He outlined the management of her case, including medications, restraints, withdrawal of nourishment, ice cold baths, and gynaecological massage. He spoke as if these treatments had been successful. All of them had been torture.

"See how calm she is," he said to Lou, as if Lydia was a child who had just regained composure after a tantrum. Lou nodded. He was satisfied, Lydia concluded, that his money had been well spent.

"Is there anything you would like to say, Lydia?" Lou asked, but she could not begin to articulate her trauma. Her capacity for communication was like a skein of yarn that had unravelled completely and lay frayed upon the ground. It would be her task in the days and weeks ahead to retrieve it, to begin winding it carefully into a new ball. Not too tight. Not too loose.

On the train, Lou produced a wicker basket that Alma had sent along for their trip home. And then he attempted another apology.

"I was wrong to send you there."

"Do I understand correctly? Are we to be divorced?"

"Yes. I have submitted the paperwork."

"In that case, I would prefer it if you never speak to me again." Her voice was raspy but her message unmistakable. It pleased her to see the look of shock on Lou's face. She reached into the picnic basket and found that her appetite was quite sharp.

Lou went directly to Gidaaki upon their return to Haliburton, and delivered Lydia into Ona's care. Fewer than a dozen words were exchanged. It was as if a slave had been freed. Lou, playing the part of a reasonable plantation owner after emancipation, accepting the consensus that his actions required correction. The war was lost.

Alma thought Ona was brilliant, the way she could bargain with men on their own terms and get what she wanted. Get what she deserved. Get justice.

"How?"

"The laws are clear concerning marriage. Not all of them are fair. Most favour men. But the law denying divorce when one spouse is institutionalized is a just one. It is intended to support the vulnerable. In this case, the steps to resolution are simple because all parties benefit in some way. Lydia gains her freedom. Lou is free to marry Catharine,

Aunt Sophia is released from further responsibility for a niece she never loved."

"But Lydia will never get back those years of suffering. How will the doctor compensate her for that abuse?"

"He cannot. No punishment would repair the damage done. Lou Kennedy is a brilliant physician, you know. This village owes him a great debt for his service. Even clever people get mired down by bad judgment when it comes to their personal affairs. Society puts altogether too much faith in courts of law to reconcile wrongdoing. If there is evidence of remorse and a willingness to do better, it is far better to put our energy into forgiveness, rather than retribution."

Alma disagrees, but remains silent. She likes to see a person punished.

~ 28 ~

Alex Smith appears at the Loyalist Lodge. He looks past Sunny Adams as if she is a servant and asks to speak with the man of the house. Sunny takes a long critical look at the figure on her doorstep until, finally, he meets her eyes.

"My husband is recovering from a chest infection and is not accepting company this afternoon," she says.

Sunny worries about the way James exposes himself to all manner of diseases when he meets with local businessmen. They arrive early for lunch, around 11 a.m., and take up the seats at the long table by the fireplace. More and more, they assume that the front parlour is their designated meeting room, their place to air grudges and propose improvements and criticize the political climate. She will pop into the kitchen and tell the cook to put the kettle on, warm up the soup, slice the bread.

"The Liar's Club has arrived," she announces.

She tries to be good natured about it. Their friendship has made all the difference to James who has no time to sulk in isolation as he once did. Instead, he is studying up on legal terms. He reads the newspapers using an easel-like contraption invented for him by Sapper. He is hungry for current events so he will know the facts when his cronies bring their rumours to the table. Sunny cannot help but be a bit fond of them, these men who commit themselves to the development and commerce of Haliburton, even though many of their ideas are old fashioned.

Their personal histories are rife with family dramas. They have been cheated out of inheritances, or lost their fiancées to despicable brothers, or suffered abuse by alcoholic fathers. There is the tailor, the cooper, the land speculator, the undertaker and the grocer. All are well-meaning. And, to a point, trustworthy. They follow her rules about chewing tobacco and cigars and alcohol. Not in her establishment, she tells them, and they comply.

But now, here comes the banker. A bully, by reputation. Even the men of the Liar's Club shunned him when he tried to join the luncheon group.

"It is a matter of importance," Alex Smith says. He does not intend to take no for an answer. Sunny is loath to interrupt James's afternoon rest, but finds herself knocking gently on her husband's door, nonetheless.

"I'll take a coffee," he says as she turns to leave. "I like it strong." It sounds threatening. Sunny is mad at herself for letting herself be browbeaten in her own home but she closes the door and retreats to the kitchen and brews a pot of very strong coffee.

"I have come to ask you to endorse my nomination for Reeve," Smith tells James Adams, getting right to the point. "The deadline is pending and I need four more signatures."

"You wish to be Reeve?"

"Yes. That is what I'm saying. Reverend Whitlock has nominated me, and the elders of the church have supported the nomination. I would appreciate your support. And possibly the support of your… friends." Alex Smith sounds annoyed at being forced to explain. His voice is strained.

"What are your qualifications for political office?"

"I was educated at Eton and went on to study at Cambridge."

"What is Eton?" James knows very well what Eton is. He understands the prestige that certain English public schools afford their alumni. But he also believes that an education at Eton is worthless for the position of Reeve in Haliburton. And he notes that "studying" at Cambridge is very different from "graduating" from Cambridge.

Alex Smith's sallow complexion reddens. "Eton College is a school in Berkshire, England. It was founded by King Henry VI. Many famous…"

"Ah. I am only familiar with North American colleges," James interrupts. "What other credentials do you have to prepare you for this role?"

"The fact that I am a bank manager, sir, as you well know, should be enough to give citizens confidence in my capabilities. If we want this community to be successful economically, we need leaders who are not afraid to levy higher taxes. Build better roads. Get aggressive with provincial connections."

Sunny knocks at the door and puts the coffee cup down on the desk carelessly, so it slops into the saucer. James says, "Sit down for a minute, Sunny. The bank manager is running for Reeve in the upcoming municipal election. He is looking for endorsement of his nomination."

"Goodness," Sunny says. "Who has nominated you, Mr. Smith?"

"Reverend Whitlock, Ma'am."

"Mrs. Adams, if you please."

"Mrs. Adams," repeats Smith.

"I don't think it's appropriate for my husband to sign this nomination," says Sunny. "Since he is also running for Reeve."

"The deadline for nominations is September 15th," Alex Smith says. "This very Friday. As of today, I am the only nominee."

"Yes," says James. "I'm well aware. Good luck to you, sir. May the best man win."

"Let me show you out, Mr. Smith," Sunny says.

"I can see myself out," Smith says.

At the sound of the front door slamming, Sunny laughs and wheels James through the door to their bedroom and they do not come out until they smell Cook's aromatic soup bubbling on the hob for the supper crowd. The next day, James will finally accept the proposal that the Liar's Club put to him weeks ago. Sunny will visit Town Hall early and get the necessary paperwork. They lie in bed and giggle like children.

Alex Smith leaves the Loyalist Lodge and walks to the church.

Reverend Dick Whitlock's office door is closed. He has a visitor. Smith settles himself in the front pew and waits. He crosses his legs and fishes a toothpick out of his pocket. Alex Smith does not like to be kept waiting, but he is anxious to get a commitment from Dick as to the theme of this Sunday's sermon. A call to action for the congregation to get involved with municipal politics. It is their duty to elect responsible officials. Who better than an elder of St. Mark's?

Smith stares up at the stained glass window and considers heroism. He sets his mind to thinking of election slogans. Something about lions and power and courage.

The voices behind Dick's office door have quieted and Alex assumes the visitor has been dismissed out the side door. He knocks twice and tries the handle, but it is locked. Some rustling and a cough and then the sound of the outer door.

"It's me, Dick," he says. "It's Alex. We need to talk."

"Wait a minute." The voice is muffled.

When the bolt on the inside of the office door finally slides open, Alex Smith glances out the window and sees the figure crossing Mountain Street. He chuckles when he recognizes the doctor's daughter and notes the high colour on the Reverend's cheeks.

"Are you counselling Catholics, now, Dick?"

"What do you want, Alex? I really must insist you make an appointment, just as I would make an appointment to see you at the bank."

"This is urgent. I need you to write me into your sermon this Sunday. It seems as if I will have some competition for Reeve after all. James Adams intends to join the race."

"Adams, eh? An admirable citizen." Dick walks out of the vestry, climbs the three steps to the pulpit and looks down on Alex Smith. "His family donated this pulpit. Beautifully carved, don't you think? It's possibly the most valuable thing in the church. James and Sunny are generous when the collection plate is passed, too."

Alex controls himself and keeps his response to himself.

"You know, Alex, that I am hoping for a window. Something to commemorate my service, here."

"Yes. I am well aware. Jesus and the little children, isn't it? That seems appropriate. You are well-loved by the children in this community."

"My fund-raising campaign could use your help." Dick Whitlock finds the raising of funds humiliating work. People expect something in return it seems. They want his rapt attention as they blither on about the weather, their health, their children. They want his active participation in local events. They want him to laugh at their jokes. What is so funny? He rarely sees the humour in the stories men tell. Should it be necessary to engage in small talk when conducting church business? No, it should not.

"I need two thousand dollars to commission the window. If you give a generous donation, I will announce your gift this Sunday."

"Never mind about the stupid window, Dick. The congregation is building you a manse. Shut up about the window."

Dick opens the large Bible in front of him and sighs. He keeps a picture tucked between tissue-thin pages in the Gospel of Luke. A picture of a pale, red-robed Jesus reaching out with delicate hands, motioning to three rosy cheeked children.

"I do not intend to give a penny toward your window. I had an interesting conversation with Sarah Langtry last week. You should know that Jesus didn't mean it literally, that the children should suffer. Seems you interfered with a little girl in Toronto. Charlotte, I believe was her name."

Dick Whitlock does not move. Except for a dripping nose, his face is like stone. "Those allegations are not true. The girl's uncle..."

"It doesn't really matter if they're true or not. It's what people are led to believe. You must champion my cause. In a delicate, honourable way, of course. Compare my community contributions to the lion," Alex suggests, looking up at the stained glass window.

"Of course," Dick whispers.

Alex Smith and Dick Whitlock shake hands limply and part in mutual dislike.

Dick slumps into the chair behind the pulpit and reaches underneath, feeling around for his fortified tonic. His toe hurts. It throbs, actually. It is confounding, he thinks, how one toe can ache so badly that it is impossible to ignore. The doctor was no help. Gout, he diagnosed. You should quit drinking alcohol, he advised. The nerve of the man! To assume he was a drinker.

~ 29 ~

Six weeks before the municipal elections in 1885, a Hoe Rotary Printing Press arrived on the afternoon train. It had been shipped via TH&B railway from Buffalo, N.Y. Seven men unloaded the crates and transferred the heavy iron contraption to an empty building behind the Post Office which was adjacent to Cook's Carriage Sales and Rentals.

While the printing press was being assembled, a sign was erected that answered many queries.

The Haliburton Chronicle
An Independent Newspaper
Publisher and Editor: A. Tucker

Aliza Tucker did not like the way her vision for the village of Haliburton was summarily dismissed. Men, it seemed, believed they did not need feminist ideas in order to build and maintain a successful municipality. They were wrong, and Aliza intended to prove it.

After her husband, Captain John Tucker, passed away, Aliza became keenly aware of her diminished position. While John was alive, her voice was respected. She stood among those who made decisions and created a sense of cohesiveness in this village where diversity sometimes led to aggression and conflict. But now she realized that all her ideas and contributions were attributed to John. Without him, her voice was silenced. There were rumblings of women's suffrage in Toronto. Sunny shared with her the sensational newspaper articles about the Toronto Women's Literary Guild, led by intelligent, women who insisted on participating in politics and in leading social change. The articles were revolutionary and exhilarating!

Aliza woke up in the middle of the night with an epiphany. She would start a newspaper. The pen is mightier than the sword. An Englishman said it, Edward Bulwer-Lytton. She intended to help him prove it by creating a forum for discussion and opinions and expertise on a variety of topics. It was Aliza Tucker's hope to provide accurate news stories that would stop the rabid speculations that led to acrimony between neighbours. When she posted an employment opportunity advertisement, a document printed on the new press, she expected that there were few in this village with the skills or the desire to apply.

Employment Opportunities

Reporter, Copy Writer, Advertising and Circulation Manager, Proof Reader

Preference given to female applicants

Apply in person

Haliburton Chronicle, Maple Street, Haliburton

Training provided

Aliza hired three women and filled the rest of the positions with her own children. Her second eldest son, Bernard, would operate the printing press. Her daughter, Elizabeth, talented in the arts, was installed as the illustrator. Aliza, herself, wrote the editorials. At four cents per copy, the Haliburton Chronicle was affordable. Aliza did not expect to make a profit on the venture, but she did hope to break even. Eventually. The printing press had been an extravagant expense. But the profits from the saw mill continued to soar and John Jr. was investigating the pulp industry. Maybe they could produce their own supply of paper.

Admiration for Aliza Tucker grew with her newspaper. Women writers were encouraged, and at first, they submitted traditional columns. Recipes, wedding announcements, poetry. Aliza understood she had to introduce controversial issues tucked in among news of rummage sales and bake sales. It would take time to help women develop an interest in politics.

The schoolteachers wrote updates on the curriculum and posted names of high academic achievers to motivate students. Lou Kennedy wrote a health column called Doctor's Orders. He ended each article with a quote from the town's namesake, Thomas Chandler Haliburton: "An ounce of prevention is worth a pound of cure."

~ 30 ~

Ona stood aside, holding open the flap of leather that served as a door so the doctor could have a look. Lou agreed with her conclusion, that the girl had pushed a foreign object, probably a peeled willow branch, deep inside the vaginal canal. The object had pierced her uterus and it appeared that she would not survive.

"She has the symptoms of advanced sepsis, otherwise I'd attempt a hysterectomy. What is her name?"

"I don't know. She won't say her name. I'm not even sure what language she speaks. She's fair. Maybe Finnish? The McGee brothers brought her here. Angel found her curled up and sleeping in their duck blind. They're pretty shook up."

"She'd be what? Twelve years old?"

"I'd say so. Same age as Mary when I found her. I'd like to cut the tadger off any man who would do this."

"The great majority of backwoods pregnancies are the result of incest. Mothers die young. Daughters mature. Families sleep together in winter to survive, with consequences as expected."

"Fathers and brothers and uncles and male cousins, they do the thing that comes naturally in the woods, same as wolves and deer."

"Education is needed. The girls often have very little understanding of their own bodies."

Ona sighs. She knows this is true. Menses starts and they think they are dying. If they are lucky, some female relative or neighbour shows them how to fashion absorbent rags for the purpose and demonstrates how to wash them out. If months go by without blood, they may not realize the reason until the onset of labour.

"Too many girls like this one," she says. "What trials these immigrants have suffered." How hopeful they must have once been that Canada would be better than their homelands. No one, seeing into the future, seeing their child end up like this, emaciated, filthy, lice-ridden, no one would have ventured away from their own shores."

Lou wrapped the blankets tightly around the girl's thin body, like swaddling a baby, to quiet the shaking. He administered a lethal dose of opium and alcohol to put her out of her misery.

"Is there someone who can sit with her? She may hallucinate but I think her heart will stop within the hour."

Ona retuned with Bessie, one of the crones who had proved her patience with the dying. A big-bosomed woman, her face a mask of untold hardships. Lou stood and packed up his hypodermic syringe. He would clean it thoroughly with alcohol before using it again. It was a miracle of a modern medical invention.

Bessie lifted the girl into her lap, preparing to rock her to sleep. Lou started to replace the deerskin that served as a door.

"Leave it open, Doctor," Bessie said.

Lou nodded. It was common practice in these hills to allow the soul a clear path for escape. No one wanted a spirit trapped inside. Lou accepted a glass of Scotch from Ona. She offered him a seat by the fire beside the McGee brothers.

"How is the wee lassie?" Webby asked. When Lou shook his head, Murdoch called for his dog. Angel let him sink his hands into the thick fur around her neck.

"Good dog," he said.

"What a sad and desperate way to end up," Ona said, wishing women could be treated as well as Angel. Desperation indeed. Some girls who came to Gidaaki recovered their health, only to steal away with the first shanty man to whisper false promises in their naive little ears. Off they went, back into the bush, thinking their lives would somehow turn out different from the ones that sent their exhausted mothers to early graves.

Even the good men, Ona thought, even the best of men, the gentle and loyal men, were still, after all, men. They accepted the power bestowed upon them by the luck of gender. Somehow, Ona straddled the divide between the sexes, meeting men and women on equal ground. She wondered at her own ambiguity. Her soul, she believed, had not been assigned a gender. It seemed to be an advantage.

Bessie approached the cloister and nodded. Ona rose and walked away from the warmth of the fire. She felt a presence behind her and turned to see Murdoch following her in the gloaming. She was filled with love for the feminine heart in him, the trait he kept well-hidden at such a cost. Murdoch wordlessly helped Bessie and Ona move the little body to the meadow behind Ona's cabin. He took up the shovel to make a grave. Angel sat nearby and stood watch, a sad-eyed sentry.

Bessie lit a small bundle of sage. The young girl's spirit drifted up with the smoke. Perhaps Kateri would meet this wee lass beyond the cold stars.

It was seven years ago, after a winter storm, that Ona strapped on her grandmother's ágimag, the snow-walking shoes fashioned from tamarack branches. She tramped through the woods with a pack of supplies, to investigate a cabin with no smoke. It was a shock, but no surprise to discover a woman tucked in bed, cold and stiff. Ona pulled back the covers and there was a baby boy, sucking on his dead mother's breast. As she reached for him, she heard a scraping sound behind her and jumped. Crouched in the dark corner was a girl wrapped in a filthy quilt.

"Oh, child! You scared me."

The girl nodded but said nothing. Ona thought she may be a deaf mute, but by spring, she was a lively chatterbox. Her name was Mary. She was twelve and pregnant.

So many Marys.

~ 31 ~

It is Thanksgiving, a national holiday in Canada since 1879. Meaning a Monday off work for labourers, bankers, and schoolchildren. But not for railwaymen.

Trains arrive and depart from the village at regular intervals. The cool days of autumn bring hunters and artists and seekers of beauty. Sugar maples have turned a brilliant crimson against the backdrop of yellow beech trees. Black spruce trees stand out like church steeples against hillsides of oranges and reds. Milling about on the platform, people want directions to tourist cabins, and hansom cab rides to hotels and inns.

The local population has recently responded to these demands, realizing there is money to be made from touring visitors. Young lads line up along York Street with horses and carts. Housewives bake cakes and wrap buns stuffed with meat. A pretty entrepreneur fills jugs with cucumber water and charges a nickel a glass. No one will pay that, she is told. But it is unusually hot for this time of year, and as the autumn sun beats down on the park beside the station, she has made three dollars.

The barkeep at the new tavern sends his daughter to the station to escort single gentlemen to his establishment. She stands strategically near the exit ramp, holding a hand painted sign.

Cold Beer and a Sandwich. Twelve cents.

It is half past six o'clock, just after the arrival of the evening train, when the wind comes out of nowhere. A gust, strong enough to steal the hair ribbon from the barkeep's daughter and send it sailing. She screams and chases it. Papers fly, horses rear, hats disappear. Turkey vultures and ravens ride the thermals high overhead, omens of some imminent apocalypse.

The sky darkens north of town and thunder rolls like an arriving locomotive. Quiet little Head Lake erupts in white capped waves. In their panic, people on the platform cram into the station. Some fall on the tracks as the rest of the crowd surges back onto the train. The shouts of the conductor, the engineer, and the station master disappear into the atmospheric vortex. Children cry. Ladies scream. Men shout. Their collective terror is sucked up into the coming gale.

The storm lashes the windows of the station and rocks the train upon the tracks. For the better part of an hour, lightning bolts descend on the village and surrounding forests. Up on the ridge, Ona huddles in her cabin. She counts heads. Twenty-one souls, crouching close together, mothers making soothing sounds to comfort the babies, crones murmuring magic spells of protection. Even so, lightning strikes the tallest pine on the ridge, a giant, hundreds of years old. It splits with a terrible sound. The smell of sulphur fills the cabin. The roof, Ona thinks, may be on fire. But rain tramples over their shelter like a herd of elk. Then silence.

In the highlands, a storm does not pass away. It gets caught among the hills, bouncing around and circling back. Thunder echoes along the ridge. Boom. Boom. Boom. Until it weakens and dies. It is fully dark when Ona creeps out of the cabin. The older children follow her, alert to danger like little fox kits, ready to flee. The world has changed, but they have survived. Cautiously, they wander around the cloister, gathering fallen branches.

"Toss them on the hearth. We will have a bonfire," Ona tells them. The full moon, orange and celebratory, rises through the branches of the broken pine. The hunter's moon.

Ona sees a lad with a lantern, climbing the trail.

"Doc sent me to get you," he says.

She fills the pockets of her long leather vest with a few necessities and follows the lad down to the village. The air has a deep chill now. As they walk through the streets, they pass damaged roofs and upended carts and horses roaming without riders. The lad takes Ona to the livery where Dr. Kennedy kneels over Clark Cook, the owner. A fallen beam from the stable has crushed his leg.

"Ona," Lou says, seeing her waiting. "There are people hurt at the station. If you could possibly..."

"Of course. I'm on my way," she says, turning to go.

"And, Ona," Lou sits back on his haunches and wipes his brow. "Jane is not at home. I don't know where she is. Hannah thinks she went to the bridge at Head Lake Park to meet a friend."

Ona nods. "I'll keep an eye out."

Where was Jane? She told Lou she was meeting friends for a picnic by the lake. She rarely made plans with children her own age, so her announcement that she needed some baked goods to share made him glad. She was a quiet girl, oddly interested in grown-up discussions and decisions in the house. Jane loved Catharine and Gloria, but now there was little Ross, a new brother. Lou had married Catharine in a private civil ceremony. Was Jane struggling with loyalties now that Lydia has returned to Haliburton? It occurred to Lou that Jane could possibly have objections. That she might be confused.

Lefty proved to be surprisingly calm in a crisis. He opened a closet in the station where a stretcher was kept with medical supplies like bandages and iodine. By some miracle, a doctor from Kingston who was vacationing at a cottage nearby, offered his services. He soon took charge, mobilizing helpers and reassuring the injured. Most injuries were limited to cuts and bruises.

James Adams and his wife opened their parlour. Except for some missing shingles, the Loyalist Lodge escaped damage. Sunny served tea and scones to any who wanted refreshment. She made up an empty room for a couple who were newly homeless.

The chaos left in the wake of the tornado subsided. Nothing more to be done until the next day. Lou went home, only to find Hannah wringing her hands. Jane was still not home. Lou knocked on several doors to interrogate Jane's friends, but all the girls insisted that Jane had not been with them that afternoon. At first, he assumed they were lying. Covering up something they didn't want their parents to know about.

Hannah reported that Jane left the house with a basket of butter tarts and lemonade at around two o'clock in the afternoon. Gradually, Lou had to accept that Jane, his daughter, had not been honest about her plans. He was unaccustomed to the feeling of panic and he did not like it one bit.

At the station, Lefty was just about to turn in for the night when Reverend Dick Whitlock limped in, demanding to know when the next train was leaving. The man's eyes were glazed like a drunkard's.

"It's past midnight, Rev," Lefty said.

"But. Look. It's so bright."

"Full moon."

"I have urgent business in…"

Lefty figured the Reverend had got a bad knock on the head. "Sorry, Rev. Next train won't get through until the day after tomorrow. There's forty or fifty trees blocking the tracks between here and Kinmount."

There would be no service until crews cleared rubbish and debris from the rails. The telegraph lines were down. No communication from Lindsay. But Lefty did not anticipate the extreme reaction from

Dick Whitlock. He did not expect the man to pull a knife on him and demand transportation out of town.

Lefty made the mistake of laughing. He barely jumped out of the way in time to miss the tip of the knife as it whizzed by him. Reverend Whitlock was stronger than Lefty gave him credit for. The knife stuck in the wooden bracket of the ticket wicket.

"What's your damn hurry, Rev?"

Reverend Whitlock's skin was covered with a film of perspiration. He let loose a cry of utter panic and turned to the door, only to find it blocked by Dr. Kennedy. Whitlock fell to the floor and begged forgiveness from the Lord.

"You fucking son of a whore!" Lefty yelled, kicking the Reverend in what he hoped was his kidney. "What is your god-damned problem? You insist on getting out of town like the devil is chasing you. Then you try to stab me with a knife. And now you're waking the dead with your belly-aching. What in hell is wrong with you?"

The Reverend turned on his side and curled into fetal position, whimpering softly.

"I'm sorry for what I did. Forgive me, Doc. Forgive me. I never meant to hurt her."

Lou felt a surge of ice water flooding his veins.

"Where's Jane? What have you done with her?"

Whitlock covered his face and moaned.

"Answer the man," Lefty said and kicked the Reverend's foot. His sore toe, as a matter of fact. That resulted in such a howl that Lefty kicked it again.

"She wanted to join the church. I christened her, as you should have done. God forgive you. God forgive me. She's in Jesus's care, now."

Lou sat in the chair in the corner of Jane's room. She was badly concussed, but not dead, as Dick Whitlock had believed. Lou found her in the church in a glittering sea of shattered glass, looking for all the world like a martyred saint. He lifted her from the wreckage, light as air. There was something dreamlike in the walk back to his office. Moon shadows made the village strange.

Hannah was awake. She assisted him as he treated Jane's lacerations, none too deep, and set her broken leg. Lou wakened her hourly and checked her pupils, but her vital signs were normalizing.

This was his fault. His negligence had deprived Jane of a mother. Lou let himself remember the young version of Lydia who had enchanted him with her free spirit and ended up seeking solace from gypsies and tramps and Reverend Dick Whitlock. He let himself remember Catherine, once youthfully vibrant and now careworn. He let himself consider the women who were tethered to rough cabins by the loyalty of their vows and by motherhood and by a lack of options, and sorrowfully admitted that he was no better than the men who gave little thought to the suffering of the women under their protection.

Men lied. Women believed them. What possible motive did Whitlock have? What kind of man was he? His mind raced into very dark places.

What could Jane have been thinking? She rarely expressed opinions, so he didn't know. Then again, he didn't inquire. He leaned forward to take her pulse and felt satisfied. Then he saw the corner of a notebook tucked under her pillow.

I am in my bedroom. Father is sitting in the chair by the window. I cannot remember him ever coming in here. How odd.

Hannah is fussing about with my bedclothes. My leg is aching. A deep ache that reaches up into my hip, up into the left side of my chest.

"Why can't I turn over, Hannah?"

Hannah does not answer, only dips a washcloth in a bowl and wipes my face. It's as if I have not spoken at all. Am I dead? I remember the storm. I was in the church. Why was I there? There was an explosion of coloured glass. Is Hannah laying me out for burial? She has experience in this task.

It's dark. I feel the pressure of someone sitting on the bed beside me. It seems like a dream. Then a soft, cool touch on my forehead.

"Shh. Rest yourself, my darling girl."

"Mother?"

"Yes, it's me. You're healing well. You'll be right as rain, soon enough."

"How did you get here?"

"I'm always here with you."

"I didn't know. I'm sorry. I thought you were gone. I didn't know. Why didn't I know that?"

"Knowing is a tricky thing. You can know things and then un-know them. Like when you were born, you knew things about your secret journey from whence you came. But then you must forget those mysteries to make way for new things you need to know. The mind is not like the train that takes you back and forth along the same track. The mind is a river that floods and goes dry and changes course. Knowledge can change too. Sometimes you are so sure you know a thing, you would stake your very life on it. And then, one day, you learn that none of it was true. You learn that the books were wrong and the teacher was wrong and the church was wrong and your parents were wrong. And you must break away and forge your own little stream of knowing things."

Catharine tiptoes into the room, tying the belt of her dressing gown.

"I heard you talking, Jane. You're awake! You scared us! We haven't heard your voice in three days."

"Mother?"

"It's me. Catharine."

"Where's Mother? She was just here. I want my mother!"

"I need to get my things," the Reverend Dick Whitlock begged.

"Consider yourself lucky that you have your head attached," Lefty told him as he pushed him into a boxcar.

"Surely you can't expect me to travel in here. With the pigs."

"Don't rile them. They're on the way to the abattoir and they ain't happy about it. A pig bite hurts like the devil. Like I said, tracks will be open in two or three days. Make yourself comfortable."

"But where will I..."

Lefty pulled the door shut and latched it.

"...go to the toilet?" It didn't matter. His britches were already soiled. The Reverend Dick Whitlock found the farthest corner from the pigs and sank into it. There was a bit of air circulating from vents high above him and he could smell smoke. Something was burning. He wondered if he had left the gas lights on in the church.

He nodded off. When the sliding door finally opened, his neck was stiff and his pants were crusty. The sun, angry and red, stared him right in the face, so he couldn't tell who his rescuer was. He crawled on hands and knees toward the light.

"Thank you. Thank you. Thank you."

~ 32 ~

The gun was heavy in Gordon's coat pocket. It weighed heavily, too, on his mind. Not because he regretted accepting it from Mr. Smith. He didn't like Smith, but he liked his expensive shoes. His pretty house. He wanted those things for himself. In the past he had taken advise from Lorenzo and Lou. An immigrant and a wife-stealing doctor. Each sly in his own way. Each looking out for himself. Not that he hadn't occasionally benefitted from their suggestions. But that was all in the past. The future was up to him.

People learn. People change. Gordon was ambitious. He wanted to end up on top. Show Lorenzo that he wasn't a screw-up husband for Maria, dependent on her to pick up after him and correct his mistakes. On the farm, he was worse than useless, and she was brilliant. To watch her, short and heavy and lecturing the babies in Italian, you wouldn't guess the things she could accomplish in a day. The garden, the laundry, the meals. Oh! Maria was a good cook. But she was a peasant. Always the hem of her skirt tucked up in her waistband, revealing stout legs and thick ankles. Always a towel slung over her shoulder for baby messes. Always dark, damp curls escaping from her kerchief. He was embarrassed when people mistook her for his servant. Sometimes he didn't correct them. Maria didn't know any different.

The farm was a successful little backwoods enterprise, no thanks to him. He was an outsider in his own home. Italians coming and going and laughing and crying and swatting kids and then hugging them so hard you'd think their heads would pop off. He wanted to move his family to the village. Away from this swarm of foreigners. Get Maria out of her dirty old aprons and into some fine frocks and fancy bonnets. It was a dream he could achieve now that Mr. Smith had chosen him to be his right-hand man. Maria didn't need to know about the gun.

But before he even has a chance to water the horse and put the wagon around back, Lorenzo and his brother-in-law, and the two Salvatori cousins, Rizzo and Tony, are on his front porch with their arms crossed. Two more cousins are crossing the yard. An ambush!

"Where's the gun?"

"What gun?"

Maria comes out crying into a dish towel. Always the drama!

"In your coat pocket!"

"You don't trust me? You following me?"

"You damn right! Since the day you marry my sister, I watch every move you make. Maybe she loves you. Maybe, I love you too, like a brother. But that don't mean you not stupid. You got no sense when it comes to people. Who do you trust? You trust family. That's it. Everybody else out to screw you one way or another. Rizzo been tracking your night work. What kind of digging does a man do after dark? That rich prick paying you to do his dirty work. He picked the perfect guy. You're young and strong and greedy."

"What do you mean, greedy? I'm not greedy."

"You're greedy," Angelo says.

"Looking for the easy way to get rich," Luigi says.

"Time for you fellows to get off my porch, talking like that. Get out of here."

"How much money he givva you?"

"None of your business," Gordon says.

Lorenzo grabs Gordon by the lapels of his canvas coat. Maria scolds her brother and swats him. Lorenzo yells at her. She yells back.

"*Andare a casa,*" she tells them.

Gordon hates Italian. If he never hears another Italian word in his life, it will suit him fine. But he knows one thing. Maria's Italian relatives are as honest as the day is long. And he suspects... no, he *knows* they are right. Alexander Smith has chosen him to do some dirty work. Something worse than digging ditches. He can't really deny it any longer. And today? When he accepted the gun, he accepted a promotion.

Inside, Gordon puts the money on the table. A pile of cash.

Maria picks it up. Counts it.

The youngest baby starts to cry. She puts the money down and spits on it, and washes her hands in the bucket, scrubbing them hard like she just touched something diseased.

"*Coglione,*" she says, turning away.

When Maria married Gordon, Lorenzo warned her he was a screw-up.

"Look at you, Maria, doing all the work," he said.

"People learn. People change," she said. A woman must defend her husband. The father of her children. But she knew it was true. She did everything. The cooking, the cleaning, the farm chores. Still, all she had to do was look at her gorgeous babies, and she knew she did the right thing marrying Gordon Murphy. She was no beauty. And as hard as she tried, she could not learn English. It didn't work in her mouth. Who else would have married her in these backwoods? Lorenzo's half-wit cousin? The dirty old Roma tinker passing through selling soaps and brushes?

Yes, it was a wife's duty to stand by her husband. But when Lorenzo started harassing Maria, telling her that Gordon was associating with a criminal, she felt fear.

~ 33 ~

From the ridge, Ona watches the weeks and months and seasons unravel. She considers the fallen leaves all around her. Listen! The scurrying, burrowing, and hunting of small animals below her feet. Only the top layer is changeable, prone to the whims of wind. Fire. Human folly.

"Lydia," Ona says, sensing her approach. "Come. Sit. You look rested."

Lydia is wrapped in layers of shawls as if she is greedy for warmth. "Yes. Look. My hands have stopped shaking. My heart has slowed. It was like a bird in my chest, trying to get out."

"That was bad medicine. Are you drinking the trillium tea? And eating the dried partridge berries?"

"Yes. Molly has already discovered snakeroot and skullcap and stinging nettle growing plentiful by the wells."

"Harburn was covered in ice, once, and the wells were draining whirlpools."

"The wells are haunted," Lydia whispers.

"Indeed, they are, Lydia. Nokomis said the very same. Spirits are plentiful where you now live. They won't harm you."

"I have seen evil, Ona. It does not exist in the forest." Lydia pauses. "But I have a burning chunk of evil in my own head. Behind my eyes. The pressure threatens to blind me some days."

"Willowbark is best for headaches."

"This malady, I fear, is from an injury inflicted upon me as I slept. A hot coal inserted there by Satan. Whole chunks of my past are rewritten or erased. I grasp and grasp at things I should know. My birthdate. My daughter's name. And. Most tragic. I have lost the ability to read."

Lydia reminds Ona of the old aunties, crooked and battered yet still strong.

"Think not on what you have lost, Lydia. Look at that beech tree. See how it is bent. See how it is scarred. See how a branch was ripped off in the recent storm. Still, it grows and thrives." She takes Lydia's hand and places it on the sun-hot rock between them. "Do you feel her? *Talamh Màthair*? Mother Earth?"

"Yes." Lydia bends down and lays her face upon the rock. She is still for so long that Ona thinks she may have fallen asleep.

"Up, Lydia. Dark comes early. Help me light the lamps. Up you get."

Far off, a train whistle sounds. A loon responds.

"Ever the competition between man and nature," Ona says.

Molly waits in the cloister. She smiles and stands up when she sees Lydia coming.

"You ladies must stay the night," Ona says, glad of the company.

Gidaaki is lonely these days. It has a history of ebbing and flowing over many generations, and now a time of emptiness has arrived. Since the trains came, Ona has sensed the shift and accepted the inevitability of it. Like the season of bare branches. Like the empty wells at Harburn that once bubbled with retreating floodwater. It is all part of the cycle. The forest is creeping back to claim the out-buildings, covering them with vines. Gidaaki was a marriage of nature and progress for a time. A marriage like her grandparents had.

Ona prepares her cabin for overnight guests. She warms the squash soup. She takes extra blankets out of the cedar trunk. She stirs the coals in the fireplace and piles on some nice dry applewood. Then. A knock at the door and Mary pops her head in.

"Ona," she calls, unable to contain the excitement in her voice. "A visitor is here." Mary holds the door wide, and an old woman enters. Deep are the wrinkles etched in her face, made more distinctive by the dancing shadows of Mary's lamp.

"She gave the boys a scare. They thought Kateri walked out of her grave."

"Do you know me, Daughter?"

"I know you." Something burns in Ona's chest. She has imagined this reunion a thousand times but the joy she expected is absent. Her arms cannot embrace this woman, her mother. They hang at her sides like stone. "I gave up hope of your return."

"You have been loyal, Winona."

"Call me Ona. Everyone does."

Exhausted from her travels, the old woman falls asleep in the chair by the fire, her mouth hanging open, her hands restless in her lap as if she is knitting. Molly serves the soup and the three women sit in tension-filled silence. The sort of silence that is crowded with unspoken words and difficult memories.

"Mothers," Lydia says, finally. Ona sighs. Molly clears the table and covers the old woman with a blanket.

Time has collapsed. Ona is reunited with her mother, but it seems the lost years are a chasm that cannot be crossed. Meg was only eighteen when she made her choice. The decision to leave her baby. The women are strangers. "It was like a walk in the woods, Winona. I saw two paths. One path was the rough forest trail back to you, littered with fallen branches and the hazy fog of hardships. The other path was protected. My husband made promises and the path looked..."

"Easier?"

"Yes. Easier. I was selfish. I thought I deserved some easiness. Fate is a funny thing. I went to Ottawa thinking I could track down your father. I met Ellwood instead, and let him fall in love with me. What did it matter if I didn't feel the same passion I had with Jacques? Here was a man of means who was off to make his fortune in New Zealand. Coming back to Gidaaki seemed a decision destined for sorrow. I did not want to be a dutiful daughter, and I was not really prepared to make the sacrifices needed to be your mother. I chose the adventure of travel and chance. Forgive me."

"Kateri mothered me."

"Yes. I owe her a debt of gratitude. I wish…"

"That you had written? Our postal service is quite reliable."

"It was always my intention to come back and thank her myself."

"She did not require your thanks. She never blamed you or said a word against you. Her love was unwavering. Until her last breath she expected you to return to her."

"And I have. You must bury me at her side, Winona."

"Call me Ona."

"I wanted to see you, too. You have been curled in my heart all these years like an infant who never grew up. An ache. Seeing you as an adult, the ache is dissolving."

"Is it?" Ona hears the resentment in her own voice but cannot seem to temper it. Is this really her mother, or an imposter? Of course, it is Meg, so similar to Kateri except for a weak and shallow voice like a creek strangled by beaver dams.

"That was a thoughtless thing to say. The ache is as sharp as ever. But I am relieved to see you survived without me."

"Survived."

"I'm sorry, Winona, that is wrong. You've done so much more than that. Gidaaki has been in capable hands. There is much of my mother's determination in you."

"Nokomis inspired and guided me."

"She disapproved of me. Something in me is hard to love. My children... you have siblings, Winona. My daughter and son do not speak to me. I am estranged from them."

Ona stands and excuses herself. She walks out of her cabin and follows the path to the lookout. A sister and a brother! Denied her.

"Why do I care?"

The clouds above are pregnant with snow. "Let winter come," Ona whispers skyward. "Let it come and freeze this hurt thing in me."

Back at the cabin, Ona expects to find her mother dozing. She sleeps easily and often. But Meg is wrapping a deerskin shawl about her shoulders. "Take me to the high meadow, Winona. It's time to visit the people I left behind."

Slow and solemn is the walk. They stop first at a sunken hollow covered by pale green reindeer moss. Meg knows who is buried here, even without a marker.

"Did my mother ever speak of me?"

"Nokomis never talked about the past. She left it behind her like dreams at dawn."

"She named me Miigwan. Because I was tiny and light as a feather."

"Miigwan. Not Meg?"

"Miig for short. Father named me Margaret McLeod, after his mother. But he called me Meg. Miig and Meg. It was typical of the compromises my parents came to over their many differences."

"Can you guess where your father's grave is?"

"The cairn that is large enough to be the burial site of ten men?"

"I had a lot of help burying him. So many wanted to say goodbye. Some were fond of him, but most, I think, wanted to make sure he wouldn't sleepwalk."

"Even Father, with all his stubborn determination, could not dig himself out of that cairn," Meg says.

"We must have a toast to the old bodach." Ona lets Meg take her arm, and they follow a path toward the bush line. "Do you recognize this broken boulder?"

"This must be Kateri's grave. We climbed here as girls."

A seam of blue sky appears in the west. The women watch it turn pink. Then purple. Meg reaches into her pocket and pulls out an acorn. "I left something precious behind. A baby girl. You are my unlikely acorn, buried and forgotten by me, the greedy but forgetful squirrel." She takes Ona's hand and places the acorn in her palm. "I want to plant something here, Winona, in this place where my childhood soul still runs and climbs and sings. This place where my own daughter is guardian and steward. Let me build something for the women and children you care for. I have money. Father would be astounded at the money to be made in raising sheep."

Meg cackles like Kateri, and the sound lets a trickle of water through the dam in Ona's heart. "What sort of place would you build?"

"Let me contribute to the hospital you are planning. Build me a wing that offers hospitality and comfort to all who need it. Call it Gidaaki. Please accept my offer, Winona."

"I wish you would call me..."

"Ona. I know. Everyone does. Everyone but me. I have made many mistakes. But naming you Winona was not one of them."

Ona has imagined her mother's return many times. Here is how it goes. A ragged traveller wanders into the cloister, full of regret and apologies. Kateri always implied that Meg was a lost soul struggling in a hostile universe. But now, it seems clear. She invented that prodigal version for Ona's benefit.

~ 34 ~

December 1885

A stone boat was a type of sledge for moving heavy rocks. The oxen at the Highland Golf Club made countless trips pulling stone boats as the McGee brothers cleared their property. Fieldstone fences and foundations and fireplaces appeared until a visitor might be forgiven if he believed he was in Scotland. The brothers even built a stone pier at the lake so golfers could come by boat.

The golf course was a secondary income for the McGee brothers, a seasonal business that sometimes broke even. In the meantime, Murdoch improved his butchering skills. Loin chops, bacon, tenderloins. Once feared for his size and stern gaze, he came to be known as a man of good-hearted generosity. He never let a bit of meat go to waste. Folks experiencing hard times could count on a handout. Or a hand up, as he said. Keeping people fed made him glad.

Consequently, the brothers were often treated to drinks at Crook's Tavern.

"Those boys have a bottomless thirst," old Jake Crooks told anyone who would listen. Lots of men, big working men like the McGee brothers, found a glass of ale revitalizing after a day of labour. Jake Crooks set out salt shakers on the tables in his pub, and men added it into their steins to replace what they lost through sweat.

"Let me give you some advice," Jake warned newcomers. "If those red-bearded brothers challenge you to an arm-wrestling match, just say no. You canna' beat them. If you try, and lose, which you are sure to do, pay your debt."

Ale was a fuel that accelerated Webster McGee's competitive nature. Recently, when a traveller tried to squelch on a bet, Webby invited the man to a wrestling match with one of Murdoch's hogs. He was never seen again. Did he end up as pig feed? Inquiries were made some months later by a family member of the traveller who wondered what had become of him, the last letter having been mailed from the Haliburton Post Office. The Justice of the Peace refused to interview the brothers.

"I am not paid enough to risk making enemies of such barbarians," the JP said. He handed the case over to the Itinerant Magistrate.

The Magistrate held court at the Orange Lodge on the third Tuesday of every month. He travelled from town to town, delivering justice to backwoods criminals. Typical cases of the time included squatting, poaching, theft, assault, and public mischief. Occasionally, there might be a murder case. But usually, a murder in the backwoods was the result of a drunken brawl or a jealous rage, and the guilty man would regret his actions after he sobered up. If he had half a brain, he'd hop on a train bound for one of the western provinces. It made more sense than going peaceably to the jailhouse in Lindsay to await sentencing.

The Magistrate made half-hearted enquiries. "Was there a murder," he asked Jake Crooks, "…or did the poor fool wander off and drown himself in the river?"

Jake understood this manner of questioning and answered accordingly. "If he did drown himself, or leave for parts unknown, he won't be missed around here."

"So, you met the traveller?"

"I did."

"And what was your opinion of him?"

"A small-time swindler with a pocket full of ill-gotten monies. I cannot see any positive outcome if you pursue the case. If the man is dead, his own foolishness contributed to his demise. The pigs in question have long ago been slaughtered and distributed to various households throughout the village. It would cause some anguish, I believe, if the McGees were accused and people were forced to wonder if the pork they purchased for such a good price was tainted by human flesh. No doubt Murdoch and Webby were the last to see the man alive, but if you interview them, you will find that their cognitive abilities, though quite sharp when sober, function at increasingly low levels when drunk. It is entirely possible that, even if they are guilty, they have no memory of the incident."

"Thank you. That is very helpful."

"It's always a pleasure to serve a representative of the court," Crooks told him with sincerity.

"Oh," said the Magistrate, as if it was an afterthought but which Crooks suspected had been the main purpose of the visit. "The death of the bank manager."

"Mr. Smith."

"Mr. Alexander Smith. Yes. What relationship, if any, would the McGee brothers have had with him?"

"Other than they were the ones who found him?"

"Yes. Other than that."

"None to speak of, Your Honour. Mr. Smith never took a drink down here at this end of town. He never arm-wrestled the McGee brothers to my knowledge."

"So. No bad feelings between the two parties?"

"Sir. Your Honour. There was bad feelings between near everyone and that asshole. The McGee brothers wouldn't have crossed the street to save his life. But I doubt they would have wasted any effort to kill the man. If they did, they would have had to get in line for a chance, and I can't think why they would bother. Smith had it coming from a dozen different directions."

~ 35 ~

On the climb up to the Nunnery, Gordon fashions a walking stick from a poplar branch. The leaves underfoot warn Ona of a visitor.

"I thought it was about time I came to introduce myself," he says. The lilt of his Irish voice echoes back to him in muted tones from the walls of the cloister.

Ona motions for him to sit. She pours some kind of hot refreshment into a cup and hands it to him.

"I hope you will forgive my intrusion," he says. "I seek advice. Maria suggested I come."

"How is Maria?"

"She is well. I'm lucky to have her, so I am."

"Ah. You are suspected in the murder of Alexander Smith, I understand? She must be worried about your liability."

Gordon nods. "The Magistrate is making enquiries."

"You were working for Mr. Smith. He paid you to bury evidence of his criminal activities."

Gordon does not try to lie. Ona knows things. She is like his own Celtic grandmother who could not be fooled.

"Yes. I only wanted to better myself."

"You can better yourself now, by making a map of all the property lines you altered. All the graves you moved, all the deeds you burned. The bones want to go home. Do that and redeem yourself."

"Or perjure myself."

"No. You didn't murder Alexander Smith."

"You know who killed him?"

"Aye. And forty wild horses couldn't drag their name out of me."

Gordon reaches into his coat pocket and pulls out a stack of bills. And something weightier, wrapped in brown paper. "Smith…"

"Yes?"

"Smith gave me a gun. He wanted me to kill the nun called Mary. He wanted me to kill her boys, too," he admits. "I know why. He thought Mary had something that could incriminate him. We dug around her old abandoned cabin for three days looking for a gold piece with his initials on it."

"The tie pin is in safe keeping," Ona says. "Should you not turn this weapon over to the Magistrate?"

"I'd rather give it to you. Along with this money. My wife won't take it. And here." Gordon hands her a book with a black cover.

Ona tucks the gun into one vest pocket as if it is nothing more significant than any household utensil. A cup or a spoon. She takes the money and puts in the other pocket and pats it and says, "You are doing the right thing, lad." Then Ona opens the notebook and exclaims over the labelled diagrams. "Well done."

Gordon follows Ona to the far promontory where the town spreads out in the bare, stark aftermath of autumn glory. His eyes fall on the bank building where he entered by the back door after dark and met Smith in echoey dimness. He feels ashamed. Shame is nothing new for him. It is dark and dank like the confessional in his childhood parish. It follows a man around, accumulating with every new screw-up. But standing here beside Ona, he feels somehow forgiven. A thousand Hail Marys could not give him this sense of peace. Smoke rises from chimneys and trails west toward the lake.

"Events tend to drift up here," Ona says.

"Like woodsmoke?"

"Yes. And wishes, maybe. Or regrets. We all have them." Ona turns to him then. "By the way, Gordon. Do you happen to know what Alexander Smith's middle name was?"

Since Murdoch gave her the tie pin, Ona and Mary have been amusing themselves with possibilities. A.S.S. Alexander Simon Smith? Alexander Sebastian Smith? Samuel? Silas?

"I have no idea."

"Och. Well, it doesn't matter."

~ 36 ~

Clarissa Smith was calm when Clark Cook came to her door. Spooky calm. He gave her the bad news about the body down in the gut and offered to retrieve it. For a fee. Unless she wanted to make other arrangements.

"Do what you must," she said, and closed the door.

"I never seen a widow take it so well that her husband died," he later told the fellows at the Mercantile. It was nearing Christmas and Alma was away up to Harburn helping Lydia Kennedy prepare a winter pantry, so Miles was tipping whiskey in everyones' coffee cups. It was a wet, gloomy, miserable day and they all felt the need to commiserate.

"That may be," said Sapper. "Seems like Mrs. Smith always has a bad taste in her mouth, her thin lips is twisted so. But, I s'pose anyone married to that bastard would be bitter. With good cause, is all I'm saying."

"She never cried, nor carried on like some women do."

"A course not. She's got money. It's not like she'll fall into poverty like most wives when their man dies. She'll hie back to the city, I imagine."

"Maybe. Maybe not. She's got a male visitor pretty regular, according to what Lefty has noticed."

"Geez. Another suspect in the murder case?"

The men laughed. The suspects were adding up. In fact, there had been at least four confessions right here in this very store. Around this very stove. It got to be a sport near-about, making up some new version of the murder. Clark Cook had slipped up one night when he was in his cups and revealed about the head coming off. And he may have mentioned the window putty on his scalp. There were limits to professionalism.

Miles made the rounds one last time. He topped everyone up, finished the bottle with a swig, and announced a toast. "Here's to Alexander Smith, Esquire, may he burn in Hell."

"And may his killer get to heaven, half an hour before the devil knows he's dead," said Doc from his usual seat on the seed bags piled against the back wall.

~ 37 ~

"Jane!" Hannah begged me. "Take Gloria outside. She's getting underfoot!"

Hannah was tired from wash day. She still had to take in Ross's diapers from the line. Both Hannah and Catharine were short tempered.

A precocious child, is Gloria, with a pretty smile and curly hair so you cannot stay mad at her for long. A handful, says Hannah. Which is a loving way to say she's a brat. Hannah hints that my father, being a doctor, has ways and means of preventing pregnancies and, if he is concerned with Catharine's health, he should use them. Catharine has not been herself for months, and I worried that she might become like Mother, moody and irrational. But one day last week I heard her singing and she kissed me, and apologized for ignoring me and asked me to recount all the things that she missed.

"I wish I had known, sweet, girl, that you were troubled. I wish I had kept you away from that awful man," she said.

Father, for his part, seems happy to fill the house with bawling babies. The next one is already giving Catharine heart burn. That means the babe will be born with lots of hair, Hannah says.

"I am getting too old for this," Hannah told Catharine when she announced there would be a newborn next summer. Father points out that he will gladly hire a nanny if one is required but Hannah scoffs. "A nanny is nothing but another mouth to feed," she says under her breath. She loves the little ones, and they adore her even when she is gruff with them. It's a mystery why some women are not gifted with children when they are so well suited to raising them.

I do not call Catharine "Mother," because, of course, I have a mother. It is a complicated tale. When people ask after my mother, sometimes they mean Catharine and sometimes they mean my real mother, who has changed her name back to Lydia Ramsey. So, for all appearances, we may not be related.

I have been to see her up at her cabin in Harburn, a long and bumpy buggy ride from town. We are shy with each other. She lives with Molly, a mannish sort of woman.

"Tucked away from prying eyes," says Hannah. "An odd pair. None of my business."

Gloria is my half-sister. I imagine people whisper about us when we go around town together. Anyone can see, by looking at us, that Gloria will be the beauty and I will fade into the woodwork. Completely unremarkable. I expect people are already predicting I will be an old maid. The boys at school do not even bother to tease me. They ignore me. I am a terrible judge of character, as well. How humiliating that I was infatuated with Reverend Whitlock. That I was flattered by his praise.

"You have an uncommon memory for poetry," he told me. "And a clever way of connecting historical events. What a lovely companion you are." I won't be ever again so easily fooled by words. But the experience has left me distracted and unsure of myself. Why is it easier for me to get along with adults rather than people my own age? The boys, so crass and immature. The girls, so full of themselves. They trade notes and whisper intimacies in the classroom, careful not to include me.

I am not normal. I do not fit in. Mrs. Crockett at the store makes time to listen to me. I help her stock shelves and sweep the aisles after school rather than go home. Strange how a peppermint candy and a kind smile make it seem that everything will turn out all right. She thinks it is Mother I worry about, and I do not disagree. I am not prepared to bare my soul and tell about what happened on the day of the storm. I cannot even write it in my diary.

"Your mother was never the raving lunatic people made her out to be. She was just a woman who refused to conform. Hold your head high. Don't acknowledge any of it. Don't add fuel to their little fires, or they'll flare up and burn you."

Alma lets me come with her when she visits Mother up at the cabin. I admitted to her that I am uncomfortable up there. Molly is so protective. She hovers.

"Give her the space she needs to settle in, Jane," she says. "She has to learn a new way of living. Not as a young girl, nor an orphan with a wealthy uncle. Not as a doctor's wife. Not as a patient. All those Lydias are dead and gone. It will take time. She told me she feels like a prisoner reprieved from the gallows at the eleventh hour. She only wants to breathe the air of freedom."

Freedom. Indeed. Lucky her. Meanwhile, I am the one trapped in a village that considers my family wicked.

So, when Gloria disappeared, the first thing that came to mind was that God was punishing us. Gloria and I were down near Head Lake, collecting pine cones for our Christmas wreath. While I filled my apron, she wandered away. Really, I am not careless. She was ducking under the skirt of the pine tree by the bridge and I heard her merry giggle. But after I dumped the cones into my basket, she wasn't there.

Gloria is a wee imp. She has been taking advantage of me since my leg was broken. My pace is slow. She knows I cannot chase her anymore. I called out her name and begged her to wait up but there was no reply. Could she have slipped on the muddy bank of the lake and drowned? Why do I always think of the worst possible outcome! There were no telltale rings in the cold water. The surface was like mercury, ready to turn to ice. How could she vanish? I stood in utter stillness, hoping to hear a branch move, or a frost-crisped leaf under her shoe. And then I panicked, screeching loud enough to scare a tree full of grackles out of their roost in a nearby maple.

You must be vigilant with young children. A thought occurred to me about her real father. Did Gordon McIntee ever think to scoop her up and take her out to the Sawyer Road settlement? Never mind the gypsies who were said to kidnap young children. Never mind the wolves.

I led the search party to the place near the lake where I had last seen Gloria. I expected to be chastised, but the villagers quickly made plans and dispersed and I was alone with nothing to do but wait.

After a while, I heard five short whistle blasts. Somehow, I put one foot in front of the other and moved forward. I felt as if I were in a trance. My mind was frozen in fear. I saw two men running up Victoria Avenue and cutting through the school yard and others were not far behind. I could hear the words. "A body!"

I dropped to my knees and felt myself sinking into icy wet muck, but could not stand. Could not save myself.

There was a commotion and more people shouting, and then, Alma Crocket was lifting me out of a puddle too small to do the mercy of drowning me.

"Come along, lass," she said. "Let me get you to home, Jane."

"Gloria? Is she dead?"

"Lord, no! It's a pile of bones they found. A tramp, maybe. Not your sister."

Lou often wondered, as he travelled from one sick bed to the next, why he managed to escape tragedy. Certainly not as a reward for good deeds, although, as a doctor, he saved lives that otherwise would have been lost. But that is merely his profession. Collecting successes through a career is any man's goal. A mason builds so many stone walls. A constable nabs so many criminals. A cobbler replaces so many soles. It adds up, or it doesn't. And Lou tried not to allow himself any more pride in his skills than the barber or the cooper or the merchant.

On the afternoon that Gloria disappeared, Lou needed help. If you had asked him before that day who might show up to help if he were ever in trouble, he would have named a few close associates. Never would he have described the crowd who arrived on foot, running out of the taverns as if they were ablaze. Never would he have guessed at the wagonload of Italians who organized a thorough search of the hillside behind the schoolhouse, Gloria's own true father among them.

Miles Crockett launched his punt and started dredging the waterfront with weighted nets. Others followed along, wading into the freezing water with long sticks. There were eighty searchers out looking for little Gloria in the November dusk.

Murdoch McGee and Angel found her. "Give me something the lass wore recently that still has her scent on it," he told Hannah, standing at the back door of the doctor's house. Hannah gave him Gloria's soiled night dress. The bitch sniffed the little nightgown and strained immediately at her leash, leading the McGees straight up the Scenic Lookout trail. Webby followed Murdoch and the dog with a lantern, hard-pressed to keep up with his belly full of ale.

"There she was, sitting on Murdy's lap," Webby said later when he was interviewed by the Chronicle reporter. "She was patting Angel's head and saying, Doggy."

Gloria was hardly the worse for wear. She was as comfortable with those rough McGee brothers as if they were two favourite uncles. And they were taken with her, tying a handkerchief around her scratched ankle and pulling a thorn from her hand. She only started to cry when she realized she had ruined the suede on her pretty new boots.

"Saint Nicholas will bring you a new pair," Webby promised and then he started to cry himself. The three of them were weeping when the doctor arrived and he joined in, emotions spilling out all over the place, sloppy and uncontrolled.

Lou hugged Gloria hard and scolded her and something shifted inside him. He felt it, physically, like a twig snapping. Perhaps he had hardened himself to loss over the years, watching people die. Babies and children among them. It seemed he had never seen such beatific faces as those big McGees and their howling bitch, Angel.

There was a great gathering on the doctor's front lawn, wanting to see Gloria returned safe to her mother. Wet and dirty, Protestants and Catholics, drunk and sober. Such a place to belong!

After Hannah bathed Gloria, Lou and Catharine tucked her into a warm bed. They stood together, admiring the miracle of her dark curls and beating heart. Then they went to the wee lad's bed. Ross was his name, after Catharine's clan. He was a calm babe, fair and loving. Jane's door was closed, as usual, but Lou opened it anyway. He had no wish to disturb her, but he felt desperate to see all his family safe, under his roof. Jane was sitting at the window, her notebook in her lap.

"Goodnight, Jane."

"Goodnight, Father." She was sad. Anyone could sense it.

"I hope you do not blame yourself, Jane. All is well."

"Father? Who did they find in the woods? The body. Who is it?"

The time of sparing her was over. Lou decided to be truthful with his daughter. To treat her like an adult. If she asked for the truth, she would have it. Otherwise, she would hear it somewhere else and know her father to be untrustworthy. The bones had been picked clean but, around the neck, an unmistakable white collar. Partly decomposed, the black cloth of a cassock. Close by, a silver cross.

"We think it must be Reverend Whitlock," Lou told her. He expected her to cry. After all, he had read the rapturous descriptions she had written about him in her diary. She had fancied herself in love with the man.

"I thought he left town. Everyone said he'd been put on the train and sent off. He did me no harm, Father," Jane admitted.

"But he might have." Then, worried Jane might feel responsible, he went on. "Someone, it appears, interrupted his departure. Reverend Whitlock was disliked by a lot of people."

Jane nodded. His lonesomeness was part of her original attraction to him. She had read The Hunchback of Notre Dame.

"He was lonely," she said.

"Lonely men do not look for solace in children, Jane. They must seek adult companions."

"I know. There was something wrong with him, Father. He wanted me to be a girl in the Bible. A girl that had an unclean spirit. It was like acting except that..."

Lou remembered the Reverend's mania on the night of the storm. "What happened, Jane?"

"He showed me a picture of Jesus and some children. '*This is me*' he said, pointing to Jesus. '*And you are the little girl.*' Then he did a strange thing. He filled a bowl with water and made me wash his feet."

Lou had heard of such men who came to believe themselves the Messiah.

"I was scared, then. He started chanting. I tried to get away and he pushed me down. That's when the tall man pushed him away from me. And then the window exploded."

"A man was there? What man?"

"Just a man. Not from around here. He didn't say anything, but he stayed with me until you came."

"I didn't see him."

"Yes, you did. He helped you carry me home."

Catharine listens in the hallway. She is expecting her third child in June, the first to be legitimate from birth. She is Mrs. Kennedy now, but she cannot rid herself of the uncomfortable feeling that Lou's first wife wishes her harm. Lydia lives nearby in Harburn. Something startling happened that has Catharine quite unsettled. She was wakened in the middle of the night. Believing it was Lou, home late after a call, she slipped back into a deep sleep. But in the morning, Lou was not on his side of the bed. His pillow was uncreased. The quilt and sheets were smooth. She thought she must have been dreaming, until she noticed that the hand mirror and brush and comb were missing. Lydia's monogrammed set. Gone. She rushed to check on Ross and Gloria because she suspected Lydia may have entered their rooms as well. They were rosy-cheeked and sleeping comfortably. Nothing in their rooms had been disturbed. But it could have been otherwise. Catharine began to think about the evening Gloria ran off. Maybe she was lured away? Maybe Lydia was not cured?

When the buzzing starts between Lydia's shoulder blades, she lies down on an ancient rock on the shore of Delf East Lake and melts into the landscape and stays still until the danger passes. The doctors, she suspects, put some kind of insect inside her that hums and thrums and tries to lure her back to the asylum. She feels better today, after pulling every single lock of Catharine's hair out of her brush and burning it. What a terrible stench.

~ 38 ~

Clarissa Smith had little experience with love. Or even friendship. In the city, there were organizations that made it easy to know people. Church, benevolent societies, card clubs. There were art galleries and museums. Society women had full calendars. And if one's husband had a brief affair, it was of little concern. Men were to be forgiven for lust. Wives were relieved, happy even, to retreat to their own boudoirs after dinner.

Clarissa was surprised, then, to find herself rejuvenated by an unexpected infatuation only a few weeks after her husband's funeral. A tender lover who brushed her hair and stroked her bare arm with fairy-like fingers. He read aloud to her from romantic books.

Clarissa had a sister long ago who climbed into her bed at night to tell scary stories. Together they did naughty things, like sneaking cookies and spying on their nanny and the gardener kissing in broad daylight behind the summer kitchen. But Chastity died of a fever when she was sixteen and Clarissa thought she would never have that kind of intimacy with anyone, ever again. Then Timothy Bailey, the teller at the Dominion Bank, knocked tentatively on her door one afternoon. He was consumed with the burden of information. Information he felt it was his duty to impart now that his boss was in the grave.

"There are two boys," he told her, after they exchanged some pleasantries about the Christmas concert and the weather and the health of Timothy's mother.

Clarissa knew right away who he meant. One of the boys looked so much like her own son that, if he had not been such a ragged lad, she might have believed Percival had come home on the train. She wondered briefly if her imagination had invented the boy, because she was reading Mark Twain's book, The Prince and the Pauper. But there was no mistaking the lad's paternity. It had to be Alex's son.

Timothy related the story of Mary, as he remembered it. How she appeared in the bank demanding money for her boys. He handed Clarissa a receipt for two hundred dollars.

"I only bring this to your attention because of the forensic audit."

"A forensic audit?"

"Yes. Mr. Austin, the bank president..."

"Yes, yes. I know Elmer Austin. He suspects something amiss with the books? He suspects that Alex has stolen money?"

"Misappropriated funds, perhaps."

"But how? Alex was so meticulous with records and..." Clarissa stopped and examined the receipt in her lap. Money was indeed transferred from her own account to the account of a woman. Mary Hammond.

The account was in Alex's name, but it was Clarissa's money. Now, here was proof that Alex mishandled her inheritance. For all his faults, she never thought him untrustworthy.

"So this Mary... Is she the boy's mother?"

"Yes. One of the boys. The other boy is her brother. Mary's mother entertained Alex, apparently, and..." Timothy paused. Lowered his voice as if there might be others in the house who could overhear. He quietly continued in language he considered might ease the blow of the information. "Alex became fond of the young girl, Mary, only a child at the time."

Clarissa felt sick to her stomach. Timothy came to sit beside her on the settee. He took her hand. The room grew dark. Cold. Clarissa sent Madelaine back to the city. She had no use for a housekeeper since Alex died. And the handyman, had not been seen in some time. There was a dispute about money he was owed and the woodpile was getting low.

Timothy roused himself and turned over the dying coals in the fireplace. He put a blanket around Clarissa's shoulders and slipped out the back door to chop kindling. After a smoky start, the damp logs caught and the flames seemed to revive Clarissa.

"Tomorrow is Sunday," she said, standing at last and lighting an ornate lamp. "Will you take me up to the Nunnery?"

"Of course." He looked past her out the front window and noticed big snowflakes coming straight down, accumulating quickly. "Do you have a sleigh?"

The Nunnery was not the enclave of savage squaws Clarissa expected. Mary was very gracious, all things considered. Clarissa liked her. A common enemy can do that, even for those who might otherwise be adversaries. She felt a deep kinship and hugged her when it was time to leave. Something she rarely did with women friends.

Clarissa wrapped her wool scarf tighter around her neck and moved closer to Timothy. He slowed the sleigh. The sun was warming the branches and great clots of snow fell all around them. Gus and Biddy snorted and stomped. Timothy put his arm around Clarissa.

"You're shivering."

"Not from the cold. I'm feeling such a fool. Why did I stay with him? I knew. I think I knew. All along, I think I knew what he was."

"You did what wives do. You honoured your commitment. You made a home for your family."

"Alex left telltale clues of perversions lying about the house. It was as if he intended to taunt me with tokens of other women. Locks of hair. Snippets of lace. A locket. Even, once, a letter, pleading for mercy. I think it must have been from Mary's mother. I burned it. I have been a coward."

At home, Clarissa made soup and Timothy chopped wood and as night fell, they smiled at one another, feeling the comfort of domesticity.

When Percival and Alice returned from school on the Christmas Eve train, the shock of finding a strange man invited for dinner was somewhat allayed by the change in the household. So informal and cozy. With a candled evergreen tree in the parlour and stockings and treats. And music. Timothy was fierce on the fiddle.

~ 39 ~

Public Hearing for Two Unsolved Murders
To take place March 15, at the Orange Lodge
All Citizens with information pertaining to the deaths of
Alexander Smith, and/or Richard Whitlock,
should attend and be prepared to testify.

Posters were distributed around the village. People paused to comment wherever they were tacked up; the Post Office, the message board at the train station, Town Hall, the windows of shops on Queen Street. Sometimes, the gatherings became contentious.

"Curious that so many folks know the facts of this case," Sapper said. He was leaning against the frame of the train station's ticket window, and picking his teeth with a sliver of pine.

Lefty leaned forward in time to see a guy get shoved to the edge of the platform by a local ruffian. "All them men claim to have intimate knowledge of how to kill somebody and not get caught."

"Makes a fella nervous to go to sleep at night, all them experts running around."

"Crime is on the rise. Too many hot heads looking for fights. Every whistle stop between here and Lindsay reported some kind of vandalism last month. A barn fire at Gelert. Dead livestock at Burnt River. A poisoned well at Lochlin. Seems there is a huge increase in mean neighbours and crazy relatives."

Sapper snapped his toothpick in half and flicked it onto the tracks. "When a man is wrong and won't admit it, he always gets angry."

Aliza Tucker was careful not to sensationalize her reports, but it was becoming clear that anger sold newspapers. Tavern brawls and lumberyard knife fights were of particular interest. Headlines about upcoming nuptials and rummage sales were left on the shelves and ended up as tinder. Her report of the Reverend's murder was widely circulated and she had to print forty extra copies. A man of God! Thought to have left town by train after the big storm, dead of a skull-bashing and left in the woods behind the schoolhouse.

Her own son Aubrey protested when he read the article.

"I'm not passing judgment on the man, Aubrey. Only reporting the facts."

"The fact is that God is making a footstool out of the Reverend's enemies."

Aliza felt cold. "What did you say?"

"Psalm 110. You know… your troops will be willing on your day of battle."

"Did the Reverend teach you that psalm, son?"

"Yes. To arm me against my tormenters."

"Don't repeat it, Aubrey. Good Christians don't talk like that."

"But—"

"Not every word of the Bible is true, son. The Lord did not edit the St. James version of the Good Book. Men did. And not all men are wise."

"Not every word of The Chronicle is fact, either, Mother."

"You're right. It's only my best information at the time. But I do try to sift the wheat from the chaff. God forgive me if it hurts anyone." Aliza disciplined herself against hearsay as she wrote the editorials about vigilante justice leading up to the public hearing, ironically scheduled to take place on the Ides of March. It was not a trial, because there were no suspects. Or rather, too many.

Meanwhile, Aliza covered the inauguration of the new Reeve with as much hopefulness as she could muster.

NEW REEVE CALLS FOR PEACEFUL RESOLUTIONS

James Adams was sworn in as Reeve this past Wednesday. In his inaugural address to the people of Haliburton, he spoke eloquently enough about the fractious circumstances that can tear a community apart. Four councillors stood with him, representing four wards. An excerpt from his speech is as follows:

"This country is young, but the issue plaguing us today is an old one. Aristocracies versus lower classes. Both think the others are idiots. Both have valid evidence to prove their beliefs. And yet, what's to be done other than to carry on and try to do a better job in the future? There is value in all levels of society, and nowhere is it more apparent than here in the rough territory of the Northern Townships. Every frontier must suffer growing pains. We, your newly elected municipal council, will get to work on building a foundation for a more peaceful village. The sound of horse hooves in the dead of night, malicious threats about disputed property lines, violent retributions. These things, I promise you, will become a thing of the past. With constables patrolling the village and outlying roads, you can expect incidents of vigilantism to disappear. Also, this coming year, we expect to announce our collaboration with a private citizen, who prefers at this time to remain anonymous, for the construction of a hospital. I call each and every one of you to service, to help us make Haliburton a safe village. A village with a bright future for all men, all women, all children."

Reeve-elect James Adams concluded by saying that his first duty is to establish a police constabulary for the district to address the disturbing increase in criminal activity. Until then, Adams requests that able-bodied male citizens report for duty as special constables. The volunteer program, Adams says, is called "Watch and Ward," and it has been successful in other Ontario municipalities to discourage thefts, public mischief, and anarchist activity. Training for volunteers will commence on January 8th. Night patrols will be organized on a rotating basis to set high standards for order and to enforce the law in the community.

~ 40 ~

March 1886

The Orange Lodge was packed to the rafters with concerned citizens, gossip-mongers and looky-loos. The municipal government faced a great deal of scrutiny, but James Adams comported himself with utmost dignity. It is said that when a man loses his sight, his hearing improves. Does it stand to reason that when a man loses his mobility, his intelligence improves? Perhaps. Perhaps not. There were accusations that members of the former Town Council had abetted Alexander Smith in his land transfer scheme. The bank audit was submitted as evidence and the conclusion was that Smith acted alone. The Honourable Patrick Collins, referred to by locals only as The Magistrate, listened solemnly as the bank manager's character was annihilated by one convincing testimony after another. Citizens stepped up, not because they wanted to, but because the rumours had become so wildly fantastic that they worried they would appear guilty if they did not. Timothy Bailey testified, and Gordon Murphy. Mary Hammond was reluctant to speak, but she was called upon to explain the matter of a two-hundred-dollar deposit. Alma Crockett and Sunny Adams corroborated her story. There were testimonies from several business owners. Finally, Clarissa Smith took the stand. In a strained voice, she apologized for the harm her husband had wrought.

"And, for what it's worth," she said in a concluding statement, "I offer my forgiveness to the murderer, whoever that may be."

The Magistrate banged his gavel and called for order and, not getting it, announced a recess until the following day at which time he would hear testimonies regarding the death of Reverend Richard Whitlock.

It was difficult to find evidence of the ordained minister's criminality. He was, it seemed, an ordinary man who believed his job entitled him to extraordinary exceptions. His preference of children for companionship, rather than adults, was particularly problematic, but other than the incident with the doctor's daughter, there was little proof of lasting damage. A man does not deserve a death sentence for being loathsome, the Magistrate concluded. Instead, he admonished the Anglican Church, specifically Bishop Marshall, who recommended Dick Whitlock for a position of trust and authority.

"An ordained minister must prove himself, by his actions and his moral character, to deserve the responsibilities of his post. Reverend Whitlock was unsuccessful in Toronto, and it must have seemed clear he would be unsuccessful in any pulpit. The bishop should be made to understand that it was irresponsible to send Reverend Whitlock to the end of the line, thinking he would do less damage in the hinterland than he could do in the city. That thinking ended in tragedy. It is my recommendation that church elders should, in the future, personally undertake a scrupulous background search before placing a cleric in a position of trust, including at least three references from men of reliable professions."

In the end, the Magistrate banged his gavel and declared both deaths accidental. "Their own behaviour hastened their own ends," he concluded. "These were leaders in the community, trusted to comport themselves in such as manner as to be above reproach. Mr. Smith committed heinous crimes upon other persons, incited hatred, and benefitted financially from illegal activities. Reverend Whitlock was a cocaine addict, leading to impaired judgment, inappropriate influence over minors, and association with known criminals. No further information is requested or required. Consider these cases closed. As for my recommendations regarding vigilantism, Reeve Adams has introduced policing policies to reassure the law-abiding citizens of this township that so-called Midnight Justice will end. Perpetrators will be punished to the full extent of the law."

The gavel resounded in the hall and the crowd seemed satisfied enough to leave peacefully.

~ 41 ~

Wilderness has given way to "progress." Progress has wrought conflict. Conflicts require resolutions. Teams of rational people are needed to negotiate compromises. But rational people cannot be manufactured.

In the meantime, troubles will not cease. Threats bubble up at every Council Meeting. Growing pains in Haliburton are acute now that the veil has been lifted on those who came to town with deception up their sleeves. Small grievances simmer and boil over into angry encounters at the Mercantile, snubs at church services, and fights at social gatherings. Even in the schoolyard, children re-enact the disputes of their parents and come home with black eyes and bloody noses.

Ona faces the facts. There are no human heirs for her cloister on the ridge. Gidaaki was like a quilt, and she stitched it together one patch at a time, thinking about how to match the colours and the patterns and the materials. But that dream is going, going gone. It is being systematically dismantled with the arrival of every train.

Ona can no longer feed one hungry mouth at a time. Women must have the resources and tools to climb out of poverty on their own. This requires books and pens. Opportunities to earn a living independently. Access to higher learning so they can become doctors and lawyers and surveyors. All possible. All necessary. They must insist on their right to vote and run for office. What is stopping them?

Is it possible for women to adopt the skills that empower men, while rejecting greed and power? The world does not need more warmongers. The world does not need more millionaires. The world does not need more corrupt lawmakers. At the centre of Ona's being, is tremendous fatigue. She buried her mother next to Kateri and now she wrestles with the desire to lie down and let Mother Earth swallow her, too.

But once she is gone, who will speak for the trees?

Who will speak for the lakes?

Who will speak for Gidaaki?

There is an urgency in her heart to discover a new kind of literacy. A language to support economic growth that also respects the land. Stories of construction that don't require destruction. Can civilization ever be truly civil? The answer eludes her.

~ 42 ~

December 1886

Butchering pigs could be satisfying work. Murdoch had a three-hundred-and-twenty pounder that he did not care to feed all winter. He decided to host a pig roast on the Eve of the New Year. The time had come, the brothers agreed, for Haliburton to let past grudges go. Most of the villagers were born far away from these highlands, and the journey here had not been an easy one. But now this community felt like home. Now they were building it together. Webby put a notice in the Chronicle.

Pig Roast, December 31
5 p.m. until 1887
Highland Golf Club
All Welcome
Donations to the new Public Library accepted

It was a gloomy day, with a genuine Scottish mist, when Murdoch took his twelve gauge and shot the pig in the centre of the forehead three inches above its eyes. Pigs are in constant motion except when sleeping, urinating or drinking. Murdock filled a pan with milk, a last supper so to speak, and bang. It was an expert shot. Murdoch was an ethical killer. He would never inflict undue suffering on man nor beast. He had killed to protect himself, and to protect others. He had killed to feed himself and to feed others. He had never killed out of anger or spite or jealousy. When, on rare occasions, it was his duty to supervise a man into the afterlife, he did it in such a way to limit his suffering. Just as there were honourable ways to kill, there were honourable ways to die. This pig died without so much as a whimper. It made Murdoch proud.

With Webby's help, Murdoch stuck the pig in the throat and strung him up from a sturdy maple bough. An appreciative crowd gathered to watch the skinning and gutting. Among those in attendance were the Anderson sisters. The Misses Anderson, as they were known. Beatrice and Morag. The schoolmarms. When the McGee brothers first came to Haliburton, the sisters ignored them. How disappointing that the bachelors in these Northern Townships proved to be so loutish! But first impressions are often incorrect.

Never in their wildest dreams did the sisters expect to play golf on a highland course like the brothers designed overlooking Lake Kashagawigamog. And then, to find that the McGee brothers were gentle of heart, scholarly in the histories and philosophies, and service-minded! It was a great relief, after many discouraging attempts to meet men in Haliburton, to be acquainted with Murdoch and Webby, and they shamelessly pursued the brothers all the way to the altar.

I don't want to take credit for this bit of matchmaking, but the double sibling wedding of the Anderson sisters to the McGee brothers would not have happened without a nudge from yours truly, Ladder. Dead men are more romantic than you may think. Sentimentality, it seems, is the last human failing to go.

Webby and Beatrice are a natural match. When she gets too serious, he makes her laugh with bawdy songs from the old country. She fills his heart with joy and his stomach with potato salad like his mother used to make. Better, he tells her. A lie, but still. Webby goes to church with Beatrice, just to make her happy. Beatrice works on improving her golf game. She learned the game as a girl and has a natural swing, but she accepts instruction from Webby. Just to make him happy.

Morag and Murdoch are quite a different pair, as you may suspect. They are serious. They sign on to help Ona make a list of essential books for the new library, and she is delighted at their extensive interest in Greek myths. There is to be a double wedding in the spring of 1887, at the Methodist Church. The two sets of siblings make a stellar foursome.

Epilogue

There are four loon calls. The wail, the yodel, the tremolo, and the hoot. The wails are my favourite, sorrowful like train whistles. They conjure up forgotten stories of heartbreak and betrayal, reminding me how little I knew of the world's mysteries when I was alive, and how much less I understand now, as a ghost. Listen well. My time for haunting these Haliburton streets is almost done.

Who killed the bank manager? Do you really want to know? If I tell you, you mustn't think less of the murderer. Murderess in fact. It wasn't Mary. Not Ona either, although both those women have the grit to do difficult things. No. It was the Italian lady, Maria Murphy.

Alex Smith went looking for Gordon with a score to settle. But Maria answered the door instead. She used her rabbit rifle and shot him at close range. Joseph, her eldest son, ran to Uncle Lorenzo's and Smith's body was chucked into the gut before sunset. Rico, one of the paesano cousins that worked for Gordon, had been carrying the gold tie pin in his coat pocket since they searched the Hammond cabin. It was something of value. But, in light of developments, he wisely returned it to its original owner.

Gordon never heard about the incident. Never suspected a thing. Omerta, as the Italians say.

And, what of Reverend Dick Whitlock's fate? He wasn't as wicked a man as many believed. Delusional, yes, but religion does that to believers. What a tremendous capacity humans have for denying the hard truth of mortality. His death was something of an accident. The pig farmer, you know him as Murdoch McGee, he opened up the boxcar in the early morning after the storm. His intention was only to water and slop his livestock, and clean their bedding. Instead, a raving lunatic came running at him. Taken by surprise, Murdoch bonked the man on the head with his shovel. When he saw what he had done, he slammed the door shut and went to find the stationmaster. They exchanged a few low words over cups of vile coffee from the banged-up percolator and then Lefty stood watch while Murdoch loaded the body into the back of his oxcart. Murdoch knew of the boggy cesspit out behind the schoolhouse on Victoria Street, as Morag had complained of the stench many times. He was pleased at how quickly the Reverend sank below the scummy surface. Dick Whitlock may well have rested there for eternity if it hadn't been for the unusual dry spell.

Time will tell which villages will thrive and which ones will end up as ghost towns with crumbling foundations and collapsing root fences. Haliburton, at the end of the line, shows no sign of fading away. It endures against all odds, like the beech tree which marks my final resting place. When I was first buried, it was a slender thing, hardly able to cast a shadow. But my flesh falls away, and the roots of the tree push through my bones and clutch onto granite and hold fast.

Back and forth through time I have travelled, like an inattentive student who cannot decide on his area of study. It is an exhausting curriculum, impossible to complete in one afterlife. Pleasanter to return to the peace of the grave where the earth's heart beats in layers of sentient stone. Where the past sounds like autumn crickets and summer thunder and sap stirring and snow landing on snow, one flake at a time.

Acknowledgments:

My appreciation must first go to my father who loved Lake Kashagawigamog. Haliburton, for him, was a safe haven from worries and worldly struggles. In my heart, it still is.

Steve Hill, Curator of the Haliburton Highlands Museum, found the perfect vintage photo for the cover, and the early map of Haliburton Village.

Early readers Bessie Sullivan and Deb Reed both offered valuable critiques which redirected this story through some rocky beginnings.

Leopolda Dobrzensky's book about pioneering in Haliburton, Fragments of a Dream, inspired me to write a fictional version of Haliburton's rough beginnings.

Jack Hoggarth from Curve Lake Cultural Centre, generously offered insights about the traditional territory of the Michi Saagig and Chippewa Nations. Long before the time frame of this novel, the Anishinaabe called this area Gidaaki (upwards earth – the high lands).

Even though the tracks have been torn up, Haliburton is a village that honours its railroad history, with a steam locomotive, a caboose and the original Haliburton Railway Station which operates as a public art gallery called Rails End. Thanks to local individuals and organizations for maintaining these relics from the past.

Finally, it has been a pleasure to work with Shane Joseph, publisher of Blue Denim Press. He has a keen eye for details (like Oxford commas) and no conscience whatsoever when killing off quirky characters if they don't advance the plot. Thanks, Shane for getting me back on track when I (frequently) went off the rails.

Author Bio

Janet Trull lives in the Haliburton Highlands, a land of blue lakes and rocky shores where her family has gathered for generations. She is the author of two critically acclaimed collections of short fiction, **Hot Town** and **Something's Burning**, both published by **At Bay Press** (Winnipeg). With small town settings and big world themes, her stories examine the tension between neighbours, sexes, races and generations during times of social and cultural change.

A graduate of English at McMaster University, Trull focused on literacy throughout her career as an educator. She was a Reading Recovery teacher, a Literacy Coach and a Student Achievement Officer for the Ontario Ministry of Education. Currently, she is a freelance writer. Her essays, professional writing and short stories have appeared in a wide variety of publications, including the Globe and Mail, Toronto Star, Canadian Living Magazine, Prairie Fire, The New

Quarterly, subTerrain Magazine, and Geist. Subscribers to The Haliburton County Echo recognize Trull as a frequent contributor, with nostalgic essays about skinny dips, campfires and lazy afternoons in a hammock. These are accessible on her website, trullstories.com

Janet Trull is the recipient of several awards, including a CBC Canada Writes challenge, a Western Magazine Award nomination, and a Commonwealth Fiction prize.

Terry Fallis, two-time winner of the Stephen Leacock Medal for Humour, says, *"Janet Trull knows her way around people and communities as well as the issues that hold them together, and sometimes break them apart."*

Printed in the USA
CPSIA information can be obtained
at www.ICGtesting.com
LVHW011840011223
765462LV00030B/374